BirthMark

LA PATRON SERIES – BOOK THREE
The Alphas Alpha

Sydney Addae

BirthMark
Book Three of the La Patron Series

Addae, Sydney
Copyright 2013 by Sydney Addae

This is a work of fiction. Names, places, characters, and incidents are either the product of the author's imagination or are used fictitiously, and any resemblance to any actual persons, living or dead, businesses, organizations, events, or locales is entirely coincidental. All trademarks, service marks, registered trademarks, and registered service marks are the property of their respective owners and are used herein for identification purposes only. The publisher does not have any control over or assume any responsibility for the author or third-party websites or their contents.

2013 All Rights Reserved

All rights reserved under the International and Pan-American Copyright Conventions. No part of this book may be reproduced or transmitted in any form or by any means, electronic or mechanical, including photocopying, recording, or by any information storage and retrieval system, without permission in writing from Erosa Knowles.

WARNING: The unauthorized reproduction or distribution of this copyrighted work is illegal. Criminal copyright infringement, including infringement without monetary gain, is investigated by the FBI and is punishable by up to 5 years in Federal prison and a fine of $250,000.

BirthMark

Book 3 of
The Patron, the Alphas Alpha

When you're the top wolf on the continent with the backing of the Goddess, how does an enemy topple your kingdom? By challenging you to a fight? No. By changing the rules.

After three hundred years of fighting and service to the Goddess, Silas Knight is the Patron, Alpha to the Alphas on the North American continent. As the top wolf, he fears little and has seen most things. But when he discovers someone or something has been quietly disturbing the natural order of things, he's surprised. Certain human women can birth fully functioning wolves, and that's a major problem.

Jasmine Bennett has no idea her deceased husband was a wolf shifter or that her twin sons are shifters. Her life changes when she rushes to her son's bedside after he's wounded in Afghanistan and returned stateside. Now her life's in danger because of her ability to give birth to a breed of beings she never knew existed.

Silas is discovering what it means to have a family. Unfortunately, it seems to clash at the worst times with running the Wolf Nation. Someone is throwing a series of challenges at him to remove him from office. Silas's and Jasmine's relationship is tested and the outcome is uncertain. With prophecies running rampant about the future of the Wolf Nation, and mysterious happenings,

Silas and Jasmine are stumped by the BirthMark on their sons.

This is the third book in the La Patron series. Book one is BirthRight, Book two is BirthControl and should be read first for a better understanding of this book.

Thanks, Sydney

Chapter 1

Silas Knight, La Patron of every wolf on the North American continent and possibly a few others as well, walked the wide hallway outside his bedroom to avoid waking his mate, Jasmine. She was worn out from tending the children all day and he wanted her to have a few minutes of undisturbed rest. Her day had been as long as his, but whereas he spent the day running a nation of wolves, she spent the day with four pups whose needs and personalities were as different as the days of the week. He would gladly face the rebels or pouting Alphas than handle his feisty litter all day. She had remarked on more than one occasion that the pups had his arrogant gene as if that were a bad thing.

He placed his bundle higher on his shoulder and patted his back gently. "It's going to be okay, little one," he whispered in an attempt to calm David's whimpering. For some reason, none of the doctors had been able to explain why the child was in a constant state of discomfort. Nothing calmed him for long.

"Is he going to be alright?" Tyrese, Jasmine's older son, asked as he walked down the hall toward them. He was dressed in pressed jeans and a bright red short-sleeved polo. His highly polished boots made a clopping sound on the marble floors. He had allowed his hair to grow out from a military buzz cut, and it now brushed against his shoulder.

Silas nodded and flicked his gaze over the young pup again. "He's fine, just having a hard time quieting down. Going out?"

"Yeah, a few of the guys and I are going to hit this new club in town. Supposedly it's owned by a half-breed, I wanna check it out."

Since Silas had approved the club owner's petition to open a business in the state, he wasn't surprised. He'd heard the business venture had proven to be such a success, the owner had petitioned the Alpha of Georgia to open a club in Atlanta.

"There are still some rebels in the area. Be careful. Have fun."

"I will. Always." Tyrese nodded and walked to the elevator which would take him down to the tunnels. He would have to walk a good distance and then come up beneath the condo complex to pick up his car. It was safer and away from the main houses.

David whimpered a little and Silas returned his attention to his youngest male pup. "I'm sorry you're not feeling well, but it's going to be okay." He started to hum and David quieted. Initially, Silas had thought to have the pup calmed in a few minutes, consequently pacing the quiet hall made sense. Now he realized he'd miscalculated and headed to the darkened nursery. He sat in one of the rocking chairs, continuing his soft serenade. There were five additional rockers in the large nursery along with the four cribs occupied by his pups, lining the wall. The nurses lay asleep on a twin bed behind a screen so they were close if one of the pups woke through the night. Except for David. They had a small crib in their room for when he had problems sleeping. It bothered him that the doctors couldn't find the root of his pup's discomfort. Poor thing had been poked and prodded repeatedly with nothing to show for it.

Closing his eyes, he sought advice from the Goddess. He waited until the warmth of her presence filled the room. David quieted and went still. Offering comfort, Silas rubbed his son's back as he waited for permission to speak.

"Patron." The whispery voice filled the room and touched every atom of his being. Her energy touched off sparks in the room and sent tingles down his spine. He struggled to make a coherent sentence.

"Goddess of Life, how can I help my pup…my son?" he asked, uncertain if She'd respond since he hadn't followed the normal protocols for contacting her. He continued humming old, forgotten melodies, so engrossed in the peaceful moments that when the Goddess responded on the wisps of the wind, he was startled.

"He is your seed, La Patron, you can heal him as you've healed many others."

How? He was such a tiny thing. But Her presence left as suddenly as it came. Holding his young pup tight, he sent warmth and waves of healing vitality to his son. He then placed his palm in the middle of the child's back, closed his eyes, and focused on healing the small body. When he was done, Silas waited, hoping the pup was better.

Within a few moments, David whimpered. Tired and confused, Silas placed David across his shoulder and started humming again. The child settled. Silas breathed in the sweet silence of the room and gazed at the ceiling. Last year the Goddess told him change was coming, and it had blown through his life with hurricane-force winds, upsetting everything he knew and believed. Human females and wolves, breeding, creating a whole new category of beings – half breeds. There were times he still couldn't believe it, but he'd just look in his nursery. All four of his pups, his first litter, were half-breeds.

At the thought of them, love welled inside and overflowed. Now with pups of his own, he fully understood why full-blood wolves fought packmates and would start a civil war to save their pups. As much as he had detested the idea of half-breeds before, he was irrevocably committed to saving all wolves, full and half-breeds. Part of the reason lay on his shoulder, taking small sips of air and trembling slightly on the exhale.

"Don't worry, little one. The Goddess says I can heal you, I just need to figure out how and then all will be well," he murmured, closing his eyes as he rocked.

His thoughts roamed to Tyrone, Tyrese's twin. He wondered how the young pup would react when he discovered another had challenged him for the right to lead the West Virginia wolves.

Silas decided to allow the challenge to stand since some didn't view the former Alpha as a traitor. But Silas knew better. He'd read the Alpha's thoughts, heard his hatred of the breeds, and his desire to destroy everything and everyone who stood in his way. That included Silas. The traitor died by Silas' hands and he was within his rights to choose a replacement.

The sweet scent of his mate reached him. Keeping his eyes closed, he waited for her to speak.

"Let me take him, you have that meeting tomorrow with the detective. You said he was coming at eight, it's after three now." She reached forward and took the pup from his shoulder. He might never admit it, but he missed the small patch of warmth the little one provided.

Silas pulled Jasmine onto his lap, pushed her swinging braids from her face, and nuzzled her neck. He had missed her. The birth, coupled with the fall in the cave, wreaked havoc on her body. The doctor restricted their lovemaking, due to the bleeding from the fall after the pups were born. There were still so many things they simply did not know about her physiology, neither he nor the doctor wanted to take any chances with her life.

"He's going to be fine," he whispered as she placed a kiss on the pup's brow.

"Oh?" She eyed him curiously. "Have the doctors said something to you?"

"No. The Goddess."

Her eyes widened and lit with pure joy. "What'd she say?... What'd She say?"

Pleased with her eager response, he repeated the words he had been told. "I've laid warm hands on him, sending healing energy through his body, but… that didn't work.

Don't worry, it is my top priority to discover how to heal him."

"Can't you just decree it? Make a command? Tell his body to be healed?"

Chuckling, he tapped her nose. "I'm not the Christo. I heal wolves because I'm their leader, we share similar energies. He needs something more and I will figure it out."

She nodded and stood, taking his hand. "Come on, time for bed, at least until you have to get up. I've missed you."

Gingerly he cupped her face between his palms and stared into her eyes. He read the fatigue and determination. During the pregnancy, she had made it very clear she would raise her children. And though she had nurses to assist, she spent most of her time caring for the pups. Initially, he had felt left out and they'd argued over the amount of time and energy the pups took. Based on an intensely enlightening discussion, he understood it went against everything inside her to hand her babies over to someone else to raise. It simply wasn't in her makeup. To compromise, he visited her and the pups every day in the nursery and they set aside an hour every evening for alone time, so far it worked well.

"I love you," he whispered across her lips and kissed her deeply.

She opened her link and he was inundated with a tidal wave of sweet, tingly, warmth that cascaded over him and permeated his heart. *"Love you, Wolfie."*

His chest tightened at her words and he deepened their kiss. His palms rested on her hips, he pulled her close to his erection.

Her breath hitched.

He rubbed her against his hardness, reveling in the friction. He released her mouth for a second, gulped down some air, and kissed her again.

"*I need you,*" he told her through their link. "*I miss you.*"

"*I need you too,*" she said. "*He's been quiet for a while now, let's go to bed.*

"*I'm right behind you.*"

They broke apart and he appreciated the needy look in her eyes. She placed her finger to her lips, took his hand, and led him to their bedroom.

His eyes were glued to her hips, remembering how well they cushioned his larger form. How hot and tight she'd been the last time, how she'd been soaking wet before he even touched her. His skin heated, his staff leaked as he remembered the long hard thrusts he'd given her and she'd taken them all.

She stumbled and turned, her eyes disbelieving. "When…when did you learn that?"

He frowned; he had no idea what she was talking about. "What?"

"I felt you…it was like…you were…you know…"

"No. I don't. What are you talking about?"

She walked to their bed and laid David down in the small crib before returning to him, and crossed her arms. Within seconds, their last sexual romp replayed in his mind. She leaned forward. "The difference was I felt it when you were thinking about it, you didn't just now. How'd you do that?"

His eyes landed on her full globes. His dick jumped. He grabbed her hand, leading her to the other side of the bed. "Horny." He slipped the straps of her dress from her shoulders. The dress pooled on the floor while he pulled her close, kissing her face, neck, and finally her breasts. His fingers ventured south and it was just as he remembered, she was wet and ready for him. He eyed his son, sent a silent plea to chill for a few moments longer.

"Hurry up and undress." Jasmine pulled at his jeans, unsnapping them and rolling them down.

He slapped her hand away and finished the job in one fell swoop. The heat of her mouth sheathed his dick, torturing him because they didn't have time.

"Damn, you have no idea how much it hurts me to stop you, but as good as your mouth feels, I need to be inside you." Gently he pulled away, loving the suction she provided on the way out.

She grinned, scooted back on the bed, and opened her legs, showing her bare lips and ready-to-be-filled center. His hard-staff jerked in greeting as he moved forward, grabbed her calves, and pulled her to the edge of the bed.

He loved looking at her like this when she was wild and needy for him. "This is going to be fast. But I promise to make it up to you whenever we get our bedroom back."

"Just do it...please."

He didn't have to be asked twice. With single-minded precision, he filled her in one thrust. Her body welcomed him and held him snug in her warmth. Tight muscles clenched and throbbed. He needed to move. In the back of his mind, he remembered she had given him four pups and should take it slow. He slid in and out, gentle strokes at first. But his mate didn't want gentle, and the image she sent through their link of him taking her made it clear she needed him hard and fast. Silas increased his thrusts, feeling the pleasure build. It spurred him on. He pumped harder, deeper, wanting to imprint himself on her.

A low keening sound filled the air. He placed his hand over her mouth as he continued to thrust into her through her orgasm. He was so close. She clenched her muscles and sent him over the edge. His heart pounded loud in his ears as he emptied his load into her.

Chest heaving, he sucked air into his starved chest as he collapsed on top of her. Firmly toned arms wrapped around him, holding him tight. "You are amazing. That was sooo good. Thanks. You have no idea how much I needed that."

He squeezed her shoulder, inhaled her scent, and placed a kiss on her shoulder. "I'm sure I have an idea, I've gone without as long as you have." He rose slightly, looked down at her droopy lids showing hints of light brown eyes, and her goofy smile. "You looked like a satisfied cat."

She grinned and ran her hand through his hair. "I am. You satisfied my cat…for now." She winked at him and rolled to the side.

"Watch him. I'm going to take a quick shower. Be right back." She rose slowly, majestically, and walked naked to the bath. He was sure she put a little extra in her walk knowing he was watching. Her bronzed complexion glowed, long braids slapped the middle of her back, drawing attention to her small waist and high round hips. In a word, perfection, and she was his.

Silas pulled off his shoes, socks, and pants, wiped himself, and then placed the soiled clothes in the basket. He glanced at his pup, pleased the little one had allowed him to spend time with his mate. Now if the pup would sleep long enough that Silas could hold and cuddle his mate until morning, which would be perfect.

Jasmine walked back into the room a short while later, feeling refreshed. Her heart swelled with love and pride at the picture on the bed. Silas lay sprawled on his back with David on his chest. Silas's long black wavy hair lay across the beige pillowcase like a dark cloud. Long lashes and perfectly arched brows complemented blue-green eyes that rarely missed anything. The man was gorgeous and big. His body lay diagonally across the bed and there was little space left except on either side of him. She pulled on a pair of panties and tank top before joining them in bed. She deliberated whether or not to move David from Silas' chest and lay him beside her so she wouldn't have to get up when he whimpered later on. But she didn't want Silas to think she didn't trust him.

Initially, she had been terrified for her son's life. Normally, in wolf culture, if a child was born sick, he would be put down. She had kept David with her at all times, not even allowing Silas to be alone with him.

During a long discussion, which covered a lot of new couple problems, he'd given his word that David was safe. Watching the rise and fall of their chests, she offered a small prayer of thanks that they were both hers.

"Come to bed, I need to hold you," Silas said, opening his eyes. "And I thank the Goddess for you as well. Now bring that fine ass over here so I can get some sleep."

Jasmine chuckled and strode to the bed, ready to fall in his arms. "Hmmm, just so you know, you fail at sweet-talking."

"Hmph," he snorted.

She lay on the custom-made bed next to him, her back to his side. His arms pulled her close.

"I'm going to let Rose deal with the human police detective tomorrow. She's not Jacques, but she's doing a decent job running my office. This will give her some practice dealing with the law," Silas said into the quiet.

She missed his assistant. Jacques had been with Silas for decades, but once he was compromised by Arianna's lure, he didn't trust himself around Silas or the pups. Silas had thought the news of one of his pups being named after Jacques, and that Arianna was dead would be enough for his friend to return. So far, Jacques had turned down all offers to reclaim his old job but did promise to visit soon to meet his namesake.

Jasmine thought of her daughter-in-law, Tyrone's mate, and agreed. "She's smart, a quick learner, and will represent your interests pretty good. Will she still work here when Tyrone takes over as Alpha? Is there an Alpha house, like a governor's mansion or something? Where will they live?" She had wondered about those things ever since Silas told her of his decision to promote her son.

He rubbed her shoulder. "First off, he has been challenged."

She stiffened, not liking the sound of that. "Challenged? Explain."

Silas's grip on her shoulder tightened a bit. She knew he didn't like her tone, but she didn't care for her son being challenged over something he didn't ask for.

"Another wolf wants the Alpha position and is willing to fight for it."

"I thought you appointed the Alphas. What happened to that?" She sensed his frustration through their link, but this was her son and she wanted to know why things were being handled differently.

"I appoint Alphas, but if an Alpha has been trained by me and does not have a position, he can challenge anyone for an open spot. The wolf challenging Tyrone completed Alpha training three years ago and has been serving another Alpha since then. He is within his right to make this challenge."

She calmed a bit but was still worried. "This isn't one of those to the death things, is it? Because Rone didn't ask to be Alpha and he shouldn't be killed because you offered him the position. You could've offered it to one of the Alphas who were waiting around."

He released a long sigh but didn't say anything. There was a lot she didn't understand about wolf politics, but since she and Silas had …this connection, she had been trying to ask questions so she wouldn't be in the dark.

"You are right. I could've chosen one of the other Alphas. There are three who don't have a territory, not including Cameron, who would have been my first choice a year ago. But, with the surge of half breeds, plus wanting an Alpha I trust implicitly at my backdoor, I picked Rone. The fight is not to the death, but it will be brutal. Both wolves are highly trained and fight well. Tyrone does not have to accept the challenge; he can step aside and allow the challenger to take the position. However, as the ruling Alpha of this state, the challenger can demand Tyrone leave West Virginia and never return."

Her eyes shot open. "What? That's not fair. You would allow him to ban Rone?"

"Allow it? No. But he is within his rights to do so. All of this will be explained to Tyrone tomorrow, well, later today. The choice is his, but I think he will fight. He is mated to a strong bitch and will not want to appear weak in her eyes."

"Weak…" Jasmine sputtered leaning up on her elbow. Her eyes narrowed at him. "How would that make him look weak? He didn't ask for the position –"

"His Patron chose him for the position, which is an honor."

She snapped her jaw closed, hearing his voice change. They were dabbling in wolf politics and she had somehow stepped into a pile of goo, offending him. Returning to the pillow and the warmth of his side, she remained quiet, her mind in turmoil. Her boys were adults, she understood that, but they were still her sons.

"He will be fine, sweet bitch," Silas whispered, spooning her. "Stop worrying."

She wiggled closer as she snorted. "Like you're not worried over Cameron. You send a search party to the woods every day looking for any sign of him and are dejected every day they return with no news."

"That's because he's out there somewhere. I feel him but cannot locate him, it's frustrating." His clenched fist rested on her hip and she rubbed it until he relaxed it again.

"Admit it. There are times when worrying over those we love happens whether it makes sense or not." She squeezed the arm draped across her chest thinking of David who had been returned to his blanket on the opposite side of the bed. In a little while, she'd move him beside her.

"Perhaps." He kissed the top of her head.

Just as she'd thought he had drifted off, he spoke. "The next time you speak to the human breeders, leave our link open. I want to hear what they have to say. Plus, there are some questions I want asked."

That surprised her. Not him wanting to eavesdrop, that was becoming their new normal, but wanting to be involved with her questioning was unusual. "Why haven't you talked to them yet?" She knew Julie and the other woman had talked to some of the Alphas already. The third woman, Anita, died before they made it back to the compound. According to the others, she had been sick for a long time. The shock of being hit with the tranquilizers, and then falling on the hard unforgiving ground had been too much for her heart. She never woke up.

"I've been waiting for them to settle, to open up more. They talk to you. I know they have been explaining how your body works and other things dealing with human breeders specifically, but I want to get to the bottom of this."

She frowned. "Bottom? What do you mean? What do you want me to ask them?"

"How did this start? Humans and wolves mating, having pups. It's been going on a long time and I need to know the origins. What's the purpose of mixing the races? Is there a master plot, some type of end game I should know?"

She hadn't thought about that, but then again, for the most part, the changes in her body grabbed most of her focus when she talked to the women. They had years of experience and had explained a lot of what she could and couldn't do. But Silas had a point, maybe they knew more.

"When I was pregnant, and even when I was attempting to rescue you in the caves, they tried to stop me. They wanted to keep the babies safe for some reason. I need to talk to them about that."

"That's a good place to start, just let me know when you're going to talk to them…" he yawned. "So I can sit in on the conversation."

She nodded. "Give me David."

He passed their sleeping son to her and she placed him on the bed next to her before falling asleep.

Chapter 2

Submerging his human side, Tyrese stepped into the club and looked around for Brad and Hank, two of Silas' top security men. He hadn't walked far or been inside long before the hair on the back of his neck stood up. Someone scoped him out pretty hard. He inhaled, analyzing scents. There was a mixture of full-bloods and some half-breeds as well as a few humans in the building.

Cautious, he headed to the bar and ordered a beer. Once he had his drink, he turned and searched for his admirer. His eyes landed on a tall, dark-complexioned wolf sitting alone at a table across the room. She tipped her head to him, her long dreads moving slightly across her shoulders. Even from that distance, he could tell her eyes were an unusual shade of brown, like sherry or whiskey. If he had time, he'd circle back around and check her out. He nodded and continued his perusal of the place. The beat of the music vibrated through the floor. The dimly lit interior was a smokescreen for the humans because wolves had excellent night vision. A mixture of smoke, beer, body musk, and …sex filled the air.

He looked up, the structure had a second floor and the patrons on that level danced close to the rails. At least he thought it was dancing, the more he watched the less certain he became. Many of the participants wore strips of clothing and some were naked. Inhaling again, he realized the scent of sex came from upstairs.

"Nice place, huh?"

Tyrese glanced at the short red-headed bitch standing next to him. By the smell of things, she was either in heat or close to it.

"It's okay," he said in a non-committal tone as his eyes flicked over the band of cloth covering the tips of her breasts while the other strip covered her ass and pussy. There was no question why she was here tonight; she was headed to the second floor.

She inched closer, her body heat and heady scent teased him. "Going upstairs?" she asked in a sultry voice that had him considering taking a climb to the second level.

"Maybe. I'm waiting for some friends." His eyes flicked over her once again; he was interested but not enough to forgo his plans. Tonight he and Silas' bodyguards were putting their pro-active plans in action. Hank and Brad still blamed themselves for not protecting Silas when the caves, which he had been rescuing Cameron from, collapsed and he was pinned beneath the earth. Everyone was on high alert, searching for potential threats to the Patron and his growing family.

She scraped her fingernails across his chest. "I'll see you up there," she whispered huskily. He watched her swing her ass, barely covered by the cloth, slowly toward the stairs and stop. Slowly he dragged his gaze upward to see her smiling at him. Taking another pull of his beer, he winked. If Hank and Brad didn't show in ten minutes, Tyrese would go upstairs.

"What are you doing here?" An unknown voice hissed the question from beside him.

Tyrese eyed the man standing next to him before dismissing him, positive the bug-eyed man wasn't addressing him.

"So, they don't trust me. I'm not forgiven. They sent you to watch me," the man sounded frustrated. He looked around the room as though waiting for someone to emerge from the shadows.

Tyrese still hadn't responded. He glanced at the khaki pants and white short-sleeved shirt the dude wore and was reminded of elementary school uniforms. The gelled back hair, pasty white skin, and hook nose promised this guy would stand out in any crowd. He moved a few steps over to distance himself. The omega rolled his eyes and followed him.

Who the hell was this dude? Just as Tyrese was about to tell the guy to piss off, he spoke.

"Okay, okay... I'm Boggs. Sorry about the attitude. I don't know much about this area, so they were probably right to send one of their own to keep an eye out." This time he eyed Tyrese. "I thought I'd met all the Bennetts, but I don't know you. You're not from Oklahoma are you?"

Hearing his last name on the lips of a weird acting stranger grabbed Tyrese's attention. Boggs had been in contact with the Bennett pack? That wasn't a good thing even if they were Tyrese's kin on his father's side. The Bennetts had gone rogue and were out to destroy the Patron and his family. They were his enemies.

"No." Tyrese scanned the man to see if he could detect a lie. He inhaled deeper to catch a scent of deception and came up empty both times. This guy truly believed the crap he spouted.

"But you smell like a Bennett. Where'd they dig you up from?" The omega acted as if they were friends and Tyrese had no clue who the full blood was.

What were the odds of being picked out of a crowd and identified as rebel kin on the one rare occasion he walked into a club? Slim, yet that's what just happened. It reeked of subterfuge and Tyrese wanted no part of it. He took another two steps to the side.

"I'm not going to stand here and chat with you," Tyrese said roughly.

"Right…right. Sorry about that." He looked around. "The contact's supposed to meet me here in a few minutes. I guess I'll just grab a seat and wait."

Contact? What contact? What meeting? Were the rebels planning something in West Virginia, this close to the compound? Tyrese wondered. Although alarm bells blared in his mind, he knew he had to follow this lead if he had the opportunity. That was the real reason he was here in the first place. Instead of asking what the meeting was about, he said, "Stand here. They'll come to you."

"Good…that's good." The man inhaled. "I'm a little nervous. This is my first job and I want to prove my loyalty to the pack. So when I got this tip, I offered to follow through, you know what I mean? If this information is good, it could tip the scale in our favor, you know what I mean?"

"Hmmm," Tyrese said, thinking fast. He needed to get word to Hank and Brad to stay away so he could follow this lead. He reached out to Tyrone.

"Rone? I need you to contact Brad and Hank, tell them to take a seat somewhere in the club, check around to see if they hear anything, but don't come near me, okay?"

"It's late, Rese."

"I know. I'm meeting them at a club. Get the message to them. I don't want this to blow up in my face."

"What? What's going on?" Tyrone asked, alert.

"Can't say right now. Get the message to them."

"Okay, but stay open. I'm monitoring and if you shut down, I'll be on my way with an angry Rose."

Tyrese sighed through the link. *"Cut the jokes, I'll leave it open. You might hear something I miss. But my wolf is live, human down."*

"Okay."

"Hey, you wanna dance?" The dark female who'd been eyeing him earlier asked the guy standing next to him. Her whiskey-colored eyes flashed at Tyrese and then returned to Boggs. Tyrese wasn't sure how he knew, but he did. This woman was the contact.

"Only if you're doing the monkey."

Tyrese wanted to roll his eyes at the corny line.

"Who's your friend?" She tipped her chin at Tyrese.

The guy looked at him for a moment and then spoke. "Bennett. Call him Bennett."

She gave Tyrese another long look and nodded. "Come over here, we can talk." She turned and walked at a quick clip toward the back of the club and then down a long hall. The sounds of revelry became muted. The clicks of her heels were amplified on the concrete floor. Her reddish-black dreads were in some twisty style that brushed against her shoulder blades. Tyrese eyed her firm round cheeks in appreciation. Muscular, well-formed thighs and calves were encased in tight-fitting jeans. She stopped in front of a door and opened it.

Boggs entered first, and Tyrese waited for her to enter. They stared at each other for a moment, but he wasn't going in that room until she walked in. Finally, with a thoughtful look, she strode into the room and took a seat at the short rectangular plastic white table.

Immediately, Tyrese checked for listening devices, escape routes and any signs of danger. He'd once been trapped in a small room in the local hospital. Silas had constructed the room in such a way Tyrese was able to stand in a small space behind a wall. He saw and heard everything in the larger adjoining area without anyone knowing he was there. He knew from firsthand experience that things were not always as they seemed.

Instead of taking a seat, Tyrese crossed his arms and stood next to the door they'd walked through. Not for a moment did he believe it was the only exit, but it was the only one he knew of right then.

She glanced at him and then gazed at the younger man seated at the table. "Talk to me."

"Whoa, wait a minute." Boggs threw up his hands and shook his head. "We're supposed to exchange information, not me give up what I have with nothing to show for it. I've come a long way, and they're counting on me to give a full report later on. What do *you* have?"

She glanced at Tyrese again. He remained passive, didn't move or acknowledge her furtive glances. "He's making me nervous. Can he step out?" Yeah, like Tyrese believed that. This woman was a pro who would play Boggs like a new guitar if he weren't in the room.

Boggs laughed. "He's a Bennett, they are all like that. I know you've heard of them." He looked at Tyrese.

Tyrese shook his head, signifying he wasn't going anywhere. There was a chance he'd learn something worthwhile. "His pack sent him along to make sure everything went smooth." He paused, leaned back in his chair. "Now what information do you have for me?"

"There's going to be an Alpha challenge soon. The Patron wanted a breed to take over the spot and we're not going to allow that to happen. There's a plan in place to make sure the breed dies even though this isn't supposed to be a fight to the death."

"And this interests me how?" Boggs drawled, obviously not interested in local politics. But Tyrese tensed and he knew Tyrone listened closely.

The woman glared at the hapless man. "There are those who believe the Patron has gone soft. He killed our beloved Alpha because he believed we were better off without breeds. Then he insults us by placing a breed to govern us." She slapped the table. "No. We won't allow it. That's why we convinced Serrano to challenge the breed."

"You? You brought in another Alpha to challenge the Patron's choice?" Boggs' brow rose. "Wow…that's awesome. You plan to kill the Patron's choice."

"He will die in the fight. And then a full-blooded Alpha will rule our state."

Awesome was not the word Tyrese would've used, but he let it pass.

Boggs smiled sadly. "Everyone knows the Alpha position in West Virginia is token since the Patron resides here. I still don't see how your information can assist our cause."

"La Patron will be at the fight."

"So will his security, not that he needs it. You cannot win against the Patron in combat, everyone knows that."

The female shook her head and dropped it into her hands. "Imbeciles, they send me imbeciles," she murmured and then gazed up at Tyrese. "Okay Bennett, I'm done talking to him, he's…he can't see past his ass."

"Hey!" Boggs yelled, his face a mask of anger. She waved him down while holding Tyrese's gaze.

"Why do you think what I said is important?"

"If the Patron is at the event, he is not at home where his pups live."

There was silence as she smiled at him. Tyrese burned with anger but kept his face blank.

"Holy shit."

She glanced at Boggs, who looked wide-eyed at her. "I see why he's here," she said with a smirk. "You are right. It's impossible to win against La Patron without leverage. The only leverage you'll have against him is his pups. From our intelligence, he dotes on his litter." She eyed Tyrese.

Boggs stared at the wall, his mouth moving as a grin split his face. "Take the pups, you rule the Patron." He looked at Tyrese with a maniacal gleam. "Fuck yeah, we can do that. It'll bring him to his knees. Then we can demand he destroy every half-breed, or better yet, make them serve us. Full-bloods rule." He jumped up and offered Tyrese a fist bump, which Tyrese ignored.

"What do you need from us?" Tyrese asked the young woman ignoring the petulant look on Boggs's face.

"Yeah…I was…I was about to ask you that," Boggs said, returning to his chair and slumping forward.

Tyrese couldn't believe anyone had sent this fool to gather information. He must be a rook, and the knight or bishop was on their way or something.

"We would like…" her hand went to her ear and she listened for a moment before standing. "I'm sorry gentlemen, there is a disturbance in the front of the building and I must leave. But I will contact you again so that arrangements can be made." She stared at Boggs. "I am aware we have not completed the bargain. I have shared information, but you have not. The next time we meet, be prepared to answer some questions."

"Sure. No problem," he said, with an offhanded wave.

She nodded. Tyrese opened the door and followed them out of the room. "Where's a safe exit from here?" Boggs asked.

"Follow me." She strode down the darkened, narrow hall and around a corner. She pushed open the door. Without pausing, the young man followed. Tyrese shook his head as he stopped, and inhaled. He scented several full-bloods outside the door. Tyrese waited with his arms folded across his chest and his legs apart to see if they planned to come for him.

"You coming?" the female asked as she returned to the door.

"It depends."

"On?" She tilted her head with a smile.

"On what the others want? If I have to fight my way through some type of initiation, I want to know about it beforehand. Otherwise, I'll pass." He leaned against the wall, fully prepared to return to the front of the club or fight his way through. Either way, he knew Tyrone was with him.

She laughed. "That's good."

A tall, muscular man with long gold dreads walked up next to her, grabbed her by the waist, wrapped his hand in her hair, and kissed her hard. Her arms wrapped around the thick neck and pulled him closer. They broke apart smiling.

"You're done here, baby," the large man said, patting her on the butt. "Go home, put the pups to bed." She leaned forward, kissed him again, and walked off. Tyrese and the large wolf watched her leave.

Then they eyed each other. "Bennett huh?"

Tyrese nodded but didn't speak.

"I'm Leonidas, but call me Leon. My parents had high hopes, but I'm just a simple wolf." He grinned, showing long fangs.

Unimpressed, Tyrese nodded.

"Bring the small one," Leon said, watching Tyrese. Two large men dragged a struggling Boggs to the entry. "He must be a decoy; no one can be as stupid and clueless as him. You're the messenger?"

"Who are you?" Tyrese asked.

"We're representatives of the resistance in this area. We were told the leaders were sending someone to check things out since the last uprising was a disaster and many brave lives were lost."

Tyrese pointed to the struggling man. "He's the rep. I'm here to make sure everything's above board." Tyrone spoke through their connection. *"Let him talk, I want to hear their plans. Plus, we're merged,"* he said as if Tyrese couldn't feel the extra energy.

"You're shitting me," Leon said. "We almost killed him for being stupid enough to walk outside without scenting the air. Even our pups know to do that."

Tyrese shrugged but remained silent.

Leon's golden brown eyes narrowed. "We almost killed him, what would've happened if we'd done that?" Tyrese knew the only reason they hadn't was because of him. He was the unknown factor in all of this. He pushed away from the wall and stared at Leon.

"You'd die." He spoke without rancor and allowed the words to settle. No one spoke, but they watched him closely, then pulled the man closer before pushing him toward Tyrese. Boggs rubbed his neck as he took in the air and stepped behind Tyrese.

"My bitch gave you information, what do you have?"

Boggs opened his mouth and Tyrese grabbed him before he could speak. Plotting against the Patron was asking to die a painful death. He didn't want to be identified as someone involved in a failed coup by anyone overhearing their conversation. "You never speak in the open," Tyrese growled without taking his eyes off the men standing in the door. "Find a safe room to talk or we walk."

Leon nodded and stepped back. Tyrese glanced over his shoulder. "What's your name again?"

"Boggs, why?"

"I just need a name to report, that's all. Follow me." Tyrese scented the air and stepped outside. The moment he cleared the heavy steel door, he spun and jump kicked a large man who'd thought to catch him off guard. Landing, he feinted to the right and gut-punched someone else, knocking him back a few feet. With Tyrone's energy, he jumped high, landed behind the next guy, and broke his leg. Afterward, he spun quickly, the air kissed his face as he kicked out. The loud snap in the otherwise quiet night signified the breaking of an arm or leg, he wasn't sure.

They all moved with the speed and agility of the wolf, but Tyrese had them at a disadvantage, he was fighting with his twin, and they fought dirty and always to win. In the end, he stood above a gasping Leon with his foot on the big man's neck, threatening to break it.

The click of a gun stopped him. "Back up, sweet cheeks, I have a silver bullet that'll have you singing soprano. Let him up."

The bullet wouldn't damage him the way it would a full-blood, but he didn't want to announce his half-breed status to this crew. Tyrese removed his foot, took a step back, and looked into the mocking eyes of the woman who'd been told to leave. He'd scented her just before the attack, so he wasn't surprised.

"You are fast and strong," she said with a hint of awe. Tyrese didn't respond but looked at the parking lot. There had been four of them. They all lay broken and bleeding on the ground. One by one they shifted into wolves to heal. He searched for Boggs and didn't see him at first, but a glint of steel near the cars grabbed his attention.

She had handcuffed the man to the car. If Boggs was the best the rebels could do, this war would be over soon.

"Damn, I feel like I was hit by a Mack truck," Leon said, moving slowly. The other men returned to human before trying to move. "I heard those Bennett men were vicious but damn…" He shook his head, stood, and looked at Tyrese with respect. "It's an honor to meet you, Bennett." Leon nodded.

Tyrese returned the nod.

Leon glanced at the female. "He's good. Let's finish this."

The female lowered her arm and headed to the car. She released Boggs, and together they returned to Tyrese and the other men. "Tell them what you told me," she snapped at Boggs.

"No," Tyrese said, stepping forward. "Not here."

Leon walked toward the doorway. "Let's go." He strode down the hall and opened a wall panel, similar to the one at the hospital. They filed into a different room; Tyrese could tell this was where private meetings were held. He waited until all five men had filed in, plus Boggs and the woman, before he took up his post against the wall.

"Now tell them," the female snarled near Boggs' face. That was not a good sign.

Boggs swallowed hard. "I said all I know is they are coming, but they didn't tell me when or where. They said I would know when they arrived and I should be ready for the attack."

"So they plan to come here and attack the Patron? Is that it?" Leon asked with a thread of disbelief. "Obviously, they haven't heard about the last group who tried that. I wasn't there, but I heard wolves were exploding all over the place from his anger."

"Exploding? Like an explosion?" Boggs asked, looking horrified.

"Dude, this is the Patron we're talking about, the head Alpha. How do you think he got to be the top dog? He's the baddest fucker out there. Has complete control over his energy and channels it like...let's just say you don't want him directing it at you. I wanted no part of a direct attack before, and I don't want one now," Leon said, shaking his head and leaning back in his chair.

"And kill the idea I threw out earlier about messing with his pups," the female said, staring at Boggs. "That was a test to see how ruthless you were." She glanced at Tyrese. "We want no part of messing with his litter. Make sure your people understand that."

Tyrese met her stare and then nodded.

Boggs looked at the faces of the people in the room, frowning. "So what *do* you plan to do?"

Leon leaned back in his chair, looked at Boggs, and then looked at Tyrese. "We've done all we're going to do. We want a full-blood Alpha. As far as the rest, your people coming into West Virginia..." he snorted. "You're on your own."

Chapter 3

The next morning Rose walked into the main nursery and stared at Adam and Jackie. The two babies were fast asleep. "They look like little angels," she said to Jasmine, who stood near the cribs with David in her arms.

"Yeah," Jasmine scoffed. "Asleep, even demons look like angels."

Rose laughed and walked to Renee's crib. "When's Aunt Renee and Mandy coming?"

Jasmine thought of her last conversation with her sister while she changed David's diaper and dressed him in a green and white short set. "In a month I think, during one of her school breaks. I can't remember which one." She laid David in his crib while watching Rose from the corner of her eye. The petite female had pulled her jet black hair back into a bun and wore a cute short-sleeved cinnamon color dress that made her already large eyes appear larger. Jasmine had fallen in love with the feisty Latina when her son Tyrese introduced her to the young girl months ago.

He'd rescued Rose and her younger brother Thorne from some rogues who had killed their mom. Things were a little crazy for a while, both twins thought she was their mate, and Rose wasn't sure either. They finally got things settled, with Tyrone being mated to his Rose. Jasmine was ecstatic her son had found such a sweet, loving girl and thought of Rose as her daughter. Right now, something was on her daughter-in-law's mind. Jasmine waited, she knew it wouldn't take long.

A few minutes later, Rose released a long sigh. Jasmine looked up at her. "What's the matter?"

Rose turned away, blinking fast as her shoulders slumped forward. Her demeanor concerned Jasmine. She rushed to Rose and held her face between her palms. "Rose, what's wrong? Is it Rone?"

Rose shook her head and looked off.

Jasmine relaxed a bit since it wasn't her son. "Is it Thorne? Your sister?"

"No." Rose inhaled and looked at Jasmine. "I'm being silly. I know it, but I can't get my stomach to settle down. I'm so nervous."

Confused, Jasmine's hands fell away. "Why are you nervous? What's silly?" She had no idea what Rose was talking about.

"Silas turned over the office administration to me today. I got a promotion and a raise. First order of business… handle the police investigator who's coming by in about…" she looked at her watch. "Ten minutes to ask questions regarding the death of Robert Merriweather," she said in a deep voice, mimicking Silas.

Jasmine chuckled but understood why the younger woman would be nervous. Robert Merriweather, aka Robbie, along with his partner Mitchell, had kidnapped her. Silas and Tyrese had killed both men during the rescue. Now the long hand of the law was knocking on their front door and Rose had been designated to handle it.

"Just tell him or them the truth, you don't know anything. No matter what he asks about that day, just say you don't know. I assure you, we will all back you up." She patted Rose's shoulder, wishing she could help her in some way. "Congratulations on your promotion, you deserve it. You work long, hard hours every day."

"I know, Rone was complaining the other night but I had to get payroll done." They both turned as the door to the nursery opened and one of the housekeepers stuck her head in.

"Rose, there's a Detective Jenkins here, he says he has an appointment with Mr. Knight."

Rose nodded. "Thanks, I'll be right there." When the door closed, she looked wide-eyed at Jasmine. "He thinks he's meeting with La Patron. What will I do?"

"Tell him Silas is unavailable and in another meeting. But think back, who would set an appointment with Silas and this man? Did you?"

Rose shook her head.

"He's lying," Jasmine said, already disliking the detective.

"What? You're right. I can't stand liars." Rose straightened her spine and winked at Jasmine. "I've got his number." She walked out with her head high.

Concern warred with pride. Jasmine checked on her babies and spoke to the nurses hovering nearby. "I've got a few things to do. I'll be back in a few minutes."

The four women bowed. "Yes, Mistress."

Jasmine hid a grimace as she left the room. As many times as she'd asked them not to do the bowing thing, they still did it, and each time felt awkward. Just as she reached Rose's office she overheard the rude comments from the detective and decided to stay close just in case. Listening to the disdain in his tone, her blood boiled.

"I don't understand why you're meeting with me, Ms. Bennett. You weren't in the forest the day Mr. Merriweather died. You do not know anything. If I didn't know better, I'd think you were trying to hide something, or are you covering for someone?"

"It's Mrs. Bennett," Rose corrected sharply. "And I'm meeting with you because your office called requesting an appointment to discuss the deceased. We agreed. I am answering your questions and you are not pleased with my cooperation. Tell me, Detective, just what were *you* expecting from this visit."

Jasmine beamed in pride as she listened. Although Tyrone and Rose hadn't been married according to human law, Silas had blessed their union which gave Rose the right to take on Tyrone's last name if she chose.

Down the hall she watched Silas, Hank, Tyrese, and Tyrone enter Silas' office. He stopped and gazed at her for a moment. *"What are you up to?"* he asked through their link.

"The detective is giving Rose a hard time, I'm her back up. Kinda like good cop, bad cop. In case you're wondering, I'm the bad cop."

"Never doubted it for a minute." He broke the connection and she focused on the conversation in the room.

"Robert Merriweather's parents are prominent citizens in the community and they are not going away. They are convinced he was the victim of foul play and have offered a substantial reward for information regarding his death. How long do you think it'll be before someone comes forward?"

"I hope soon, Detective. Especially if it will help that grieving family," Rose said, sounding sincere.

There was a moment of silence. "There are rumors, Rose."

"You will address me as Mrs. Bennett or this conversation is over." The chill in her voice could be felt in the hall. Jasmine applauded the younger woman for her stance.

"Mrs. Bennett, there are rumors that strange things are happening up here. I've only been on the local force for three months and no one was willing to handle this case. No one was willing to talk to Mr. Knight. Why do you think that is?"

Jasmine smothered a groan. A new cop out to make a name for himself.

"I have no idea, Detective. You need to talk to your associates, ask them why they're so reticent. I don't see what that has to do with this investigation, and since that's the purpose of this meeting, does that mean you have no more questions?"

"I'm just getting started," he snapped. "There have been sightings of wolves in these mountains, is it possible a wolf killed Merriweather?"

"I don't know, I work in an office. That's your area of expertise, Detective. Do you think a wolf killed that man?"

Jasmine sat in the chair near the door, grinning. So far Rose had put the little twerp on the defense without being rude. If Jenkins was taping the conversation, and she suspected he was, there'd be little aggression on Rose's part.

"I don't know. Have you seen wolves in the area?"

"I suppose so, wolves roam the forest, right? Was this man killed by a wolf?"

"The autopsy report says Merriweather was beaten and eventually died from his injuries. His partner, Mitchell Tyson, was found dead at the bottom of the cave with a bullet in his chest. Both men had been snacks for some of the animals roaming the forest before we recovered their bodies." He paused before continuing.

"Who do you think beat that man to death? The man you work for perhaps?"

"Mr. Knight?" Rose tittered. Jasmine smiled, the girl was working this. "No. Mr. Knight didn't beat anyone, let alone kill them."

"Why do you say that? You sound so sure."

"Because if someone disturbed Mr. Knight, he'd call the police and allow Southerland's finest to handle it for him."

Jasmine's hand flew to her mouth to prevent the bark of laughter that bit of drivel produced. She gave Rose high props for being able to speak such utter bull without laughing in his face. Silas calling on or asking human authorities for anything was a joke.

The murders occurred on Mr. Knight's property –"

"It did not and you know it," Rose snapped. "The least you can do is get your facts straight. You are not the first officer to discuss this horrible crime with us, Detective. We know the bodies were found on government-protected land. If this is a witch hunt, this meeting is over."

"Sit down, Rose. I'm not done talking to you."

Jasmine had had enough. "But she's done talking to you. I have been listening and you have completely disregarded the courtesy afforded you as an officer of the law. You need to get the hell out of here before I call security and have you taken out."

"And you are?" he asked in a condescending tone.

"The woman who is tired of listening to you disrespect her daughter." She looked at the tall, deeply tanned male with his slim muscular build with contempt. His faded blue eyes which looked as though they had seen way too much, narrowed at her.

"I have not disrespected her. You heard wrong." He waved his hand as though her words were pesky bugs, of little consequence.

"If her husband were in this room you wouldn't have called her by her first name, especially after she asked you not to. You have lied and stretched the truth in so many ways it may never see the light of day again. This conversation is over." Jasmine stared at him, telling him with her eyes and posture to get out.

"No…I am not done." He ran his long narrow fingers through his thick, unruly dark brown hair, pushing it back from his eyes. He looked at Rose and then back at her. "Look, I don't know who you are, but you can't just come in here and interrupt our discussion."

Jasmine crossed her arms and looked at Rose. "This is over, if he or his department has any more questions, they'll need a warrant, and this jerk will not be allowed back on this property." Turning, she winked at Rose. If she handled the man physically in any way, Silas would get involved and that would not be good for anyone, especially the detective. "Call Tyrone," she mouthed to Rose.

"Yes, Ma'am." Rose picked up the phone. "I need security to my office."

<<<<>>>>

Silas strode into his office thinking life with Jasmine was never dull. He hoped the detective was on his 'A' game because those two women would have him on the ropes if he wasn't. Taking a seat at his desk, he motioned to the twins and Hank to do the same. He looked out the large picture window at the forest and longed for a brisk run. It had been too long. These days it seemed he was constantly putting out fires instead of preventing them.

He gazed at Tyrese. "Okay, tell me how a night of drinks with the boys turned into a scouting expedition?"

Tyrese crossed his legs. "I was going to meet Hank and Brad for drinks at the club I'd told you about. We planned to keep our eyes and ears open for anything, but for the most part, I just planned to unwind. I'm standing at the bar and this guy walks up, starts babbling, and tells me he can smell that I'm a Bennett."

"You didn't tell me that," Tyrone said.

"It happened before I contacted you. Anyway, that's when I started paying attention." Tyrese recounted everything that'd happened.

"Where's Boggs now?" Silas asked, leaning back in his chair, digesting everything he had heard.

"Brad has him sedated in one of the condos. He won't wake him up until you clear it," Hank said.

Silas nodded. "Alpha Chan warned me that the Bennetts had left his area and were planning an attack against my mate and her sons. Seems he was right, they are recruiting, and in my backyard. Bold fuckers." He glanced at Tyrese. "What did you think of the group who met with you? Can they be turned? Or will I need to destroy them as well?"

Tyrese placed his finger to his lips, took a moment before answering. "That's a tough call. Before the fight, they were all, let's get the Patron. But afterward, they were like, we want no part of him or any plan to overthrow him. They scared Boggs shitless telling him about exploding wolf parts. I thought the dude was going to piss himself."

Tyrone chuckled. "Seems like their gripe is about the Alpha and the challenge."

Hank leaned forward in his seat. "Yeah, is there something they can do to affect the outcome of the fight? They sounded bloody confident." He flicked worried eyes over Tyrone.

Silas thought about it. Even though the twins didn't mention it in front of Hank, he knew they had merged during the fight the previous night. Was it possible Gregorio possessed the same skill? Silas wasn't sure, but he would run a scan before the fight just in case.

"He didn't when he trained here but that was years ago. Besides, it sounds as if these rogues have done something themselves to ensure he wins."

Tyrese nodded. "That was the impression I got. It was hard standing there listening to them talk about destroying my twin and taking my brothers and sisters hostage. I didn't think I'd last to the end of the meeting."

"I'm glad you did, it's important we know what's happening –" Silas looked at Tyrone, who stood and headed for the door. "Life is never dull with my mate," Silas said.

"What happened? What did mom do?" Tyrese asked, watching his brother leave the room.

"She's throwing the detective out. He offended her daughter. Rone was summoned to do the honors."

Hank and Tyrese chuckled. "She won't get in trouble will she?" Tyrese asked a moment later.

Silas deliberately flashed his eyes at him. "With who? The human authorities?" he scoffed. "No, if anyone will get in trouble, it'll be the detective. From what I understand, he's new from out west. One of the boys on the force will teach him some manners."

"Hmmm…can you read him?" Tyrese asked. "Make sure he is who he appears. Seems stupid to walk into somebody's house and deliberately bait them."

Impressed with the line of thinking, Silas had Tyrone bring the detective near the office so he could scan him. Silas' scan wasn't as good on humans, but he could get a decent amount of information. A moment later Silas had Rone escort the detective out. He sent a message through their link to Alpha Jayden in Maryland to make some inquiries while he waited for Rone to return to the office.

"He's angry, swears he will get an order and make us all come downtown to answer questions. According to him the Merriweather's have clout and will use it. Blah, blah, blah…" Tyrone said dryly as he re-took his seat. "Now, about this challenge, are you sure I can't kill this guy? Because I don't want him sniffing around later causing problems."

Silas wasn't surprised at the level of confidence in the young pup. Both of the twins were tall, brawny, and top-notch fighters; few could beat either in a fair fight. Pity his mate couldn't hear her son, perhaps she wouldn't worry so much. "It's not a deathmatch, but as Alpha, you can ban him from the state."

That seemed to placate the young man. Silas turned to other pressing matters. "I don't like having rebels this close to my litter. We will work out security rotations and I will scan every person who works on this property. I will take no chances with the lives of my mate or pups. Is that clear?"

"Yes, Sir." The men all answered as one.

"I'll scan Boggs. I cannot fathom sending anyone as inept as you described to do reconnaissance work. He may be a plant or have a bug implanted in him somewhere."

"That makes more sense," Tyrone said, slowly drawing out his words. "That way they can listen to everything, possibly see things without setting foot on our territory. If he's captured…" he shrugged. "They care nothing for him. No big deal."

"Like the game of chess, he's just a pawn," Tyrese said. "First in the line of fire and expendable."

"Can you scan him while he's under or does Brad need to bring him out?" Hank asked.

"I want him disoriented, that way he won't shield. I don't want to alert them that we have him and are accessing his memories."

"What if…what if there's something more?" Tyrese said looking at him with a frown. "What if he's locked and loaded?"

Silas's gut tightened at the implication. Had the rebels become that savvy? He wasn't sure but didn't want to chance it. "Internal explosives?"

Tyrese nodded. "Could be, I mean think about it. Suicidal bombings are not that rare. He mentioned something about proving himself to the pack. What if this is his way to do that?"

"But he'll be dead and won't know if he proved himself," Tyrone said.

"Suicide doesn't make sense to me so I can't answer that," Tyrese said.

"Didn't you scan him?" Tyrone asked.

"Just a handheld scan at the condo. It didn't go off," Tyrese said. "It'd be just my fucking luck the bastard's loaded and the scanners didn't pick it up. That's a whole 'nother set of problems."

"Most def," Tyrone said morosely.

As long as it was a possibility Silas would treat it as such. He contacted Brad through their link. *"Is there a way to move Boggs to the bomb shelter in the basement?"*

"Yes, Sir. I can do that right now. You want me to keep him hooked to the IV?"

"Yes, if possible. The most important thing is to get him to the basement, lock him in the bomb shelter."

"Yes, Sir."

Silas released a breath as he looked at a worried Tyrese. "Hopefully this is just a precaution. I can scan him once he's secured."

"Understood. This whole thing smacks of a Trojan horse kinda thing. Him picking me out, the meeting, the information they gave him isn't a secret per se, then the fight."

"The fight was real," Tyrone interjected.

"Yeah, that was real, they would've beaten me to a pulp if they could."

"Or they were trying to call your wolf. Maybe they wanted to see your wolf," Hank said. "Humans remember faces, wolves remember scents and a wolf's scent is his signature. If I wanted to know who you really were, I'd track down your true scent."

"That's something to think about," Silas said and then paused to listen to Jayden's report. He thought about the information for a minute and then looked at the men in front of him.

"I asked Alpha Jayden to do some research into Detective Jenkins for me a few minutes ago. Some things in the man's mind disturbed me. First off, he knows we are wolves. He knows I'm the Patron. He knows you are breeds, and the reason he knows this is he's a breed himself."

"What? I didn't smell anything," Tyrone said, looking at his brother, who shrugged.

"I smelled his wolf. It's a timid thing, scared and starved. Initially, I wasn't sure what animal he was until my wolf confirmed it. That's the first thing I need to find out, why no one detected his wolf. He should have scented Jasmine and immediately known who she was, but he had no idea. So I have a malfunctioning half-breed with a sick wolf whom we can't scent. That's... that's major."

"No way I'd have allowed that bastard around my mate," Tyrone said with feeling.

"He was with my mate as well," Silas said, tamping down his anger. "But here's another thing. He's from Washington state, a small town in the mountains called Dalista. There's a decent-sized pack living nearby. It's the pack we discovered when we confirmed Arianna's story."

"The one where the bitches abused her?" Tyrese asked.

"I don't have all my notes, but I believe that's the one," Silas said, wondering what Jenkin's end game was. This placed a different spin on things. The Detective's wolf was so weak; Silas was unsure how much of the man he could control through his animal.

"You think he ever shifted?" Hank asked.

"Is he Arianna's seed? Is he here for revenge?" Tyrone asked.

"Do we take him out? Will he suffer from an accident?" Tyrese asked.

Silas's brow rose at the blood-thirsty suggestion although he shouldn't be surprised. Of the two, Tyrese was by far the most volatile with everyone except family, or more succinctly, his mom.

"What?" Tyrese asked, looking at Hank, his brother, and then Silas, who stared at him with raised brows. "That man was in this house, talked to my mom with my brothers and sisters in the same building. Now I find out he's not who he claims? That's family, and I'd take the motherfucker out in a heartbeat over them."

"Amen," Tyrone said, offering his twin a fist bump.

Silas closed his eyes and completed a search of the house, seeking out any devices Jenkins may have slipped past the metal detectors or his highly trained security. Finding nothing, he glanced at Tyrese, who sat calmly in his chair with his legs crossed, hot tension flowing off him in waves.

"Let's hold off on sending Jenkins to meet Arianna in the after-life for a mother-son reunion for a while. I have some questions he may be able to answer. I may need to pull his wolf and strengthen him first."

"Capture him, pull his wolf, and keep him for a while?" Hank said, grinning. "I like that idea. Where do you want to keep him?"

"Near the training compound. His wolf is timid, so he might be skittish. Let Froggy work with him, he has the best success dealing with injured animals," Silas instructed.

"Yeah, Frogs has a nice touch," Hank said. "When do you want this done, Sir?"

Silas leaned back in his chair and thought of everything he had committed to do this week. "After I check Boggs out, I'll let you know. Maybe by the end of this week. I have to make sure they give him hell at work first, so he'll be in a real pissy mood. Maybe his anger will trigger his wolf."

"If you need help, let me know," Tyrone offered Hank.

Silas received a message from Brad and released a sigh. "Okay, Boggs is incarcerated in the bomb shelter. Brad still has him connected to the IV, so he's still out of it. I'll check his body while he's out and if he's clean of explosives, we'll bring him out slowly and I'll read his mind."

Chapter 4

Silas, Tyrese, Tyrone, and Hank entered the bunker beneath the guest condominiums. Brad waited in front of a heavy steel door and bowed at Silas' approach.

"Is he still knocked out?" Silas asked, pointing to the door.

"Yes, Sir. You can view his vitals from here." Brad pointed to a small closet-sized room behind the much larger, steel and concrete-reinforced one. "He's sedated, Sir."

Silas glanced at the screen and threw out his senses, trusting them more than the electronic devices. He couldn't get an accurate read through all the thick walls.

"Open the door." Silas stepped out of the way so Brad could get past him to carry out his request.

Tyrese and Hank flanked him while Tyrone bought up his rear. He withheld a sigh at their hovering, but let it go. The twins were just as bad as Brad and Hank, who had been with him for over a decade.

"A little room, please." He glanced at them and focused on the room. He stepped closer, stuck his head inside. There was a soft swishing sound, humans probably could not hear it, but his wolf did. Silas jumped back and slammed the door shut. The clicking of the automatic lock had just engaged when a loud boom shook the area, sending sprinkles of dirt from the ceiling to the floor.

Silas lost his footing and fell on top of Tyrese, who pushed him aside and covered his back. Hank crawled over and covered the rest of him. Once again, Silas wanted to yell. Since when did he need protection? But he'd read the remorse in Hank's eyes when he'd returned from being buried beneath the caves, and no matter how many times he explained that it wasn't Hank's fault, the guilt remained. But still, this was bordering on ridiculous. His very name, Patron, signified he was the protector, the one who offered safety, yet his security detail treated him like he was an untried pup.

He pushed against the floor and stood, shaking his men from his back. He had more important things to deal with. Someone penetrated his defense. He needed to get on top of this pronto. Even now he heard footsteps running in his direction.

"*Silas? What happened?*" Jasmine asked, trying to hide her nervousness.

"*Someone sent in a Trojan horse, but thanks to Tyrese the damage was contained.*"

"*Tyrese?*"

"*Your boys are fine. There was only one death and it wasn't any of mine. Rest easy, take care of my litter. I will come to you after I clean up this mess and some other things."*

"I need to see you are okay."

He looked around the area, the walls seemed okay, but he wanted an engineer to come and verify that. *"Call me in an hour, I'll try to meet you for a quick kiss, but my day just got busier."*

She sighed. *"I know. I'll make it a quick kiss and a fast grope."*

He laughed. *"Later."* He searched the area for Brad but didn't see him. "Brad?"

The man wasn't in the small room or the open hall. He looked at the twins and Hank, who were sitting up slowly, rubbing the back of their necks. "Where's Brad?"

"He's not in that room?" Tyrone asked.

Silas stared at him with a raised brow. "No, that's the first place I looked," he snapped. "Find him," he yelled to get them moving faster. The three men jumped up and scattered, searching the halls. Silas looked at the door and shook his head, Brad had been on the outside when he opened the door for Silas to look in, hadn't he?

A sick feeling rose in his stomach. He walked toward the door as though tethered by an invisible string and opened it. The smell of burnt flesh, acid, and blood pinched his nostrils. What had they used to make that bomb? He wondered as additional scents assaulted him. There was nothing left of Boggs. Every part of the unfortunate man painted the walls and dripped from the ceiling. Silas stepped back when heard a shout from Hank.

"Found him." Silas heard a curious scraping against the concrete and went to investigate. Hank dragged a bloody, unconscious Brad into the hall and released him gently onto the concrete. "He got hit with something in his chest that torpedoed him down the hall. He hasn't shifted yet."

Silas looked at Brad and searched for his wolf. The animal whined and snapped to break free. "Easy…easy," Silas said softly as he pulled Brad's wolf. The animal whimpered and lay on its side for a moment. Silas walked over, stooped, and placed his palms on both sides of the wolf's head to hold him steady. Closing his eyes, he sent a steady stream of healing energy into the animal. The damage to Brad's chest had been severe, he'd probably need to rest for a day or so, but after that, he should be fine.

He removed his hands and stood slowly. The room shifted for a second before he got his bearings. Tyrese didn't touch him but he did take a step closer. Silas straightened and looked at Brad lying on the floor. "Take him to his room so he can rest. Let him stay wolf until he crawls into bed. He can shift later."

Hank nodded and snapped his fingers at the wolf. The wolf didn't move, instead, he looked at Silas and then at Hank.

"Go with Hank now so you can heal. I need you at one hundred percent." The wolf whined but stood slowly. As he walked off, he looked back at Silas repeatedly as though asking him to reconsider. Once the wolf and Hank turned the corner, Silas looked at the room and then at the twins.

"When I looked inside, it activated whatever was inside Boggs." Tyrese's brow rose. "I heard a soft whirring noise, which I assume was a trigger."

"No…" Tyrese said as his finger tapped his jaw. "You were the trigger. Whatever was inside Boggs, was attuned to you specifically. Damn it," Tyrese growled as he smacked his fist against the wall. "We didn't pick up on it." He looked at Silas and then Tyrone. "They have a device that we cannot detect until it's activated."

"Not good," Tyrone added, staring at the door to the room.

Silas agreed. How had the Bennetts come up with such a sophisticated device? Remembering his short visit with them not too long ago, he wouldn't have thought they had that much brain power between them collectively.

"Something's off," Tyrone said. "I met my kin and I don't see them doing this." He looked at Tyrese. "Think, did Boggs say the Bennetts sent him, or was it the rebels?"

Tyrese frowned in apparent concentration. "He was nervous, said they didn't trust him. He wanted to prove his loyalty to the pack. Claimed I smelled like a Bennett, but he never came right out and said the Bennetts sent him."

"I bet someone else sent this guy."

"Someone working alongside our dear kinfolk?" Tyrese asked Silas.

"Could be, or it could be whoever started this whole fucking game," Silas said, pissed they still had no clue who'd started breeding humans and wolves and why. "The guy in the caves who took Jasmine said he had two offers…"

"That's right," Tyrese said. "One to save mom and one to kill her and her pups. He said two men offered him a deal if he'd kill mom. I wondered why he told you that. He had to know it would be his death warrant."

Silas had wondered about that as well. When he'd found the man, Tyrese was right behind him with a gun pointed at the guy. So it wasn't as if he'd had a chance to escape. "You think someone's trying to organize the rebels? This seems like a coordinated effort. They gambled one of you or one of my inner circle would show up. Then this guy shows up on a kamikaze mission, starts a conversation, says enough to get you hooked, and then allows himself to be taken by you and brought into the compound."

Tyrese ran his hand over his face. "When you say it like that, I feel like a damned sucker. I should've picked up on... something."

"It was a precise plan with lots of players. They tested you, made sure you were the real deal, and then served Boggs up for a death mission. Poor guy probably had no idea he was packing whatever that was inside him," Silas said, slapping Tyrese on the back.

"So the woman and those guys, they were a part of it?" Tyrone asked.

"Probably," Silas said. "They followed Tyrese last night and watched him and Boggs enter his condo in town. From the reports I have, they are still watching the building."

"I bet they try and break in to look around," Tyrese said, smiling.

"If they do, they won't be leaving. That unit is set to destruct," Tyrone said.

"Yeah, but they're probably feeling pretty good since this bomb went off. And knowing you were the only possible trigger might make them over-confident," Tyrese added.

"We need to know what was in that explosive and find a way to detect and destroy it. I don't want to think what could happen if that thing was placed inside a lot of wolves and they were sent out to play or fight. It would be a disaster. Too many people would get hurt." Silas looked at the twins. "Get the cleaning crew and forensics down here. I want this area treated as a crime scene. I want everything tagged and bagged. Tell them to find some clue as to what was in that fucking bomb and how we missed it."

"Yes Sir," Tyrone said, whipping out his phone to call Rose.

"I want to talk to one of the people from the other night. Make it happen. Find him or her and bring them to that room after it's clean." Silas looked at Tyrese. "Got that?"

"Yes Sir."

Silas walked out and took the lift to find Jasmine. He was ready for that kiss and grope.

Chapter 5

Jasmine stood waiting in the hall to meet him. Her eyes roamed over his tall frame searching for anything out of place. She knew it was overkill; she had already examined him through their link and on a mental plane, knew he was fine. But still, she needed eyes and hands confirmation that he was okay. Flashes of him buried beneath the rubble hit her at the most inconvenient times, reviving the breathtaking fear she had felt that day.

Once he reached her, he pulled her into a tight embrace and just held her for a few seconds. Inhaling, she breathed him in, basking in his earthy scent, watering her dry areas. He opened his link and breathed her in as well. Thoughts of her warmth filled him, causing him to open as the rarest flower. She smiled at the imagery and held him tighter.

"I love you," she whispered, kissing his shoulder.

He pulled back, his eyes twinkling as they looked down into hers. "If you're going to say those words, your kisses should be on my lips."

"I agree." She leaned up as his mouth slanted across hers and delved into hers. He tasted so good, like coffee with lots of cream. His hand eased down her backside and squeezed as he broke the kiss.

"I said I wanted to grope you," she complained good-naturedly while rubbing his rear cheeks.

"Yes you did, but then I got to thinking of this voluptuous –"

Laughing, she covered his mouth as Rose walked by chuckling. "Silas, behave," she whispered.

"This is me behaving," he said, squeezing her again.

"I know." She stepped back and gave him one last look over. "Okay, you can go back to work now, I've gotten my fix."

He grabbed her and pulled her close. "Maybe you have but I haven't, let's go to our room for a quickie?" He rubbed against her, allowing her to feel his desire.

She looked at him with true regret. "Sorry I can't. I'm on my way to talk to Julie and Siseria while the babies are taking a nap. Miracle of miracles, they are all sleeping at the same time. You know how rare that is?"

He pulled her toward their bedroom. "That's because they want Daddy to bury himself into Mommy. Come on, you don't want to disappoint our pups, do you?" He looked at her with a saucy grin and winked.

"Using your kids to get laid? That's low, Silas." She slapped his chest and ran around him, headed down the hall. "Keep your ears open for this and the other..." she pointed to his crotch. "I'll take care of that later. You can count on it."

He shook his head and walked down the hall toward his office.

"Don't pout baby, it's not attractive," she teased through their link.

"I'm not pouting."

"Yeah, yeah you are," she countered. She made her way through the underground tunnel to the security complex, pretending she didn't see the guard following her.

"What do you plan to ask these women?"

She smiled at his change of subject. The man did not appreciate being teased. *"We went over this last night,"* she chuckled. When he didn't join in she rolled her eyes and answered seriously. *"I will discuss human breeders and see if they have any information regarding how the mating began."*

"There may be something else they know, but I'll wait and see how the conversation flows. Is Jarcee behind you," he asked, referring to her behemoth guard. She would swear Silas had grabbed this guy off a farm somewhere, he was that massive. Standing at almost seven feet, he was as wide as Tyrone and Tyrese standing side by side. It didn't make any sense. Silas said he was some type of rare wolf breed. She believed it.

"Yes, he's behind me. I'm almost there, don't distract me."

He snorted but didn't say anything.

Her guard strode in front of her, nodded, and proceeded to unlock the gate leading to the security wing of the estate. Once he swung the gate open he stood to the side, allowing her to walk in, and then relocked it behind them.

They walked in relative silence, the sounds of their footsteps clicking on the concrete the only noise. Jasmine touched her voice-activated recorder and inhaled. Collectively, these women had information that was critical to the health and well-being of their children. That meant she would be as ruthless as her mate to gather the data.

Beads of sweat graced her forehead from the hotter temperatures in the tunnel and the lengthy walk. She rubbed her palm against her pant leg as they stopped once again. Jaree punched in a code and they entered the much cooler section where the women were kept.

Her security guard opened the door, walked in, and did a sweep. He returned and waited for her to enter. She thought about asking him to wait outside but knew that wouldn't fly, and Silas would be pissed. So she motioned for him to stand near the door as she walked further into the area.

"Julie? Siseria? Are you ladies decent?" she called out and sat in the overstuffed visitor chair facing the cells. Each cell had a bed, shower, sink, and toilet. She watched as the women rose from their beds slowly, blinking against the light until they saw her.

"Jasmine?" Julie said hesitantly as she scooted to the end of the bed. "How have you been? I see you've had the babies. That's wonderful." She paused. "Are they all okay?"

Jasmine thought the framing of that question was strong, but before she could answer, Silas spoke through their link. *"Tell her they are all fine. I don't want them to know about David."*

As if she would tell them that, she scoffed. "They are well, how are you?" She looked at the thin woman and wondered if she had lost weight since her capture or if she had always been that thin.

"Eh…I'm as good as can be expected." She tipped her jaw at Jasmine. "For a prisoner."

Jasmine nodded and glance to the next cage. "And you Siseria? How are you?"

"Same as Julie, same as Julie." The woman's eyes darted around the room as she rocked back and forth. Jasmine stared a few moments longer, wondering if the woman's mind had been broken from mistreatment at the hands of wolves.

No one spoke for several moments. Jasmine was content to let them start the conversation and then she'd lead it in the direction she needed it to go.

"How many children did you have?" Julie asked.

"Four."

"All the same? Boys? Girls?"

"Two of each."

Siseria gasped. Julie shushed her.

Jasmine watched but didn't say anything.

"Are you going to breed more children?" Julie asked.

"I don't know. I have to think about it."

"That's the trick, you know," Julie said, moving closer to the edge of the thin mattress. Jasmine got a good look at her face for the first time and gasped softly.

"What happened?" Silas asked.

"Nothing, I just saw the claw marks on her face."

"Oh yeah. I heard about that. Ask her what she means by the trick," Silas said.

"No, I don't know what you're talking about," Jasmine said, looking Julie in the eyes.

"Thoughts. They are the trick for regulating our bodies," Julie said softly. The claws had slashed from the side of her eye down to her chin, splitting her upper and lower lips. The wound had healed leaving the lip split and deep marks on her face. Jasmine wondered why it hadn't healed cleanly.

"Thoughts," Jasmine said, tearing her gaze from Julie's eyes and looked at her brutalized face.

"Yes. Think back on when you were impregnated with the Patron's seed. You had to have thought of children, maybe remembered fondly when your sons were younger, and a desire was birthed from that. It would have set your pheromones in action preparing your womb to conceive. You control your body. When you want children again, just think about it and give your body permission."

It couldn't be that simple. "Birth control pills, IUD?"

"Won't work. The only birth control for us is in our minds. We use untapped energy from our brain and focus it inward. It's not that much different from what the Patron does. Although from what I've heard, his energy levels are off the charts," Julie said emphatically. "But back to breeders, most don't know how to tap into their natural energies and think they don't have a choice. Not that it's easy," Julie warned. "Women have a natural desire to reproduce. You have to fight against that for this to work."

Siseria nodded. Her limp, dull blonde hair barely moved. "Julie's right."

I need to tell mama about this, Jasmine thought as she watched the woman lick her lips repeatedly without taking a break. *What's wrong with her?*

"*What?*" Silas asked.

"*She keeps licking her lips.*"
"*Ask her.*"

Normally, Jasmine would never ask such a personal question, but time was of the essence and she needed to be sure the woman didn't have some kind of infection or something. "Why do you keep licking your lips?"

"Huh?" Julie said.

Jasmine pointed at Siseria. "She keeps licking her lips. Why?"

"She wants to breed but is fighting the need."

Jasmine jerked back and looked at Julie. "What? She wants babies and is fighting it? Why the hell is she doing that?"

Julie crossed her arms and pursed her lips. "Because we are committed to never birthing pups again. Things are escalating and we don't plan to be casualties of war."

"What the hell are you talking about and what does that have to do with her wanting to have sex and get knocked up?" Jasmine asked, exasperated with the circles in the conversation.

Julie's hands flew up and waved around the room. "All of this is for the cause, Jasmine. I was recruiting you for the side of good, but you…" she pointed at Jasmine and sniffed. "You choose the animals. Well, you're going to wish you had listened to me. Just wait," she said self-righteously.

Jasmine leaned forward in her chair and pointed. "You wanted me to give you my babies. Hell, I don't know you. Why would I give a stranger my kids? You crazy."

"To save them. To prepare them, you selfish bitch," Julie yelled.

Glaring at the woman, Jasmine jumped up wishing she could just smack the woman and leave, but that wouldn't get them the answers they needed. She needed to be mature about this. Her security guard made a step in her direction, she waved him down.

"Prepare them for what?" Jasmine asked in what she hoped was a calm voice.

"Good girl." She heard Silas say.

Julie laughed and lay back on the bed. "I'm not telling you."

Gritting her teeth, Jasmine glanced at Siseria and then at Jaree. She arched her brow. Somebody in this room was going to tell her what she needed to know today. "Jaree come here."

The large guard strode forward and nodded. Jasmine glanced at Siseria. The woman had stopped licking her lips and stared hungrily at the tall blond man with mint green eyes who stood in front of her.

"Stop… shoo, go away you big wolf," Julie screamed, jumping off her bed and running to the bars between their cages. "No Siseria, no." She reached for the other woman and failed, but that didn't stop her from trying. "Leave her alone, just leave her alone."

"Go back," Jasmine said softly to her guard, feeling guilty at the look of longing in Siseria's eyes. "Step outside for a minute, give her a chance to pull it together."

He looked at Siseria and then at her before opening the door and taking a step outside. She noticed the door wasn't closed tight but doubted the women would pick up on it.

"Prepare them for what?" she asked Julie again.

"I can't tell you." The woman sounded genuinely regretful.

Jasmine nodded. "Siseria, what did y'all want to prepare my children for? If you don't tell me, I'm going to call three men in here and they will not leave until you are breeding. Is that what you want?"

"Stop it, damn you. Can't you see she's weak?" Julie yelled.

Jasmine thought of her four kids upstairs in bed and the bomb that'd went off less than an hour ago. The lives of everyone she loved were in jeopardy. *Weakness worked for her.* "Siseria, why do they want my babies?" she asked again in a more demanding voice.

"They are going to determine the future of the war. If we can teach them the ways of Nicromja, then the breeds will defeat the wolves. But you have sons and daughters, that complicates matters. We don't know which will lead. Your house may be divided."

What the hell? "Who or what is Nicromja?" Jasmine asked.

Siseria smiled. "He is our Patron."

"She answered your questions, now leave her alone. Siseria lay back and rest. Be easy," Julie said, but Siseria didn't respond. She continued sitting on the edge of the bed, looking straight ahead and licking her lips.

"A Patron like Silas?" Jasmine asked, not liking the idea of two of them walking around.

"No. Silas is a toy for his Goddess. Ask the Goddess who Nicromja is."

Puzzled, Jasmine leaned forward. "Why ask her, don't you know?"

Siseria looked her in the eye, Jasmine gasped at the raw pain she saw reflected there. Whatever was going on with this woman was taking a serious toll. "Who changes life from the seed? Humans? Wolves? No. We are pawns in this game. It is being played on a chessboard none of us can see."

Jasmine froze as the wisdom of the softly spoken words settled on her. "Okay." There wasn't a whole lot she could say to that.

"Silas ask your Goddess about Nicromja."

"Most definitely," he said tightly. *"Get more information about the pups."*

"Babies," she corrected automatically. Inhaling, she glanced at a wound up Julie as she spoke to Siseria. "What makes you think one of my children will determine the outcome of the war? Why can't it be one of yours? Or Julie's? They're breeds."

"Siseria, shut your mouth. Do not answer her," Julie gritted out.

Siseria looked at Julie and then at Jasmine. "I can't tell you the answer." She looked down and away.

Jasmine nodded. "Jaree?"

He stepped inside. "Yes, Mistress?"

"Please remove her and take her to an empty cell in the next block." He nodded and walked toward the cells.

"You are a horrible person, Jasmine. How could you do this to her? If he touches her…you know what will happen," Julie screamed.

Siseria watched the big guard approach and Jasmine would swear she was drooling. He reached for Siseria's cage and Jasmine stopped him.

"No, not her. The other one." She pointed to Julie and the woman went ballistic, running around the small space trying to escape Jaree's long reach. She was no match for the huge man and within moments he had the struggling woman over his shoulder. He nodded to Jasmine as he removed the screaming woman from the room.

Jasmine brushed her pants to give Siseria a second to collect herself. "Now, please answer my question. Why did the baby have to be mine?"

Siseria closed her eyes and swallowed hard. For a moment, Jasmine wasn't sure the woman would answer. "The child had to come from the Patron's seed since this will be his ultimate downfall. The egg had to come from a human capable of birthing wolves because the child must be a half-breed. Your Patron is over 300 years old and favored by the Goddess, yet his seed never took root because he despised humans. You are his Eve and your babes are the forbidden fruit that will destroy him."

Gut punched, Jasmine pinched the bridge of her nose for a few minutes before eyeing the woman. The words rang false and Jasmine lashed out. "You are lying to me. You made this up so Julie won't be mad at you." Jasmine stood. "Our deal is off. Jaree," she yelled.

Siseria jumped up from the edge of the bed and ran to the bars. Her knuckled turned white beneath the pressure. "Please no…please. I can't take it. As much as it pains me to admit it, I'm not strong like her or the others were. I have told you the truth…except…"

"Except what? Because I need some good news after that bombshell you just dropped."

Siseria looked up at her. "Everything is fluid and depends on a series of combinations. Choices made, the environment, people we meet. That's why we wanted the children to control all those things."

Jasmine looked at the woman and then looked at the wall, her mind racing. "So basically what you're saying is that in the right environment, none of what you predicted will happen," Jasmine said, pissed at the level of adrenaline coursing through her body from that whack announcement.

Siseria licked her lips and looked around the room before speaking. "Here's the thing you have to remember. Jacob and Esau were twins, yet they divided a nation. There is potential to do both good and evil in every person, it is how the seeds are watered that make the difference. A wise king said there is nothing new under the sun, this is an old game being played out, the difference is the players."

Jasmine considered everything the woman said and could tell by his silence Silas was as well. *Basically, she's saying this is out of our hands, we are all pawns and must play the game to survive,*" she said to Silas.

"You believe she's telling the truth?"

Jasmine eyed Siseria, who had returned to the edge of her bed and was licking her lips again. Her eyes flicked all over the room, it gave Jasmine the creeps. *"Some, but not all."*

"I agree."

"I definitely don't like your destruction being the result," Jasmine said.

"That part doesn't sit well with me either."

"If what Julie says is true and we control our bodies, why are you in such a bad state?" Jasmine asked the twitching woman.

Siseria wrapped her arms around herself tight. "My mate is near. He always finds me and he's close. I can sense him. He's close and I can't block him out."

"What?" Silas yelled. *"Leave now, Jasmine."*

The woman made her nervous. "Jaree?"

"Yes, Mistress?"

"I'm ready to leave now," she said, heading toward the door.

He waited until she was close and led her out the room. Jasmine glanced back at the chair to make sure the small listening device she placed in between the cushions couldn't be seen. Once they had cleared all the gates and were back in the tunnels she gave Jaree his instructions. "In about an hour, have Julie returned to her cell and I want every conversation between those two monitored."

"Yes, Mistress." He picked up his phone and made the arrangements.

Jasmine pondered Siseria's predictions during the walk back to her living quarters. Part of it was common sense; aside from the occasional mad scientist you see on TV, God was the only one to successfully change human biology. If some kind of cosmic chess game was being played, there wasn't a whole lot they could do about it other than hope to be on the winning team. Silas would get more information from the Goddess and they would take it from there.

But this thing with the kids. The Jacob and Esau reference, that bugged her, and she couldn't put her finger on the reason why. Was it because David was sickly and the rest of the kids weren't. But Silas said David would be okay. So he wouldn't always be sick. What was it Julie and Siseria said…something about a sign or a mark? None of her children had any distinguishable marks.

She cleared the elevator and walked toward the nursery. When she stepped inside she wasn't surprised to see Silas and the twins sitting in rocking chairs, holding babies while a nurse changed Renee.

"Hey, guys." She strode to Silas and met his lips for a kiss, then she placed a kiss on Adam's forehead.

"I don't want anyone to know about the conversation with the human breeders yet, not until I talk with the Goddess. We are ramping up security because of the bomb. I'll tell you more about it tonight," Silas said through their link.

She nodded and went to greet the twins.

"Hi, Mom," Tyrone and Tyrese called out. She leaned down to Tyrone and he kissed her cheek while Tyrese reached over and kissed the other side. She brushed David's dark curls from his forehead and kissed him, and then turned to kiss Jackie in Tyrone's arms.

"Everything okay?" she asked as she took a seat.

"Yeah, everything's good. We have our best planning sessions after we spend a little time with the pups, so we'll be doing some brainstorming as soon as Hank gets here to handle Renee," Silas said.

"Well, I'll go do a little eavesdropping on our guests and see if I can learn anything useful." She leaned down and brushed her lips across Silas' as she sent him a message. *"I don't want to be your Eve, but the idea of walking about naked with you is all kinds of sexy."*

He coughed and cleared his throat as she headed for the door. *"I have a rising boner with my son in my lap. You will pay for that, sexy Mama."*

She looked at him over her shoulder as she reached the door. *"I'll hold you to that, Wolfie."*

He sputtered through their link as she left the room and headed for Rose's office. Rose was on the phone when she walked in.

Chapter 6

"Thank you, we appreciate any assistance you can give us in this matter." Rose hung up and looked at Jasmine with a grimace. "Detective Jenkins is turning out to be a royal pain in my ass. He's got the Merriweather's thinking the Patron was somehow involved in the death of their son. So the police chief can't close the investigation without serious blow-back right now. I told the chief, Jenkins is not permitted on our property without a warrant and the chief agreed."

Jasmine sat in one of the smaller leather chairs facing Rose. "Didn't Silas read Jenkins?"

"I don't know," Rose said. "Did he?"

"Silas, did you read Jenkins?" Jasmine asked through their link.

"Yes, why?"

"Rose just talked to the police chief and Jenkins is stirring up a pot of mess with the family of the dead guy. What'd you find?"

"He's a breed but his wolf's sick. I've got some things in the works to deal with Jenkins."

"Hmmm, you might want to step it up because he's gunning for you."

"Who isn't these days?"

Jasmine didn't have an answer for that and left it alone. Instead, she sent a wave of warmth through their link to remind him he wasn't alone. She was glad he had Tyrone and Tyrese to help him with some of the madness.

"Jenkins is a half-breed," she told Rose.

"What?" Rose jerked back, her eyes widening. Frowning, she said. "I didn't smell his wolf."

Jasmine shrugged, glad she lacked that ability. "Silas said the wolf's sick." Her thoughts traveled to the women in lockup. Silas didn't want anyone to know the things they'd discussed. But her spidey senses were tingling, something was off about that entire conversation with Siseria. She couldn't put her fingers on it and it was going to drive her crazy until she figured it out. She needed to find a spot to listen to Julie and Siseria's conversations. Julie would be back in the cell soon, she needed to get situated before that happened.

"I need a room to listen to the women downstairs. I left a bug in the chair."

"You didn't have to do that," Rose said. "Those rooms have audio and video in place. I can set you up in a secure spot where you'll be comfy. Have you had lunch?" Rose asked, rifling through a steel box of what sounded like keys.

"No, not yet." Jasmine wondered why Silas hadn't mentioned the surveillance equipment before. Not that she told him she planned to leave the listening device Tyrese had given her yesterday, but he could've listened and watched the monitors instead of through their link.

"I'll have the kitchen prepare you, what? Sandwich? Salad? Pizza?" Rose stood, holding a ring of keys.

"Club sandwich and some of those sweet potato fries with a bottle of water will be good, thanks. I appreciate it," she answered, standing as well.

Rose tapped the small device in her ear and placed Jasmine's lunch order as they stepped into the hall and headed toward the elevator. It always amazed Jasmine how certain rooms in this wing were warm, comfortable, and inviting, and other areas were cold, sterile. The moment they turned the corner, the hallways changed. There were no pictures on the walls, no wallpaper, instead, pearl gray paint coated the plaster and concrete floors. It felt like walking in a time capsule.

Rose glanced over her shoulder at Jasmine. "I stopped by the nursery and saw Rone holding Jackie, he's a natural. We want to have a litter once he settles this Challenge. I'm a bit nervous." She licked her lips and looked at Jasmine just as the elevator arrived.

They stepped in and pushed the button for the level above the tunnels. "Silas chose Rone to be Alpha of West Virginia, which means he has faith Rone can do the job. I have confidence in them both." She said, hoping she hit the right tone with the right amount of assurance because it took everything within her to believe those words.

Rose visibly relaxed and smiled.

Relieved, Jasmine breathed through the tightness in her chest. "This way." Rose pointed down the hall once they left the elevator.

The room they entered was small and could fit four adults; five would be tight but doable. There was a bank of monitors on three long consoles. Rose turned on all the screens and showed Jasmine how to pan the hidden cameras to see everywhere in the cells and the halls outside the holding area. Next, she taught her how to deal with the sound equipment.

From one of the consoles, Jasmine could talk to the women, to change the temperatures or the lighting in both the cells and the hall outside those rooms. Jasmine was impressed that the lights could be dimmed, and even that wasn't too dark, but they could not be turned off.

"Has anyone been in here lately, messing with their room?" Jasmine asked, remembering the women were beneath a mound of covers when she had first arrived to talk to them.

Rose typed in a few keys and looked at the screen. "Hmmm, someone has been watching them the past four days around the same time, between nine and ten at night."

"Does it tell you who?"

Rose tapped a few keys and waited for the information to display. She gasped. "Shit. What the hell is going on?" She looked at Jasmine. "It's Thorne. My brother has been spying on these women."

That didn't sound right to Jasmine. "Is there any way to playback what happened last night during that time?"

"What's wrong?" Silas asked with a long sigh.

"I'll let you know tonight," she said, reminding him of his promise to tell her what's been going on later.

"Jasmine, it doesn't work like that. Now tell me what's going on? Did you learn something?"

"Shhh. I have to listen. I'll let you know later." She shut down their link knowing it would piss him off. But she wasn't ready to throw Thorne under the bus until she discovered his role in all of this.

"I got it," Rose said with some hesitancy. "Uh…this is my brother, do you want me to step out?"

She looked at her daughter-in-law's red face and her heart squeezed. "No. Turn it on."

Rose pushed a button and at first, there was nothing. Jasmine leaned back in her chair and placed her hands over her stomach, glancing at the clock. Five minutes until Julie returned to her cage.

"You have everything you need?"

Jasmine sat up and looked at the monitor. Julie was lying on her cot and Siseria paced the small cage. "Yes, young one, we are fine. How is your sister? She is well?"

"Yes, I wish I could help her more but she won't let me visit her anymore. She says it's too dangerous," Thorne said. Jasmine could hear him but there was no visual. His voice was a timbre between adolescence and manhood; Jasmine had teased him about it last week. She glanced at Rose. The woman was frowning at the conversation.

"Things are speeding up. The signs are all around us. You must be careful you are not caught young one. Your service is necessary for the cause. Tell me of the children," Siseria said.

Jasmine blinked at the vibrant woman on the monitor. This was no bumbling, nervous ass.

"I have only seen them once. The boys are as I told you before, Adam and David. The girls, Jackie and Renee."

"She did that right at least," Siseria spat. "Gave them good biblical names of men who changed history, both strong leaders, but…which way will they lead?" she whispered, searching the floor for answers.

Goosebumps rose across Jasmine's flesh. She opened her link to Silas but didn't say a word.

"You think one of the boys will lead, why not one of the girls? My sisters are strong, they are leaders."

"No doubt you are right, young one, but we have the names of the leaders, it will be the males. They must be watched. No harm can come to them. When will your sister arrive?"

Jasmine started and looked at Rose. Her skin had lost its color. Jasmine stopped the tape. "Rose, are you okay?"

"He's …my brother has been…he's been talking to Lilly." She looked shell-shocked. "My twin, Lilly, that's who they're talking about. I've been seeking her through our link and never gotten a response. But she's somewhere close. Thorne's seen her, talked to her. What's going on?" she asked Jasmine brokenly.

"Rone's on his way. I think Rese and I need to see those tapes as well. Record whatever is happening live in Julie's cage, we'll get to it later. Right now I need to see how much our security has been compromised," Silas said, sounding weary.

Her heart hurt for him and Rose. Silas couldn't allow this to pass. Thorne would be called in to give an accounting for his actions.

"I can't believe this," Rose whispered. "We were never really committed to their cause. Mom kept so much of it from us that...all we ever knew were bits and pieces. Lilly and I played the role to keep peace with mom...but it was never real to us." She looked at Jasmine with tear-filled eyes. "Please don't kill my brother. I don't know what's going on, but he wouldn't betray me, us. There's something wrong here."

Jasmine reached over and squeezed her hand. "I promise your brother will not die because of this." She shut down the link behind Silas' growling. "I have some questions I'd like to ask because the Siseria he's talking to is not the woman I talked to earlier today. I'm wondering if there's some kind of game they're playing. He could help me understand that," she said, changing the tone of the conversation.

"Now that you mention it, she did seem arrogant, bossy. I thought you said Julie was the one in charge."

"I know. That's who talked to me most of the time. I thought she was the leader. Now, I think I got played. These two are playing a deep game with us. They wanted to be here in the compound, close to my babies."

"I picked up on that too. But why?" Rose asked, then stood and rushed into Tyrone's arms as he entered the room.

"You okay?" he whispered, holding her tight. His lips brushed against her forehead. Jasmine smiled as she watched her baby, now a man with a family, take care of his woman. Her heart warmed with pride at the man he had become. She wondered what Davian would say if he could see Tyrese and Tyrone now. Probably try and take credit, the asshole.

"Yeah, shocked, disappointed, but, I'm okay." She laid her head on his shoulder and stood there for a moment. Tyrone's eyes met Jasmine's. This was not good. Silas might be tolerant to a point, but not when it came to the safety of his pups. For the most part, she was right there with him. This was special because of Rose and Tyrone, but Thorne needed a good explanation to avoid Silas' wrath. He wouldn't die, because she had promised, but he might wish he had.

A few seconds later Silas and Tyrese entered the room. Jaree and two other guards stood in the corridor and the blinds were drawn. Jasmine knew without asking that Hank and Brad were lead security with the babies and that they had been moved to a secure location.

"Rose, I am going to ask that you do not contact your brother or give him a hint of your distress. I need to talk to him, and my mate," Silas' eyes flicked at Jasmine, "has already given her word he will not perish because of this. I have sent security to bring him to my office where I will talk to him, do you understand?"

The tension in the room was volatile. The heat of it brushed against her skin, reminding her of when she had first met Silas. The man could blow out the walls of a room with his anger. But this was a family matter, and even though having a family was new to him, she had faith that they would work through this just fine. She looked at the twins and sensed their inner turmoil.

Tyrese had saved Rose and Thorne from an attack by rogue wolves and brought the teen into the compound. After what happened with the spy who'd exploded earlier today, she knew her son was feeling some kind of responsibility for what happened with Thorne as well. Tyrone was scared for his wife's mental being. Rose held a high-security level and was privy to most of Silas' personal and private information. If her brother was selling them out, then she could become a suspect as well. And Silas…her man was nearing the end of his tether with so many things flying at him at once. She rubbed his arm and smiled when he glanced at her.

The tic in his jaw stopped and the air in the room lightened a bit.

"Yes Patron, I understand," Rose said quietly.

Silas pulled up a chair and sat next to Jasmine, taking her smaller hand in his. "Tyrese check the mechanics of this thing, I want to be sure it hasn't been tampered with."

Tyrese nodded, took some sort of device from his pocket, and turned it on. A few moments later he grinned. "Got it. Let me fix a few things and we should be ready."

"What was wrong?" Tyrone asked, still standing near the door and holding his mate.

Tyrese looked at his twin and his grin widened. "Smart kid. He fixed the system so the women would know whenever someone was watching or listening in. A small beep emits in the cell every time you turn on the equipment."

"So they'd know not to speak freely. Makes sense," Tyrone said.

"Yeah, let's hope we discover something that will answer some of the questions piling up around here," Silas said, squeezing her hands.

She leaned over and kissed his cheek. Their eyes locked for a moment and she was pleased his eyes were now a lighter shade of blue and not the dark blue they had been when he had walked in. "Love you," she mouthed.

He smiled crookedly. *"You should,"* he said through their link. *"I let you get away with way too much."*

"Hmm, I wonder why?"

He shook his head. *"Hell if I know."*

She punched his shoulder.

"Tyrese get this thing started before your mother hurts me," Silas said, straight-faced.

There was a pause and Rose laughed. Next, the twins joined in. Jasmine just shook her head and leaned against him for a quick kiss.

"It's ready," Tyrese said, tapping a few keys. "I'm recording their current conversations on that monitor over there and I've cued this one to replay Thorne's past conversations with the women. There are only three. So this is relatively recent."

"Good, glad we're getting on it early. Start with the first tape and bring it forward. I'm interested in how they recruited him," Silas said as he waved to the empty chairs in the room. "Rose, Rone, sit down, I need all eyes and ears on these screens in case I miss something."

"I wanna hear what Julie has to say when she comes back in the cell," Jasmine said, releasing Silas' hand. She scooted her chair closer to the monitor displaying the cell area. Picking a pair of headphones, she placed them over her ears and panned the camera for a similar view as when in the room with them. Rubbing her hands together for warmth, Jasmine watched Siseria lay on the bed looking up at the ceiling. The sound of footsteps caused a reaction in the woman on the bed.

Standing, Siseria pulled herself into a stooped position and resumed the same vacant expression she had worn earlier with Jasmine. When Julie became visible, Siseria played the role of an ashamed, weak woman.

"I hope you didn't say anything," Julie snapped.

"I didn't. I was scared," Siseria whimpered. Her actions sickened Jasmine now that she knew what was going on.

The guard opened the cage and Julie walked in, scowling at a cowering Siseria. He locked the cage and turned to leave. Siseria looked at him hungrily, even reaching out a hand to touch the man until Julie yelled, "Stop, you don't want to do that."

Siseria snatched her hand back from bars and started licking her lips. The guard shook his head and strode out the room.

"Now what bitches?" Jasmine's eyes flicked from one woman to the next, neither spoke nor moved.

"He's gone," Siseria said, stretching as she straightened. "You okay? They didn't bother you did they?"

"No, I just got some rest. Wasn't too bad," Julie said.

"Come on, come on, talk about me," Jasmine murmured.

Julie sat on her bed facing Siseria. "She looked good, I thought he was abusing her. Harming her and the babies in some way."

Siseria shrugged. "You're right, she looked good, at least as far as we could tell. Women hide scars all the time, there's no telling what's truly going on with the two of them."

Jasmine flinched at the spasm of pain that crossed Julie's face at the mention of scars. "You are such a bitch," she murmured to Siseria.

"None of the children are marked. Isn't there supposed to be a mark?" It seemed like Julie had taken her time alone to reflect on some inconsistencies. Good for you, Jasmine silently cheered.

"Yes, everything we've been taught says the child will have a birthmark. But really, do you expect her to tell us the truth about that?"

"It's not just her, the boy also said he overheard the nurses talking and there was no mention of birthmarks."

"Did anyone ask the question, are there birthmarks on any of the babies?" Siseria snapped. It was obvious she didn't appreciate this line of questioning.

"I don't know but people talk. If there was a mark, I believe someone would have said. Maybe the child's not in the first litter. Maybe he's in the next."

Siseria marched to the side of her cage closest to Julie. "Is that why you told her how to control her body? We are not supposed to help her. She refused our offer."

Julie shrugged. "She made a valid point, she did not know us. Very few women, rational women anyway, would have responded differently."

"You have changed your mind about our cause?"

"No. I just don't think the path we are on is the right one. More flies with honey, that kind of thing. For instance, since we do not want harm to come to her babies, why aren't we helping her? The easier she controls and understands her body, the more likely she will listen to our suggestions on how to raise the new leader."

"You suggest we become her friend," an angry-sounding Siseria bit out.

"We are already her friends, she just doesn't know it. Why antagonize the only person who can assist us in reaching our goals."

"She sees me as a retarded fool," Siseria said, turning away.

"No. I see you as a liar," Jasmine said softly while watching the drama on the monitor.

"That is who you showed her. I am at peace with my mission, but I fret over the lack of progress. The rebellion is growing—"

"The number of breeds outnumbers them three to one," Siseria said smugly.

A look of sorrow graced Julie's face. "They won't all fight in this war, many still hide in fear of their lives."

"The Patron's hiding his pups like full-bloods have been doing for decades. Once the Patron shows the world his litter of pups, the breeds will come out of hiding and unite. When everyone knows the Patron's pups are half-breeds and he accepts them, we will begin."

"The war you mean," Julie said, not sounding as happy over the idea as her cellmate.

"Of course, that's the beginning of the Patron's downfall. It's what we've worked for all these years." Siseria returned to the bars and looked at Julie. "What's wrong? Did someone say something to you while you were in the other room? Let's talk about it."

Jasmine held her breath waiting for something monumental.

"No. I have been thinking and going over the little bit we know of this cause. It's been going on for so long I have forgotten the origins and what we believe."

"Julie!" Siseria sounded shocked.

Julie waved her down. "It's true. I don't even remember Nicromja and what his role is in all this. It's like fairy tales being passed down through generations."

Siseria's hand flew to her mouth and she looked up as though an appearance from an angry deity was imminent. "Careful Julie, that's blasphemous."

"No, it's not, and stop being so dramatic. All I said was I don't remember him or her or it. It has been a long time since anyone has remotely connected him to this mission." Julie sighed and scooted back a bit. "I want to help those children. I want them to survive the fallout unharmed." She looked at her partner. "That has always been my assignment."

Siseria nodded. "I know. Just as you know my assignment is different, and one I will die completing."

A chill slid down Jasmine's back at the woman's words. She sat staring at the woman who had all but admitted to being a part of Silas' demise until her knuckles cracked beneath the pressure. She hadn't realized she was gripping the arms of the chair until Silas covered her hand with his.

"It's okay. Others have tried and failed, before. We will survive to see another day," he said through their link, easing her fears.

Jasmine released a sigh and continued watching the monitor. "Separate them. Leave Julie in her cell and place Siseria in the bomb shelter or something similar. She needs a 'come to Jesus' moment, maybe she'll find it in the silence of that space."

Silas nodded and gave the instructions to the guard near the cells. Jasmine watched as Siseria spun around at the sound of the guard and sunk into her persona. Without answering Julie or Siseria's questions, he opened the cell, tore the dress from Siseria's quivering body, and scanned her with a device. There were a few sharp pins in her hair that he removed and placed in a bag. Her slaps and punches against the huge wolf went unnoticed as he identified something that wasn't visible. He picked up the naked female and carried her away.

Everything had happened so fast. Julie stood looking at the closed door open-mouthed. After a few moments, she slid down the bars and sat on the floor with her face in her hands. Jasmine turned off the audio as the sounds of weeping filled her ears. She split the screen and watched the two guards take a screaming Siseria through the tunnels and then to the bomb shelter.

By the time they reached the shelter, Siseria was crying and begging them to release her. Heedless to her cries, they dumped her in the barren room, fresh from its recent scrubbing and disinfecting.

Faint sounds could be heard coming from the room, but Jasmine hardened herself against it. Tyrese touched her shoulder. "Her ultimate assignment is to destroy your mate. She mentioned it on one of the other tapes. She's locked and loaded like Boggs. Only this time we're going to get a chance to look at it before it blows. You did the right thing, Mom."

Jasmine's heart raced. She couldn't swallow past the sizable lump in her throat. "I was talking to a woman with a bomb inside her?" She felt nauseous.

"I'm sorry, Jazz," Silas said. "You know I would never allow you to be in any danger. That's why what you did is so impressive. On a visceral level, you sensed she was the dangerous threat and separated her from everyone in the compound. I filled the room with gas before she could trigger the mechanism. Right now I'm pulling a team together who will be able to identify and hopefully disable the device. We need to understand how to detect these things before we allow anyone else in or out of the compound." He kissed her gently. "Thank you. I thank you and my people thank you."

Choked by the intensity of his gaze, she tried to speak and couldn't. She nodded and leaned forward until her head rested on his chest. The strong beat of his heart eased her fears.

"Sir," Tyrone said quietly.

Silas sighed as he looked up. "Thorne's gone?"

Tyrone exhaled. "Yes. They can't find him."

Silas nodded, patted Jasmine's shoulder, and stood up. "Make copies of those tapes and place them in the safe in my office," he said to no one in particular and left the room.

Jasmine stared at the sad faces in the room and knew nothing she said would make a difference. They were responsible for bringing Thorne into the compound, and by extension were responsible for his actions.

"I'm sorry," Rose whispered before turning her face into Tyrone's chest. He closed his eyes and held her tight.

"We have to find him," Jasmine said, looking at her sons. "The only way to protect Thorne is to bring him in. Rose, can you reach him?"

"La Patron said not to," she looked wide-eyed at Jasmine.

"*Silas?*" Jasmine reached out to him and wasn't surprised he was with the babies in the nursery.

"*Yes?*"

"*I want Rose to contact Thorne and tell him to come to the compound. I want Tyrone to meet and run a scan over him and then take him to lock-up for questioning. Is that okay?*" Jasmine asked, watching Rose and Tyrone hold each other's hand tight.

"*Jasmine, you can't get involved with these things.*"

"*I'm your mate and that's what we do. You are not accustomed to dealing with family matters, I'm an expert at it, so I will lead in this arena for us. Okay?*"

He sighed and her heart ached for him. His plate was past full, it was overflowing. "*Okay. Let me know when he's here. I want to question him myself.*"

"*Okay.*"

"*And thanks for asking instead of just flying solo and telling them to call him in without talking to me.*"

"*You welcome, Wolfie.*" She cut the connection and told the three of them what she and Silas agreed to.

Rose reached out to Thorne and was so surprised when he answered her immediately that she dropped the connection. Inhaling, she contacted him again.

"Thorne? Where are you? I was looking for you, haven't seen you around much." Tyrone relayed the silent communication between brother and sister to his mom and brother.

"I went out for a run in the woods. It's nice, I went all the way to the big mountain, I'm on my way back. You inviting me to dinner? I'm hungry."

"Yeah right. Since when have you wanted to eat my cooking?"

He laughed. *"Good point. I'll be over to see you as soon as I shower and put on some clean clothes. I can grab a bite to eat on the way. How's Rone and Rese?"*

She looked at Jasmine, frowning. *"Both are good, working all the time. That's why you should visit me more, I get lonely."*

"Sure you do, with all those people in the main building, don't make me laugh."

"Yeah, but they're not my baby brother, though."

"True...true. I'm back on the grounds, going to take that shower, see you in a few." He pulled out the link.

Tyrone was the first to speak. "He sounded fine. I detected no deceit or guilt."

Tyrese tapped his earpiece. "No, don't let him leave the grounds if he attempts to flee, otherwise, just stay out of sight. He is meeting Rone in a few minutes."

Tyrese looked at his brother. "You need to scan him before he comes to the main building. No offense," he looked at Rose. "But we don't know where he's coming from, or if he's been tampered with. We don't know how these bombs are being inserted, I don't believe Boggs was aware he was loaded, but Siseria is."

Tyrone stood. Jasmine and Rose both protested. "Why does he have to do it?" Jasmine asked, afraid for her son.

"I can do it," Tyrese said, standing.

"No," Rose and Tyrone said at the same time.

"Look, we are trying to keep this in the family," Tyrese said, exasperated. "Silas is only going to allow us so much leeway. Two people entered the compound wearing explosives on my watch. I'm not taking any chances now, not with anybody. As far as I'm concerned, to enter this area you will be scanned, me and everybody in this room included." He glanced at Jasmine. "Except you, Mom," he said sheepishly.

"Hmm, well thank you, Sir," she said in a dry tone.

"I'll be back in a few," Tyrone said. He kissed Rose on her forehead and left the room.

Jasmine gave Silas an update and promised to let him know when Thorne was secured.

She exhaled and grabbed Rose's hand. They sat quietly waiting for the all-clear from Tyrone.

"He's clean," Tyrese said ten minutes later, releasing a breath.

Rose exhaled, and bending from her waist, placed her forehead on Jasmine's shoulder. Jasmine rubbed the younger woman's back and murmured words of comfort.

"I don't think I've ever been that scared before," Rose whispered and slowly lifted her head, wiping away her tears.

Jasmine cupped her daughter-in-law's face in her palms. "There's nothing wrong with being scared, almost every great thing that was ever done in this world happened when people were scared. We just keep moving through our fear, that's all."

"Rone and Thorne are in the room in the tunnel. He contacted Silas, he's on his way."

Jasmine stood.

"Uh…Mom?"

She looked over her shoulder at Tyrese. "Huh?"

"Silas doesn't want you or Rose down there. He…uh…told me to escort both of you upstairs."

Jasmine stared at Tyrese for a moment, trying to decide if she was going downstairs to intervene on Thorne's behalf, which would cause her son, who has already had a hellacious day, problems. Or go upstairs and deal with Silas' heavy-handedness later. She shut down the link between them and nodded to Tyrese. Silas was on his own, he'd learn soon enough dealing with family was no easy task.

"Fine, son. Let's go."

Rose's brow shot up.

Tyrese's eyes widened and then he smiled. "Thanks, Ma. It's been a rough morning and I haven't had lunch yet."

"My lunch never arrived, so we can have lunch together since you're on babysitting duty."

"Mom, that's not fair, I love spending time with you. It's no duty." She slapped his arm and walked out of the room.

Chapter 7

Silas walked into the lower office being used to interview Thorne. The young man sat at the table eating and laughing with his brother-in-law, Tyrone. The sight ticked Silas off and the heat of his anger filled the room, causing the walls to expand outward a bit. The lights flickered off and then came back on. Thorne's long hair moved as if it was being blown by a strong wind. The young man and Tyrone held on tightly to the table, but it began to slowly slide. Silas cut their communication channels, so neither man was able to contact anyone. He knew Rose would be angry, but he was Patron and he would not allow these infractions in his compound.

"Thorne?" Silas said, and the young pup rose from his seat. Wide-eyed, he stared at Tyrone as his feet moved toward Silas. When he was two feet away, Silas made him fall to his knees.

"I am going to ask you one time and you will tell me everything, do you understand young Thorne?"

"Yes...yes, Sir. Please Sir, I understand," Thorne said, crying.

"Why did you contact the human females from the surveillance room?"

"Oh shit...shit...shit. I...." He wiped his lips. "My sister asked me to contact them. She wanted to know if they were okay."

Silas looked at Tyrone, noticed the deep scowl on his face on behalf of his mate, and asked another question. "Which sister?"

"Lilly. She is with her mate in the caves. He is hurt and she cannot leave him." The pressure in the room eased. Rone and Thorne both gasped for air.

Silas sat forward, the human women forgotten for the moment. "Who is your sister's mate? Have you seen him?"

"No, Sir. I don't know who he is, never met him. She won't allow me or anyone to get close. Lilly's mean, a real fighter. If she says no, then it's no."

"Where is she?"

"I don't know, Sir. She contacts me sometimes, asks how Rose is doing or how I'm doing. Twice, I took some medicine, just some bandages and antiseptic, along with two blankets, bottled water, and a few bags of jerky, and left them near this big rock for her. She was supposed to pick it up later. This past week she asked about the humans, but I don't know why. They just talk about their stupid cause."

Silas wondered if Lilly had found Cameron. He knew the man wasn't dead; Silas still sensed his wolf but couldn't lock on him. "Why didn't you tell Rose or Rone about this?"

"Lilly told me not to. Plus, Rose is busy with everything; I didn't want to bother her." Silas looked sharply at Tyrone, his message was clear. Keep the boy busy and close to home or else. Tyrone exhaled and nodded.

"Stand up," Silas said, feeling the sting of his separation from his mate. He hadn't realized when he'd shut her out; she had shut him out as well. When Thorne stood, Silas scanned him again just to be sure and was satisfied the young pup was clean and telling the truth as he knew it. "You are never to go in any part of this compound other than your sister's and Tyrone's wing. I am limiting your access because you are not ready to handle that type of freedom, yet. You will move in with them immediately."

Thorne bowed his head. "Yes, Sir."

Silas glanced at his watch, turned, and left the room. His security detail fell in behind him. He contacted Rose. *"Has the technical team arrived yet?"*

"Yes Sir, they are assembling now in the lower chambers waiting for you to brief them. Tyrese is on his way." Good, he wanted to talk to Tyrese and Hank about Cameron. Maybe there was some way to track Lilly and hopefully find Cameron in the process.

Silas stopped, closed his eyes at the growing discomfort behind his eyes, and unclenched his fist. This mating thing pissed him off at times. *"Where is Jasmine?"* he growled at Tyrese.

"In the nursery."

He knew Jasmine had felt the energy blast in the room with Thorne, even without their mental link. She was probably pissed over his poor family skills but…damn it.

How could he lead his wolves when he couldn't protect his mate and four pups? The enemy sat in his basement for weeks. She could've exploded and wiped out his litter, and to think a 'family member' had shared information with that bitch, it had been too much. And now he was paying for it with the backlash of his mate's displeasure.

"*Jasmine,*" he called, hoping she would answer. She didn't, stubborn bitch. "*Jasmine,*" he called again with a bite in his tone.

"*What?*" she snapped, and the tension eased in his head.

"*Don't shut me out.*"

"*You shut me out, Silas. Don't put this on me.*"

"*I know, I know.*" He released a breath. "*But we are not meant to be disconnected for long periods. I have a lot of work to do and I cannot concentrate on it when you disconnect like that.*"

"*What?*"

"*You can keep me from hearing your thoughts without disconnecting our link, love. I'll be out of your immediate thoughts but we will still be one, okay?*" This was another one-sided benefit the human breeders had that wolves didn't. A full-blood bitch had to be connected to her mate at all times and vice-versa. But the breeders, it didn't seem to bother them at all, and that sucked big time.

"*Oh, okay.*" She paused. "*That's all you have to say?*"

The tone of her voice stopped the 'yes' that was forming on his lips. He took a moment to think. "*I'm on my way to deal with the technicians; can we continue this conversation later?*"

"You better believe we will, Silas." She shut him out of her thoughts. He didn't like it, but it was better than the void he'd experienced before. Pushing the conversation to the back of his mind, he headed down the corridor to reach the lower tunnels.

"Rose, set up a meeting with the Alphas in an hour." He needed to brief them of these new threats. Hopefully, he was the lone recipient of the attack, but he doubted it.

"Yes, Sir."

When he entered the room, six men and three women stood at attention. Silas looked at Hank and the man nodded, each of these people had been scanned for devices and deceit. Silas stepped to each individual, shook their hand, and did a more in-depth search, rifling through their minds for deeply rooted deception. By the time he shook the last hand, he was pleased with the level of loyalty and commitment of each person. They were eager to begin the research.

"This way." Silas led them to the room where Siseria lay in an induced coma. The team looked at her through a large window as Tyrese spoke of Boggs and gave them folders with pictures from the aftermath of the explosion and some before. They looked at the x-rays of Siseria and all agreed there was something inside her that shouldn't be there.

"I am borrowing some equipment from the hospital," Silas said. "It should be here within the hour. It's a robotic x-ray machine. It will be operated from outside the room so you can get a better idea of the shape and size of the object. I believe you have her blood work and preliminary lab work. Any questions?"

"Yes, Sir. What is our primary task?" Passen, one of the lead doctors asked.

"It's two-fold. Find a way we can detect this device without a scanner. And find a way to neutralize it before it's triggered."

"That can take months, years," another tech said.

"You don't have months, let alone years. We are all prisoners here until you unravel this mystery. I have an Alpha challenge to preside over in a month. You have until then. If you need help, bring them in. Understand, anyone who enters this area must be personally cleared by me." He looked at the shocked faces of the people in the room. "As Patron, I have chosen you because I am certain you can do this, was I wrong?"

"No, Sir, we…we will get started right away. We must outline our strategy, where is the blood work?" Passen asked, taking the papers and walking toward the monitors.

Silas nodded and left the room, waving at Tyrese to follow him. When they stepped into the hall, Hank joined them. Silas pointed at Hank. "You're lead on this project and security detail. I want it tight. No leaks, no mistakes. Everything goes through you to me. Make sure you introduce yourself to Passen and everyone in that room."

Hank nodded. "Yes, Sir."

"Where is Brad?" Silas asked, looking around; the man should be fully healed by now.

"We rotated out at lunch," Hank answered.

Silas nodded. "When he comes down, work out a schedule with him, I want eyes and ears on this crew around the clock. Use Jaree at night when he's not guarding my mate if you need to. Any other guards you use must be personally vetted by me. Your job is to make sure they have everything they need to find a solution to this problem. I want it done quietly and efficiently, but quickly. They need to make a schedule and give it to you so we know where everyone is at all times. Two connecting rooms have been outfitted with twin beds, trunks, and a few desks for their use. The cams are active there and in the bathroom as well. No outgoing calls. I've disabled their mental links, nothing in without a security check, got it?"

"Yes, Sir," Hank said. He nodded and returned to the lab with the techs. Silas and Tyrese walked down the corridor in silence. Security guards stood in the halls to ensure no one left or entered the area without Silas' permission. They rode the elevator in silence.

Silas shuffled his priorities and by the time they entered his office he had called Tyrone in to join them. The twins each took a seat in front of his desk and waited for him to give instructions. It dawned on Silas he had never had this level of assistance before. He'd always had his Alphas and they'd do jobs for him as needed, but they'd be away from their primary responsibilities of handling their state matters. Jacques was his administrator, not someone he sent on jobs. Maybe this family thing his mate talked about was good. He looked at the twins. This *was* good, he decided.

He waved them to seats at the table as the large monitor flicked on. Within moments, the camera was active. Roll call would begin momentarily. Silas went over in his mind what he wanted to say and what he planned to keep in reserve.

"Alpha Theron reporting, Sir." Silas nodded as the next Alpha checked in. These were men he'd personally trained, each had taken his last name, Knight, and wore his crest on their shoulders. That one had betrayed him cut deep.

"Alpha Jayden reporting, Sir." Silas nodded, glad to see the man.

Within five minutes, the roll call was complete.

"Up until last year, we met on these conference calls once every two months, or if a special situation arose that needed my attention. Now it seems as though we are meeting weekly. Times are changing quickly and we, no I, was caught off guard. The human breeding phenomenon was bigger than any of us imagined."

There were some nods and verbal agreements from the monitor.

"My job as Patron is to all wolves. I control the wolf, so if a person shifts into a wolf, he merits my concern and protection." He had said those words before, but it bore repeating every time they talked because there was still some reluctance. With the overwhelming number of half-breeds being reported, most of the Alphas agreed those wolves needed to be accepted into the packs. Some merely gave lip service and did nothing to ease the way of the half-breeds. Those were the Alphas he addressed with his declaration.

"Is that understood?"

"Yes, La Patron," the Alphas and the twins said.

"Good, now to bring you current, we have run into some problems." Over the next hour, Silas explained about the bomb, eased concerns over his security, and had to defend his staff.

"This was not a security breach. Focus on what I'm saying. Someone has invested money to make an undetectable bomb. Think suicide bombing on steroids."

No one spoke as his words penetrated. "Think full-bloods or half-breeds with wolves so weak they are undetectable. How the hell did that happen? I need each one of you to see the bigger picture. Someone is fucking with us and I want to know who and I want to know why. That…" he pointed at the Alphas, "is what we should be discussing, not that other bullshit."

"Yes, La Patron."

Silas watched the monitor and realized they were beginning to see the enormity of the problem, and felt better. "Now I'm going to open the floor for discussion. Let's take the wolf issue first."

An hour and a half later, Silas and the twins left his office with an outline of a sketchy plan. Everyone agreed Dr. Passen and his team should look at Jenkins' wolf and make a diagnosis. More information was needed before they could go further. The tone of the meeting was a lot different at the end as the discussion peeled away layers of what these new threats meant to their nation.

"Change of plans, I want Detective Jenkins bought in as soon as possible and kept beneath the gym. After I pull his wolf, I want Froggy to work with him. I don't care how long it takes. I want his wolf healthy so I can have better access to find out why he's in my town."

"Rose says he's talking to a lot of humans, they are going to notice when he goes missing," Tyrone said.

Silas pinched the bridge of his nose and counted to five. Once done, he inhaled. "Fix it so that isn't a problem.

Do not bring the police to my door. This discussion is about what I want to see. I expect you to work out the details, the implementation, and get him here. No fuck ups. No excuses." He looked at each one with an arched brow.

"Yes, Sir," Tyrone said.

"Yes, Sir," Tyrese said.

Glad they understood, Silas pulled open his desk and placed a key in a lock. The blinds closed. The curtains moved inward blocking the residual sunlight. He slid back in his seat and typed a few keys on his keyboard. The screen he used for Alpha conferences rolled down and clicked into place.

A few minutes later, the interior of a large room filled with people appeared. The initial picture quality was poor. After playing with the keys for a while, the picture quality improved well enough that you could see the various eye colors of the people milling about the room.

"What was the date you were at the club and the time?" Silas asked Tyrese, who stared at the images on the screen.

Tyrese told him and Silas typed in the dates and the blocks of time. The screen went black and after a minute or so, the picture returned. Silas used the knob to pan the room and stopped on Tyrese and Boggs. They watched in silence as the black female with the long braids walked up to them.

"Hold on, can you check and see what she was doing before she met them, was she talking to someone?" Tyrone asked.

Silas split the screen so they could watch what she was doing while Tyrese and Boggs were talking.

"She's talking into a headpiece and laughing. You see that." Tyrone pointed to the screen.

"Hold it," Tyrese said. "That's Leonidas. He was in the club, standing not too far from her and I never saw him."

"Do you see any of the others?" Silas asked, searching the room.

Tyrese quickly identified the four other wolves. "I didn't see or scent them inside the club and I was constantly filtering scents. In the corridor, I knew there were wolves outside but they were unfamiliar."

Silas panned to the conference room and the first discussion. "Seriously, Boggs was a joke," Tyrone said, listening to the conversation.

"Watch this," Silas said. He zeroed in on Tyrese's and the female's faces when she mentioned killing the breed during the Alpha challenge. Tyrese's eyes flashed gold, and although the woman was facing Boggs, she noticed the flash and her lips pulled up at the corner in a grin.

"See that?" Silas asked. "She was deliberately baiting you. Look at this when you mention the pups."

Tyrese's jaw was so tight it was amazing the words passed through his lips. But her eyes glowed. "They knew who you were," Silas said. He fast-forwarded to the fight and was impressed by the speed and agility Tyrese displayed as he whipped five full-blooded wolves.

"I should've killed them," Tyrese said in a tight voice.

"No. You did right. They overplayed their hand. And even though they backpedaled at the end after identifying you, they spoke words of treason and I will now deal with them," Silas said as a burst of satisfaction flowed through him. He rewound the tape and placed the cursor on the face of each person Tyrese identified and immediately the screen filled with data about that person. Silas saved the information and sent it to his computer.

"I'm creating a file on these six people. I want to have a conversation with them. They have a problem with how I am governing, they think I'm soft." He chuckled. "Maybe I am, but they will never know." He typed in the dates from the two previous nights and had the computer search the crowd for the five faces.

"No results" flashed across the screen.

"They have not returned to the club since that night, but I am certain they have others hanging around watching. Neither of you is to visit that place until I clear it, is that understood."

"Yes, Sir," they said simultaneously.

"I sent their files to your tablets, open them." The curtains slid back and the blinds opened so that natural sunlight flooded the room. There was a knock on the door.

"Come in, Rose," Silas said, looking up as she entered the room balancing a tray filled with food.

"Jasmine sent this."

Honeyed warmth filled him. He hadn't eaten anything since this morning and seeing the platters of steaks, chicken, and ribs, he was suddenly ravenous. "Thank you." He pulled the tray in front of him and glanced at the twins as Rose left the room.

"I know both of you had lunch."

"Actually you called me in the middle of my meal," Tyrone said, looking at the meat with a ravenous gleam in his eyes.

"And I had just sat down with Mom to eat when you called me," Tyrese said, licking his lips as Rose returned with another tray filled with over-stuffed sandwiches, plates, and cutlery.

"She said you have drinks in your office refrigerator," Rose said as she placed the second tray next to the first. Silas watched her wink at Tyrone before she left again.

"I thought this was all for me," Silas grumbled as he filled his plate with a steak and half a chicken. He pushed the platter to the twins and watched open-mouthed as they filled their plates, leaving him very little for seconds. Tyrese reached for the sandwich platter and Silas slapped his hand. "Mine."

Tyrese looked at the meat-filled delicacies with longing and leaned back into his seat. They ate in silence until every morsel was gone. Silas relented and allowed them to take a half sandwich each. He polished off the rest.

Tyrone rose and went to the small refrigerator in the back of the office. "What do you want to drink?" he asked Silas.

"A bottle of water."

"A beer," Tyrese said, looking at his electronic pad. "Hmm, they aren't from around here. Now, why am I not surprised by that bit of information?"

Silas swallowed and glanced at the bios of the rebels. "They have been all over the place, haven't they?" He read through Leon's travel record; the man had been in five different countries and six different states within the past three years. "I wonder if Leon is a courier of some type, he's traveled to some interesting places."

Tyrese bit into his sandwich, nodding. "The female has him beat, though. She's been in more places, most of them hot. Plus look at her list of aliases, I wonder if she knows who she really is."

Silas whistled as he read her travel record. Tyrese had been right. She'd been to Greece, Israel, Italy, Iraq, and quite a few other Middle Eastern countries. He needed to delve deeper into her past. Brushing the crumbs from his fingertips, he sent her file to Jayden with instructions to complete a high-level background check. Being situated in Maryland had its benefits when it came to dealing with human government secrets, and something told him she had plenty.

Tyrone returned with two beers and a bottle of water. Silas looked at the frosty bottles of beer and changed his mind. Standing abruptly, he walked to the fridge and grabbed a brown bottle, twisted the cap, and took a long pull. It felt damn good going down. When he finished, the bottle was empty and he threw it in the trash. He wiped his mouth with the back of his hand and re-took his seat.

Tyrese and Tyrone stared wide-eyed at him.

"What?" he asked before biting into his last sandwich.

"Nothing." Tyrone then took his beer and upturned it. Silas watched with a grin as the young pup choked and beer dribbled down his chin and neck. When he finished, the bottle was empty and the fool was grinning like a loon.

"Your turn, "Tyrone said, pushing Tyrese on the shoulder.

Tyrese shrugged and upturned his bottle, swallowing constantly. In a few moments, he was done. "Ahhh," he said, licking his lips as he chucked the bottle in the trash can.

Silas didn't like that Tyrese finished his bottle almost as quickly as he'd finished his. "Get three more bottles," he said while fishing in his desk for his stopwatch.

Tyrone placed the ice-cold bottles on the desk and pulled off the caps. Silas brandished his stopwatch. "Let's do it again. Best time wins."

Tyrone groaned.

Tyrese grinned and Silas picked up his bottle. "You first, Rese."

Tyrese nodded and upturned his bottle. When he was done, he slammed the bottle on the desk. "Ta da!"

"Not bad," Silas said, writing down the time on the pad so they could all see it. "Rone, you're up."

Tyrone upturned his bottle and chugged. He did better this time but lacked Tyrese's finesse. He put the bottle on the desk, coughing. "I know I beat your time," he said, looking at Tyrese.

Silas's brow rose at the ridiculous comment as he wrote down Tyrone's time and passed Tyrese the stopwatch.

"Awww, that can't be right, I drank faster the second time," Tyrone complained.

"Which goes to show how slow you were on your first attempt," Tyrese said smugly. "Whenever you're ready, Sir."

Silas nodded and upturned his bottle, and within seconds it was drained. He placed the bottle on the desk and gazed at the astonished expressions on the twins' faces.

"It's a full-blood thing, you wouldn't understand," he mocked as they closed their mouths.

"Again," Tyrese said. "Let's do it one more time." Tyrone returned to the refrigerator to get three bottles.

Silas knew his body would treat the beer like water. It would have little to no effect on him. But the human side of the twins would feel the high levels of alcohol in the locally-made beer.

He looked at the files on his monitor and thought of the strategies they needed to implement. And then he looked at the two men in front of him laughing and making off-colored jokes while holding their bottles. Tyrese had been weighed down with the guilt over Boggs, even though his clarity of thought saved many lives today. Tyrone struggled with the guilt of Thorne and the possible leaks of critical intel and still chose to serve as the West Virginia Alpha if Silas decreed it.

These two men were his sons in all but blood; they served him with unswerving loyalty. That had been clear on Tyrese's face when the rebels had talked about Silas and Tyrone and his young brothers and sisters. It was a good thing few knew of Jasmine, he doubted anyone would have left that meeting alive had she been threatened.

Putting business aside for a while, Silas picked up his bottle. "Okay, who's first?"

Chapter 8

The dark brown wolf crept beneath the low rocks and tread slowly down into the ravine's dry bed. Stopping, it turned and scented the air. Certain nothing was amiss; it trotted a few feet to the low-hanging bushy limbs of the two trees that covered the mouth of the cave. The paws of the medium-sized animal pat the leaf-covered earth a few times as it inspected the opening to ensure it hadn't been tampered with or discovered. Finally, the wolf ran past the entry into the forest, stopping at one of the larger trees.

Lilly Garcia searched the forest once again, and sensing no danger, she shifted. Quickly, she stuffed her long legs into the jeans and pulled on the tee-shirt she had left in the plastic bag beneath the roots of the tree. Shaking her sneakers from the bag, she inspected the insides for bugs or worse, scorpions, before slipping them on and pushing the bag into her pant pocket. She took a moment to push her hair beneath the dark cap and pulled it down over her ears. Dressed, she returned to the entrance of the cave stopping shy of the long branches and crouched to get a better view. She remained still for several minutes before inching the branch outward. The process was excruciatingly slow in case someone watched from a distance, they wouldn't detect any movement. Once the opening was wide enough for her to slip through, she duck-walked inside and began the slow process of replacing the limbs in position.

Satisfied she had done all she could to conceal her whereabouts; she turned and took off at a run until she reached a fork and turned sharply to the left. Inhaling, she looked down, saw no movement, and sent up a prayer of thanksgiving. Slowly, she climbed down to the floor of the cave and jumped the last few feet. It was cooler and darker down here. Bending forward, she felt along the wall until she was stopped by a solid boulder. Slipping sideways, she squeezed through a small space and entered a much larger cavern. She looked toward the far wall near the warm spring and saw him.

He lay unmoving on the blankets. Inexplicable relief flowed through her, pissing her off. The whole thing with wanting to leave and not being able to without mind-numbing pain made her blood boil. She ran her fingers through her hair, removing the cap as she strode toward him.

Squatting she touched his forehead. It wasn't as warm as it had been last night. Grateful her brother kept them from starving, she stretched and then checked their meager supplies. Down to the last bag of jerky, a couple of granola bars, and an apple on its way to decay, she grabbed one of two large metal cups, went to the hot springs, and filled it with water. A small fissure in the rocks released a constant stream of steam. Lilly placed the cup on top of the steam and added a piece of the jerky into the water. In a few minutes, she'd try and feed him some broth, what he needed was solid food to regain his strength. Frustrated with the situation she ran her hand through her hair, going over possible options in her mind. Nothing worked with him unable to walk on his own. Wanting to scream at the unfairness of being mated to a cripple, she directed her energies to feeding them both.

While the jerky boiled, she pulled out her knife, cut the apple into small pieces, and sat beside him. "Hey." She pushed his shoulder. His eyes opened slowly and blinked a couple of times. She wondered if he ever really saw her, much of what he said before was gibberish.

"I'm back. I have some broth cooking, it should be ready in a few. Try and eat some of this." She placed a small bit of the soft apple to his lips. He licked it and then sucked the small piece in. Pleased, she fed him piece after piece until he wouldn't open his mouth.

"Okay." She cut off the rotten part and then finished most of it off. Standing, she moved to the steaming cup and dropped in the last bits of apple to give the broth some flavor. After wrapping her hand in her shirt, she moved the hot cup to the side and blew on it. She glanced over her shoulder, pleased he had been able to keep the apple down and had high hopes that he might be able to eat some of the softened meat.

He coughed.

Changing directions, she picked up the other cup near a smaller rock outcropping and placed it beneath the cool trickling water. Once the cup was half full, she sipped a bit to cool her throat and walked toward him.

Holding his head up slightly, she placed the cup to his lips and tipped it up. Some of the water ran down his face, which was okay since he was drinking. When she removed the cup, he groaned in protest, pleasing her beast in ways she couldn't explain.

Sip by sip, she fed him the cool water until the cup was empty. She wiped away the water from the outside of his mouth with her thumb. "More?"

"No," he whispered.

Her breath hitched. Since she'd dragged him from the collapsed cave to this place, those were his first words.

"I am going to get the broth so you can eat, and get stronger, then you can leave. I can leave." She released an aggravated breath. "We can both leave this place."

"Okay," he said in the barest whisper. Still, it was more than she'd gotten before. She touched the cup with the broth and realized it was cool enough to pick up. Over her shoulder, she looked at the crude wood splint on his leg, more like a small branch tied to it, and sighed. There hadn't been time to do more. Hopefully, he'd be able to shift long enough for it to heal.

She and carried the broth to where he lay prostrate with blistered lips, discolored cheeks, and weakened frame. For the hundredth time, she wondered who was he? More importantly, why had the fates mated her with such a frail creature? Numerous times she tried to leave him, only to discover she could not. For the time being, they were irrevocably bound and that angered her more than she could say.

She placed her hand beneath his head. Dark brown eyes, filled with pain and something she hadn't seen before, determination, gazed up at her. Lilly placed the warm cup to his lips. "Drink this slowly and then I'll give you some of the meat."

Although he didn't speak, she sensed his agreement. Sip by sip she fed him the broth and pieces of the meat. One goal, one thought filled her mind, get him stronger to shift and heal so they could leave this hole. For that outcome, she'd take all day to get food in him.

He chewed the meat, rested, and then finished it. She laid him back on the blanket and watched him for a few minutes. Pulling out a piece of jerky stashed in her pocket, she bit off a piece and asked him a question.

"What's your name?" She had asked him this question dozens of times, and he had never answered, maybe this time he would.

His eyes fluttered and opened. "Cameron."

Pleased he'd responded, she rolled the name over in her mind. It had a nice old-world feel to it. "You have a Patron tattoo on your shoulder, you an Alpha?" She waited, hoping against hope he wasn't close to the Patron. According to her brother, Lilly's twin was mated to one of the Patron's high-ranking security people who would be the next Alpha of West Virginia. She smiled. Rose mated to an Alpha. Based on what they had been told, the tattoo on Cameron's shoulder meant he was an Alpha or close to the Patron.

"No. No Alpha."

She released a stream of air, glad she didn't have to deal with that. If she had known, she would not have sent Thorne to find out if the Breeders still planned to kill the

Patron. If they were, she needed to move far away in case her mate died and dragged her to an early grave with him. She looked at him again and breathed freely.

Tonight, unrestrained relief that he wouldn't die before the sun rose, a first since she rescued him, shook her.

"Ummm," he grunted as his face morphed into a mask of pain. She reached out and touched him, pleasantly surprised that he was warm. Warmer than he had been for days.

"You will not die," she murmured, willing him to live so she could survive. "You will get better and shift so you can heal." She closed her eyes and repeated the words over and over until she felt fur beneath her hands and heard the snapping of the splint on his right leg. She jerked back once her mind caught up with her eyes and ears.

"Oh my God…" she cried as he stood gingerly and hopped a bit favoring his right leg. Every once in a while, he'd attempt to walk on it and then lift again as he hobbled around the cave.

She covered her mouth at the sight of the huge beautiful black wolf with two white stockings on his front legs. Even thin, he was…gorgeous, in wolf form, she qualified. He swung his head and looked at her. They locked eyes for a moment before he walked slowly toward her. He inhaled and then sat carefully, still favoring his right leg. He placed his head in her lap and made some chaffing sounds. She rubbed him beneath the ear and patted him gently.

Within moments he was asleep. She expected him to shift again, but he remained wolf. Instead of pushing him away, she stroked his coat and wondered what happened next. When he shifted they could leave or leave with him in his present form. She missed her sister and brother, perhaps they could seek them out before leaving the area.

<<<<>>>>

Something wet and sticky intruded Lilly's sleep. She slapped away the intrusion, and tried to get more comfortable, and found she couldn't move. Her eyes shot open as everything returned in a flash. She leaned back to avoid touching the nose of the large black wolf entirely too close.

"Back off."

He stared for a second and then moved back slowly, but continued to watch her. Standing, she grimaced as her muscles ached from the cramped position she slept in. The wolf watched closely but remained in place. She had the oddest notion he'd move quickly if she faltered or needed assistance. That thought propelled her to look around their small cave to check their supplies.

A sharp bark from the opposite side of the cave garnered her attention. She swung around and her eyes rounded. He'd dug through into another tunnel and she hadn't noticed. He stepped forward again, turned, and looked at her, emitting a soft whine.

"You want to leave now?" Eager, she bent and stuffed the jerky, two cups, and her clothes inside a bag. Just as willing to rid herself of the cave, she pulled off her shoes and clothes and stuffed them into the bag along with her hat. Naked, she tied the top of the small bag and watched him trot toward her. He sniffed between her legs. Heat raced up her face. She pushed him away before he could touch her.

"Stop that." He may be her mate, but she wasn't ready for a relationship with him.

He whined a bit, then picked up the bag with his teeth and turned away. Lilly shifted, followed him out the cave, and down a rocky path, she hadn't seen before. Every once in a while he'd stop and wait for her. The trek was slow and hard. There were times she wondered if he knew where they were going, but he never hesitated. So they trudged on.

She had no idea how long they'd been below ground when they trotted up an incline. Cameron stopped, sat on his haunches, and howled. The sound was picked up across the forest. There was an answering howl. Then another closer.

Afraid of what this meant, she backed up. Now that help was near, she wasn't so sure she was ready to deal with a mate and what that entailed. She was no coward, but she simply couldn't see how she would be happy with Cameron.

The howls grew closer.

Turning, she ran back down the incline, stopped, and peeked outside. The black wolf remained still, watching her and the forest. He yipped at her, telling her to return to him. But she wasn't ready.

She backed up and stopped. Soon he was surrounded by five wolves; they rubbed against his fur and howled triumphantly. Her heart thumped as he moved toward her and stopped midway, barking and yipping in her direction.

The other wolves came to investigate, but a low warning growl stopped them from venturing closer.

Seeing that he would protect her from the others and that he wouldn't leave, she met him halfway. Together they moved ahead of the other wolves and started to run.

Chapter 9

Jasmine and Rose stepped into Silas's office and burst out laughing. Silas smiled as well at the antics of Tyrese and Tyrone. They weren't drunk, not yet, but they were feeling relatively loose. Their laughter was infectious and Silas couldn't remember when he had laughed as much or as hard.

So when the first *"Patron?"* came through his link, he heard it but was in the middle of wiping his eye and catching his breath, and didn't address it. The second time it came, he didn't filter the link to determine who it was from, he grunted a greeting.

"Patron, this is Cameron."

When those words hit him, he held up his hand as he jumped up. *"Cameron? Where? What?..."* he shook his head to clear his mind. *"Where are you?"* Silas walked to the window and looked outside as though he could see his godson.

"In the caves. I see some light ahead and will be in the forest soon."

Silas's heart rejoiced. *"There is a crew searching for you. When you enter the forest call out to them. How's your leg?"* He marveled at how clear-minded Cameron sounded.

"Better, I'm running on it again. I'm clearing the cave now."

Silas waited to assist if necessary.

"La Patron," one of the men in the search party called out to him.

"Speak," Silas said, expecting verification that Cameron was found and okay.

"We believe we have found Cameron and are on our way to his location."

"Sounds good," Silas said before closing his eyes and leaning against the cool pane of glass. He offered a prayer of thanks to the Goddess. Over the years, he had begun to think of Cameron as his son and his absence had been a huge weight on Silas' mind.

Jasmine's hand touched his back and he turned, pulling her close to him. Inhaling deeply, he pulled in her womanly scent and allowed it to fill him as she stroked his back. "Is he okay? His mind I mean?" she whispered.

"Sounds like it."

"Eek," Rose yelled, jumping up and down in front of Tyrone, who grinned at her fondly.

Silas and Jasmine turned and looked at her. "What?" Jasmine asked.

"My sister is with Cameron. She is his mate," Rose said, her face one of shock. She looked at Tyrone and smiled. "My sister's coming," she yelled and jumped into his arms. "Thank you, Goddess, my sister is coming, she's almost here and she contacted me. She misses me," Rose said, crying while telling them what she was being told.

"Are Cameron's rooms ready?" Jasmine asked, stepping away from Silas and looking up at him.

"I have sent servants to make sure all is ready." He looked at Tyrese and Tyrone, they hadn't said much and he wasn't sure it was the alcohol. "I know we are on high alert, I will be with you when he is scanned." He looked at Rose. "They will both be scanned before being allowed into the wings."

He noticed the relief in Tyrese's eyes and understood his reluctance to bring up the matter.

Jasmine squeezed his arm "Oh, that's the nurse calling, David is woke and fretting," she said, walking toward the door. When she reached it, he realized she hadn't mentioned whatever was bothering her earlier and he was glad.

"We'll talk about tonight," she said breezily through their link as she left the room.

He shook his head at her antics. *"I can't wait."*

"But you will."

He shook his head. She just had to have the last word. Knowing his godson was close eased his spirit. Finally, something good had happened this week. He was beginning to think the whole world turned against him.

"They aren't far, you want me to handle the scan?" Tyrese asked.

"Yes," Silas instructed the search party to head to the basement beneath the gym and that he would meet them there. "Let's go, they are almost here." He looked at an apprehensive Rose. "You too, let the receptionist know you will be gone for the day."

She squealed and ran out the door. "Thorne?" Tyrone asked.

"No." Silas didn't bother to look at Tyrone to sense his disappointment. If Thorne was ever going to be useful, he needed to learn protocols and the punishment when they were violated.

"You got the scanner?" He looked at Tyrese.

"Yes, Sir. There are two more locked up in the holding area beneath the gym. Rone and I have the keys."

"Good." They stepped into the hall and a jubilant Rose joined hands with her mate as they headed for the tunnels. Silas could only hope Cameron's mind was okay and that he wouldn't take exception to being scanned. A lot changed since he'd last seen the pup. They had much to talk about later.

"Does he know you're mated?" Tyrese asked.

"I don't think so. The last time I talked to him was in the caves with Arianna. The conversation didn't go much further after they realized I was not going to pardon her for destroying my property or wolves. He thought she was carrying his pups, but she wasn't. The explosion happened and we were out of it for a while."

"I wonder if Lilly told him about the babies," Rose murmured.

Silas had no idea and remained silent. This was not the homecoming he wished for Cameron, but with the rebel attack, he refused to take any unnecessary risks.

Ten minutes later they were waiting in the bunker beneath the gym. With every second Silas grew more and more concerned. "They should've been here by now," he said, standing in the hall, leaning against the wall facing the stairs.

Rose stiffened and looked at Tyrone. Silas caught the worried look. "What's wrong?"

"It's Lilly. She's refusing to come inside. She doesn't trust us."

"She doesn't have to trust anyone but her mate. He would die before allowing her to get hurt. Doesn't she know this?" Silas snapped, heading for the stairs.

"She does…but."

Silas stopped and looked at Rose. The sorrowful expression on her face didn't bode well. "What?" Concern laced his tone. "Is something wrong with him?" He remembered the vacant spaces that had been in Cameron's mind after the fight with Tyrone. Was Cameron still sick?

"Understand that all she has ever seen of him has been while he was sick." She hedged.

Silas nodded, concern turned to understanding.

"She thinks he's a weak wolf and she wants to leave. She doesn't trust him to care for her," Rose said in a rush.

"She's a breed and won't feel the mating pull as deeply as he does. I'm afraid of what it will do to his mind if she leaves him," Silas said, looking blankly at the stairwell. "Poor pup can't catch a break. Gets wounded in the war, PTSD fries his brain, roaming the forest he runs into Arianna, kills another wolf over that bitch only to discover she was using him. He breaks his leg in a fall trying to protect her and then his mate discovers him in that fucked up condition and despises him for it."

He leaned against the wall for a few moments and threw out his senses. Sure enough, Cameron was above ground, as well as the search party. There was one unfamiliar wolf. Silas took control of Lilly's wolf and led her snapping and yipping down the stairs. A growling Cameron followed.

Silas sat both wolves down in front of him."Scan the search party, Rese and Rone, we'll do these two last." He watched Cameron's head swing toward the room the other wolves were led into and asked Rose to bring two chairs from the room.

Lilly whimpered when Rose walked off, watching her the entire time. Rose looked over her shoulder and smiled. "Be right back."

Both wolves stared at him, questions in their eyes, but he had control and wanted them right where he was. Tyrone carried the chairs and placed them in front of the wolves.

"Patron?" Cameron called him through the link.

"Shhh, your mate cannot communicate with me through her link, so it's rude for you to do it. Look at your mate, she's in a new place with people she doesn't know or trust. She needs to trust you."

Cameron's head swung to his mate and he barked. Lilly watched Rose with searing intensity as she and Silas took seats. Tyrone returned to the secure area to help his brother with the scanning. "I suppose you're wondering what's going on," Silas said, looking at Cameron. "Since you've been gone, I have been attacked by rebel forces. When you and I were in the cave, it was blown up by the rebels. They attacked the compound and tried to destroy me." He waved his hands. "As you can see, they were unsuccessful, but we have upgraded the security, and everyone entering the compound is scanned in both forms, that's why it's taking a little longer than usual."

Cameron whimpered and bumped against Lilly. She growled. Baring teeth, Cameron growled and tried to stand. Silas looked at Rose.

"Should we allow him?"

Rose smiled. "Indeed, if he can take her she might submit."

Silas released Cameron and Lilly. She headed for the stairs but Cameron cut her off. Baring his teeth, he stalked the smaller wolf, but she was no pushover. With teeth bared, she leaped forward, barely missing him. Cameron's feral sounding growls bounced off the walls and echoed down the halls. Tyrone ran out of the room to check on Rose.

Silas waved him back inside as he watched Cameron wear down his mate. He never hurt her, but he didn't allow her to have her way either. Finally, Cameron covered the smaller wolf, his teeth on her neck, and she yielded.

Cameron remained standing over her until her breathing returned to normal and she whimpered. After giving her a few licks Cameron stepped back and trotted over to Silas. Lilly followed dutifully behind. This time, when Cameron sat in front of Silas, Lilly lay beside him.

The five men from the search party waved good-bye as they exited the bunker. Silas stood and headed for the room. "Rone scan Cameron first, let him shift, and then Rose will scan Lilly."

Tyrese sat next to Silas at the table. Once Tyrone finished the scan, Cameron shifted and stood to the side watching his mate. Rose took the scanner from Tyrone and copied his movements. She ran the device along her sister's body while sneaking in hugs and giving words of encouragement. When she was done, she returned the device to Tyrone with a huge smile.

"Shift Lilly," Silas said when she didn't change immediately.

"Hold on," Rose said, and walked into the supply closet and came out with a lab coat. "We're human and wolves. The human side gets embarrassed being naked in front of strangers." She handed the coat to Cameron. He stooped and held the coat around her like a curtain. After she changed, he wrapped it around her and took her in his arms, holding her tight.

She stood unresponsive.

"I need each of you to step in this machine," Silas said to cover the awkward moment.

Rose took Lilly's hand and led her to a large x-ray device. "Just walk up there, stand, and the machine will do a full body scan in seconds."

Silas watched the two sisters. They looked related but not identical. Their dark hair was the same. Their builds were similar. Although Lilly seemed taller than Rose, that could be because she was thinner. If he had to point out the major difference between the two women, Silas would say it was their eyes. The color was the same, but there was a world-wariness in Lilly's that was not in Rose's. Thorne had said Lilly was mean, but Silas wondered what had she seen or done in her short life to make her that way. He hoped she relented and gave Cameron a chance because if anyone deserved a break, it was his godson.

Lilly nodded but peeked at Cameron, who watched hungrily from the other machine.

Silas sighed. As if he didn't have enough on his plate, now this. Then he remembered his mate was big on family dynamics and smiled. This was a job for Jasmine. He thought back on how easily she'd handled the twins when they both thought Rose was their mate. That had been impressive.

"They're good," Tyrese announced. Tyrone stood near Rose as she grabbed her sister and the two hugged through tears for a few minutes.

"I'm off the rest of the day, let's get you something to eat," Rose said, not releasing Lilly's hand.

The dark look on Cameron's face made Silas intervene. "I need to debrief both of you. Rose have food brought to the condo. They can shower, change and eat there." Cameron's face cleared some, while Rose's face pinkened.

"Yes, Patron. Just got a bit excited. It's been so long and I've missed her," Rose said, looking at Lilly with a sheepish smile.

Silas nodded as they left the room. "I understand, but some of us wait hundreds of years for mates, and need the comfort of their presence."

Rose peeked at Cameron, whose hooded gaze had not left his mate since they'd shifted. "I understand, Sir."

Lilly glanced at Silas and then at Cameron before turning to her sister. They walked through the tunnels in silence.

Silas prepared his speech for dumping these two on his mate. The beer-drinking detour he and the twins took earlier had thrown them behind and they'd be working late tonight to get everything done.

When they reached the elevators to the condo, Silas sent a greeting to Jasmine. *"How're my babies?"* Ever since he discovered how much it meant to her to call them by that label, he tried to remember to do it as often as possible.

"Fine, David's back asleep with the others. How's Cameron?"

"Not well, his mate doesn't want him and I'm afraid he'll turn feral or revert to his old self if she doesn't."

"Oh, I'm sorry. I hope things work out." She paused. *"I meant to ask how things were going with Siseria. Has the team gotten started yet?"*

"Yeah, they were pretty eager to solve our problem. Hank's handling that situation for me."

"That's good, he's steady. You've got to delegate, otherwise, you'll be ragged. Too ragged for me later on."

He perked up. The elevator was nearing the floor and he wanted her here for the debriefing. *"Meet me at the midway condo. I'm questioning Cameron and Lilly. I'm going to need your help."*

"Really?"

He shook his head and smothered his laugh at the way she rolled the word on her tongue.

"Yeah."

"Okay."

The elevator door opened and Jasmine stood in front of him dressed in a plum short-sleeved dress that hugged the delectable curves on her body and complimented her light brown complexion. Her long braids were piled up in some sexy twists that had his fingers itching to mess up. Silas's erection was immediate.

She smiled at Cameron and Lilly as they exited the steel box. *"I planned to greet him anyway,"* Jasmine said through their link. *"But thanks for inviting me. It means a lot."*

Silas understood. The last time she'd seen Cameron, she and Silas hadn't acknowledged their connection. She stood to the side and waited for Silas to introduce her.

"Cameron, Lilly, this is Jasmine, my mate, and mother of my pups," Silas said. He proudly took her hand in his and placed a kiss on the back of it.

Cameron's mouth dropped and then broke into a wide smile. "Mate? Pups? The Goddess has blessed you, La Patron. I am so happy for you." He embraced Silas and the two men held on for an additional moment. Something shifted inside Silas. It felt right having the young pup back home again.

Cameron stepped back and looked at Jasmine, gracing her with a large smile. "May I embrace your mate, Sir?"

Silas looked at Jasmine, whose light brown eyes were laughing at him. "Yes go ahead, but not too long."

Cameron stepped forward and hugged Jasmine briefly beneath four pairs of eyes. "I am so glad you have returned, Cameron. Maybe now Silas can rest at night. He has been worried about you."

Cameron looked at Silas, and the pup he once knew gazed at him with love and gratitude. "Thank you, Sir, for never giving up."

Choked, Silas nodded and looked down at his mate. Her eyes glowed. It was times like this he wished he had her alone in a room for 10, no, 20 minutes.

Hearing his thoughts, she patted his cheek and smiled. *"Only you would want a sex break instead of a coffee break. Behave, Cameron is doing his thing."*

Cameron reached for Lilly, who stood slightly behind him next to Rose. "This is Lilly, my mate," he said without hesitation as he introduced the female first to Silas and then Jasmine.

Silas kept his distance and nodded, knowing how skittish Lilly was, but Jasmine grabbed the woman in a big hug.

"I will have two daughters. First Rose and now you." She stepped back and glanced at a smiling Rose. "You never told me you two looked so much alike. Two more pretty women to spice this place up, just what we need." Jasmine linked her arms with Lilly and then Rose. The three women walked slightly ahead of the four men toward the condo. Lilly in her lab coat, Rose in a tailored suit, and Jasmine in her tantalizing plum dress. The three couldn't appear more different, but right now they were joined with a common purpose. To make the transition easy for Lilly.

"Uh…what just happened?" Cameron asked Silas, looking confused.

"Welcome to the family," Tyrese said, chuckling.

"Family?" Cameron's eyes widened a bit as he looked at Silas.

"It's a human thing. Your mate is a half-breed," Silas said as though that should explain things.

"I know that," Cameron said slowly. "But…"

"She has a teenage brother, as well. He's kind of on house arrest," Tyrone said with the smug look of a man who had intimate knowledge of the level of confusion Cameron was wading through.

Cameron stopped. "What? Why?" His head swung between Silas and Tyrone.

Silas continued walking after the women. "Don't waste time out here, you don't want to give the women a whole lot of time to talk without us being there. My mate will start asking questions before I arrive if I take too long. And I know you want to learn everything you can about your mate, right?"

Cameron ran to catch up with them. "Yes, yes I do."

They entered the room as Lilly was drying her hands before pulling out a chair to sit at the table. Jasmine glanced at him and placed a plate of food in front of the female. "Eat first. You need to regain your weight if you were larger than Rose."

"Hey, I'm not that big, am I Rone?" Rose looked up at her mate. He took her in his arms and rubbed his hands down her backside.

"Not at all, babe. You're perfect. For me." He placed a kiss on her forehead and led her to the loveseat in the living room.

Cameron walked to the table and looked around.

"The food's in the kitchen, grab a plate and put whatever you want on it," Jasmine said.

He looked surprised but walked out and did as she said. Silas settled in the chair next to Jasmine as Tyrese sat near his brother and Rose in the living area. Cameron returned to the table with his plate, sat next to Lilly, and tore into his food. He finished his first plate before Lilly was halfway done with hers. After having seconds, he placed a bottle of cold water next to his mate. She opened it without comment and drank her fill.

Silas sensed his mate was about to begin her gentle interrogation and nodded to Tyrese, who would be taping the conversation. Once Lilly pushed her plate away, Jasmine began. "Don't you want some dessert?"

Lilly groaned. "No, I am stuffed. But this should digest pretty fast. I always had a high metabolism."

Cameron watched from the corner of his eyes but didn't say anything.

Silas glanced at the clock. He needed to check in with Hank to see how the doctors and lab techs were doing, especially since he'd told them about the detective and what they needed to do. The team of wolves he'd sent after Detective Jenkins should also be checking in soon. They hadn't come up with a plan to corral the rebels from the nightclub incident, but he was waiting to hear from Jayden regarding Leon and the female. Still, he needed to get the word out in case they were spotted.

"Tyrese?"

"Sir?"

"Get the word out that I want the whereabouts of those five rebels. But no one should approach them. For now, I just want a location and any patterns. I'm waiting on some intel and will let you know when I want them brought in."

"Yes, Sir."

"Oh yeah, check in with Hank, find out how things are going in the lab as well."

"Yes, Sir."

Tyrese nodded and left the room. Silas relaxed next to Jasmine and started playing with one of her soft braids that had escaped the pins holding them in place.

"I helped Silas escape the cave-in, but Cameron, you were buried beneath the rocks," Jasmine said, looking between Cameron and Lilly. "When the men went back to get you, you were gone. What happened?"

Cameron shrugged. "I don't know. Last thing I remember, Arianna was saying the pups weren't mine and then everything went dark." He looked at Lilly.

She bit her lip and glanced at Jasmine. "I was on my way to find Rose and Thorne. Mom…she was dead. On the way, I heard him moaning in pain and I…I couldn't ignore it." She released a breath and pushed her hair back from her face.

"Then he stopped. There was nothing. Just a faint heartbeat. I remember being scared but not sure why. When I got to the cave, he was beneath the rocks and I dug him out. It took a long time because I had to stop whenever I heard voices. When the sounds passed, I'd start up again. By the time I finished and could pull him out, it was dark, so I hid him away until first light. I took some clothes from the men on the ground and made a sleigh with those and some tree limbs. We got a fair distance before the limbs broke. Luckily there was a cave nearby. I got him in there and that's where we stayed."

Silas marveled at the tenacity and ingenuity of the young bitch. The Goddess had chosen well for Cameron. He felt sure once they overcame their problems they would have strong pups and a peaceful den.

Jasmine reached across the table and covered her hand. "I'm sure that's an extremely short version of everything the two of you went through to survive. I for one am glad you are here. How long were you sick or out of it, Cameron?"

He released a sigh. "I don't know. There are flashes of images and I remember bits and pieces, but not much. Not until last night, I believe." He looked at Lilly. "The apple, was that last night?"

She nodded.

"Lilly was feeding me pieces of apple. Then she gave me something warm to drink. But at some point, she touched me and told me to get well so we could leave. An electrical charge shot through me, energizing my cells or something." He laughed. "I'm not kidding. All my senses flared and I could see and think clearly for the first time since…wow, I guess since I left for basic training. I remember shifting, and it was as if I was realigning on the inside." He looked at Silas. "Does that make sense? I mean I may not be explaining it right, but that's as close to it as I can get."

"Sounds good to me," Silas said, understanding, even if Cameron didn't, that Lilly had been the catalyst of his healing.

"The longer I stayed wolf, the stronger I became. I went a little stir crazy trying to find a way out of that cave and started digging. When I felt fresh air, I left to check things out. I must've run for miles trying to find a safe path to the top. It took a while, but after I felt confident, I woke Lilly and we headed out. I called you when I was close to the forest. You know the rest."

Lilly sat still in the chair without speaking. She appeared to be listening intently to Cameron's accounting, obviously hearing all of this for the first time.

"What's wrong, Lilly?" Jasmine asked gently.

Lilly shook her head as her lips tightened into a straight line.

"Lilly?" Jasmine's voice changed, it was a little stronger. "Head gestures don't work. You have to use words for me to understand."

"I don't want to talk about it."

"Did he hurt you?"

"No," Lilly said before Cameron could speak. "I...this whole thing. It's not, things aren't like I thought." She swallowed and glanced at Cameron. "He's not like I thought."

"That's a good thing or a bad thing?" Jasmine asked, compassion lacing her voice.

"I don't know. He has a tattoo. That means he's an Alpha, but where's his pack? Why aren't they here?" She frowned.

"His pack is here. We're his pack. He is Alpha-trained and can assume the position one day, but until then he works with me, here at the compound," Silas said.

Lilly looked at Rose and Silas suspected the two were communicating. He took Jasmine's hand and kissed the back.

"What are the names of your pups? How many do you have?" Cameron asked.

"Four. Adam, David, Renee, and Jackie," Silas said, glancing at Jasmine.

Cameron nodded, although his eyes slid to Lilly. "That is so awesome. I can't wait to see them. How old are they?"

"A few days shy of six weeks," Silas said, watching Lilly who was listening. "I had your quarters cleaned and stocked. I figured the two of you might be tired."

Lilly sat up ramrod straight. "I thought I'd stay with Rose and Thorn since I haven't seen them for a while."

"They are in a different wing but you can visit with them any time. However, you cannot live there," Jasmine said with a firmness that surprised and pleased Silas.

"Why not?" Lilly asked, obviously peeved but trying to hide her frustration.

"Because I require peace in my home," Jasmine said succinctly. "And a separated newly mated pair?" Jasmine shook her head. "You will be too jealous and so will he until the two of you settle down and mate properly. So until then, you'll be in Cameron's quarters."

Silas appreciated the firm but gentle manner in which she handled the girl. He knew he didn't have the patience for this type of negotiation.

"I'll leave then," Lilly threatened.

Cameron tensed but remained silent, wisely allowing Jasmine to handle the conversation.

Jasmine smiled and patted her hand. "Lilly, you and I both know if you could have left Cameron, you would have done it a long time ago." Lilly's face reddened but she remained silent.

"You're upset. You feel your life is out of control. I understand and get that." She inhaled and looked at Silas. "Believe me, I do. Silas and I danced a long time before honoring our bond. But neither of us were able to escape it."

"So you're saying suck it up and go with the flow," Lilly asked in an acerbic tone.

Jasmine leaned back in her chair. "Well, you could try talking, get to know him. You've never had the opportunity to spend time with him as a healthy man. He lost his parents when he was young, served in the military, traveled the world. There's a lot you don't know about your mate and a lot he doesn't know about you. Take some time, get to know him, it can't hurt." She stood and smiled. "We did and look what we have to show for it."

"Four pups?" Lilly asked skeptically.

"No... peace in my house. A frustrated mate is hell to live with," Jasmine said with a light laugh while walking toward the living area.

"I know that's right," Rose said from the love seat, elbowing Tyrone.

"Hmph," Lilly snorted.

"You can't leave him. And to be horny and angry all the time is a ticking time bomb. It goes both ways, you're going to want him as much as he wants you. I guess your systems have been a little off because of your situation. But now that his wolf is healthy... and yours is no longer worried over his survival, nature will jump-start those libidos. Save yourself and everyone else the trouble, date him if you want, but spend time talking, get to know one another or whatever else people do before admitting the inevitable."

Jasmine pulled Silas close, opened her link wide open, and kissed him, sharing her heartfelt love and appreciation for the man he was. The taste and feel of her hit his system like a narcotic. He pulled her close, needing more as her scent flooded his nostrils. The way she saw him, handsome, sexy, intelligent, strong, competent, smart, engaging - completely blew his mind. He mirrored her emotions and they flowed between them on a loop that touched off a firestorm in him.

"*I love you so much,*" she said through their link.

"*You complete me,*" he returned.

"*Always love me.*"

"*That is the only thing I can do.*"

They broke apart, gasping for air. She touched his face and leaned against his chest breathing heavily. Holding her tight, he looked around the room. The blueness of his eyes reflected in the mirror across the room. He glanced at the flushed faces of Rose and Lilly. Tyrone and Cameron looked everywhere but in his direction.

Jasmine smiled. "*The babies are awake. I'm going to the nursery. I will see you tonight.*"

He patted her on her backside and walked to the door. "Cameron, escort my mate and Rose back to their floor before you and your mate return to your wing."

"Yes, Sir."

Chapter 10

Silas waited until they left and then asked Tyrone, "Has Rese checked in?"

Tyrone glanced at him before speaking. "No. Sir. Would you like me to contact him?"

"Yes." Silas strode to the kitchen, grabbed a glass of cold water, and drained it. He poured another glass, held it in his hand for a moment, and then rubbed it across his forehead. He willed his painful erection to ease up. It didn't help that her scent remained in his nostrils, the feel of her skin still teased the pads of his fingertips. And her taste, God he hadn't wanted her like that since… last night. Jasmine was his singular addiction.

He squeezed his neck and thought of Siseria and the explosive device somewhere in her body. His hardness softened a bit. Then he remembered the rebels who wanted to destroy his precious litter. And his back stiffened. His thoughts flitted over Detective Jenkins, then the rebels who set up Tyrese and the explosion with Boggs, those situations trekked across his mind, effectively bringing him out of his lusty haze. Prepared to deal with the issues at hand, Silas stepped out into the living area. Tyrone stood in the middle of the room.

"He's in the lab. They have the x-ray of the device. He thinks you may want to see it."

Silas nodded.

"Also, Jenkins has been brought into the bunker beneath the gym. Froggy is with him. They have him sedated and are waiting for you to pull his wolf."

Silas decided to pull the wolf first so Froggy could examine the animal and create a training plan.

"He's been scanned?"

"Yes. Froggy scanned him. Says he's clear. Plus Rese scanned him a few minutes ago and locked him in. No one can access him until after you pull his wolf, not even Froggy."

Silas smiled. Tyrese was serious about carrying out his no fuck-ups decree. He snapped his fingers and contacted Tyrese. *"Do you still have those clothes you wore to the club the other night?"*

"Yes, Sir."

"I'm heading to pull Jenkins wolf and will come to the lab afterward. When we return to the wing, grab those clothes, I need to scent the wolves from the fight."

"Yes, Sir."

Silas and Tyrone strode down the hall toward the elevator to take them to the tunnels. "You think Lilly and Cameron will be okay?" Tyrone asked. "Rose is worried. She's afraid Lilly will run away."

"She would have done that already. I believe she's with him because she wants to be. It may take a little time for her mind to catch up to her heart or vice versa. But it'll happen."

"Good, because I don't want Rose caught in the middle of this." They reached the tunnel and returned to the bunker area. After clearing security, they entered the area where Jenkins lay on a cot behind a secured door.

Silas sought out the detective's wolf, but it fought the change. Eventually, he was able to pull the wolf out and it lay heaving on the bed. Watching the limp animal on the bed, Silas became concerned. The wolf should have become vocal after the change. There should be some whimpering or howling, or something. Standing close to the steel door, Silas looked through the glass and scanned the listless wolf.

As he continued the scan he grew angrier. When the scan was completed, Silas dropped his head against the steel door and prayed to the Goddess for strength. The happy glow from having his godson returned hadn't even faded before he was slammed with another possible catastrophe.

What the hell was going on?

Surely he was in the midst of some sort of cosmic test. At every turn, he was bombarded with new crises and threats. Counting to ten, he inhaled, jumped off the pity party bus, and fought like hell to be the man his mate saw.

"Call Hank, have him bring Dr. Passen here." The doctor and his team were aware of the detective's weak wolf, but there was more. A lot more.

"Yes, Sir," Tyrone said.

"Rone?"

"Sir?"

"Have them wear the hazmat gear. Something is attacking this wolf from the inside out and exposing him to air may have made it worse." Silas turned and leaned against the steel door, hoping he hadn't just escalated the wolf's death.

"I've told him and they will be here shortly," Tyrone said, standing nearby. "How bad do you think it is?"

"I'm not sure, but I think it is some kind of virus." He shook his head. "Talk about throwing the kitchen sink at me, this has been one hell-uv-a-day."

"Damn, that's…messed up."

"Yeah," Silas pushed off from the door. "It is." He strode across the hall and took a seat. As a distraction from the new problem behind the door and the other BS sitting on his desk, he pulled out his electronic pad and checked messages. There were quite a few from various Alphas seeking his counsel. Not surprising after he'd torn into them this morning.

Getting comfortable, he responded to the requests, gave his advice, and functioned as a sounding board. He had just finished sending his last response when Tyrese, the doctor, and three security guys entered the bunker. Not only did they wear the hazmat equipment, but they rolled a large incubator-looking cube with them as well.

Silas stood.

Dr. Passen, dressed in protective gear, walked over to meet him. After bowing, the doctor looked over his shoulder at the equipment. "I thought we'd take him back with us so we can run tests and use the equipment we already have set up." The flare of excitement in the doctor's eyes was hard to miss.

Silas smothered a grin. Although, not a scientist or doctor, he assumed the idea of getting the first crack at two possible weapons being used against wolves was exciting. "That makes perfect sense. I pulled his wolf and grew concerned when there was little response. After a cursory scan, I detected something wrong with the wolf's muscle tissue. Find out what it is. If it's a birth defect, I want to know the cause and ways to prevent it in the future. Or if something was administered to harm his wolf, I want to know everything. Possible side effects, is it curable, permanent, everything. Because his human side appears to be fine."

The doctor's brow rose. "A breed with a sick wolf, that's interesting indeed. So many possibilities," the doctor murmured and turned to look at the steel door. "I will get started immediately. First, I need to have some blood work done and examine his muscle tissue." He faced Silas again. "We have made some progress on the woman. The device is a small bomb. The reason it cannot be sensed is it's covered in a tissue that mimics human tissue very closely. On the x-ray, it looks like an enlarged gland, something that wouldn't be commented on or even noticed if you weren't looking for something specific. Someone went through a lot of man-hours creating that device. I have two of my best techs working on ways to detect it without a scanner. There may be some frequency or scent or something that will identify the device before it detonates."

"Good, that is great news," Silas said with heartfelt gratitude. Identifying the device was a small part of the problem. The real challenges lie in finding a way to detect it.

"Now, I want to get this wolf to the lab if that is okay?"

Silas nodded. "*Tyrese?*" he called through their link.

"*Sir?*"

"*I put the wolf to sleep. Only those of you in protective gear enter the room. Take the cube and place the wolf inside. Lock him down. I want no traces of the wolf in the air until we know what we are dealing with. Call sanitation to clean this room, but I want them in protective gear as well. They are to do a thorough wipe down in here, specifically for contagious diseases.*"

"*Diseases?*" Tyrese sounded shocked.

"*That's almost unheard of for wolves, but apparently not for breeds. His wolf is sick, possibly dying. If someone fed him something or gave his wolf an injection, I damn sure want to know about it.*"

"*Understood.*"

Silas could imagine the young pups' concern. It wasn't enough to play with the natural order of things, wolves and humans mating, having pups. Admittedly, it'd taken him a while to get on board, but he accepted half-breeds were here to stay. His entire inner circle, except for Jacques, Cameron and Hank, were breeds. But this…destroying the wolf in a breed. This was beyond over the top. There was no way someone was doing all of this to get rid of him. No, there had to be another agenda.

Maybe there was more than one player. The human female had talked about destroying him but saving his pups. But that Mitch guy said two men wanted Jasmine and the pups dead. Plus, the man never attacked Silas, Jasmine had been his target all along.

Silas sifted through all the information he and his men had gathered. No matter how he sliced and diced the data, he kept coming to the same conclusion. The Wolf Nation was under attack by two opposing factions with different end games. That one would trigger the other was a moot point at this time. He needed to go on the offensive and lock down more information.

The small team rolled the wolf down the corridor. Tyrone approached.

Silas waved him closer. "Go grab some dinner and check on your mate and her siblings. Under no circumstances is Lilly to stay in your wing. Meet me in my office in an hour and a half. I've thought of some things I want to go over."

"Yes, Sir." Tyrone left.

Silas repeated the message to Hank and Tyrese. He wished he could include Cameron in his findings, but a newly mated wolf's mind is half-cocked until he completes the mating 'dance' and secures his mate bond. Once connected via their links, the need to be close physically eased tremendously.

"I'm hungry," he said to Jasmine through their link. *"Can you make some time to feed me?"* He sent her an image from that kiss she'd laid on him earlier and the impact it'd had on him. He felt the warmth of her laughter through their link and smiled. *"The babies are up and I am on my back while they crawl over me, exploring. As babies, the twins progressed fast but not like this, must be your super sperm."*

The hazmat cleaning crew entered the bunker. Silas scanned each man to make sure their wolves were healthy before allowing them to enter the room that held Jenkins.

"*You are probably right. Normally, pups are running around about this time so there is some delay caused by their human genes.*"

"*Ha, human genes.*" She laughed. "*You're probably right though.*"

"*I am always right.*"

"*Pfft.*"

"*Most of the time?*"

"*You're getting closer.*"

He stifled his laugh, but some sound must have escaped since one of the cleaners gave him a confused look before replacing his helmet.

"*Okay, I will meet you in the nursery so that my pups will have something really tough to climb and explore. I've got a meeting in an hour and a half in my office. But I'd like to spend some alone time with you before that.*"

"*Sounds good, I'll see what I can do.*"

"*Love you.*"

Her breath hitched and he smiled. Normally she said it first, but he wanted to beat her to it this time.

"*Love you, too.*"

Despite the chaos of this day, starting with the explosion this morning and ending with a possible chemical weapon against wolves, Silas was not in despair. Oh, he was pissed, but not devastated. He understood the implications but they hadn't sent him spiraling into depression or rage. A year ago, all of those things would have happened and more.

The words the Goddess spoke last year flowed over him: *"The one definite thing is change. It's coming with a time of testing. Your obedience and service to me has not gone unnoticed. You will be rewarded, although it may not seem so at the time. Be vigilant, you'll need your eyes to see. Be faithful, you'll need your ears to ferret out the truth. Be merciful, your nose will lead you to understanding. Be courageous, your heart will suffer but will guide you to the truth. Taste the truth and embrace it, reject the lies and you will ride the wave of change. Your wolves need your direction now more than ever."*

Change slapped the Wolf Nation awake creating growling in the streets. A time of testing, She had said. After the day he'd had, he hoped this was the eye of the storm, and things tapered down. Vigilance, faithfulness, mercy, and courage, were traits required of him to ride this wave. Right now he held a serious deficit in all of them, especially mercy. His lips tightened at the thought of the woman with a bomb lodged inside her and the danger she presented to his pups. Mercy… he completely lacked that necessary virtue.

After scanning the last cleaner to leave the bunker, pleased they were all good, he locked the door and placed his seal on it. No one would be able to enter it until he removed the seal, and that wouldn't happen until the doctor could explain what was going on with the Detective's wolf.

Chapter 11

Jasmine lay on the floor with David on her chest. She stroked him to ease his frustration. At least she thought he was frustrated over his inability to sit up like the rest of his brothers and sisters. The three of them had been fed and bathed. Now they sat nearby playing with blocks and an assortment of too-large-to-swallow toys.

At six weeks, her babies looked like six to eight-month-olds, sitting up, scooting, and crawling. At first, it boggled her mind. The twins had developed fast, but this…this was like babies with a fast forward button pushed to its top speed. The doctor said Silas' genes might cause the babies to develop at a wolf pup rate rather than a human's, even though they appeared human and couldn't shift. She would have to come up with some explanation for her mother and sister, but for the life of her, she hadn't been able to think of a single thing.

Plus, if Julie was right, and the woman certainly believed she was, one of these four would lead the wolves after Silas. She looked at each child and realized they all had the personality for the position.

Adam tossed a plastic block at his sister, Jackie. Before it reached her face she'd batted it down like an inconsequential bug and continued putting the wood pieces in the correct slots. He pouted a bit and then picked up another block and aimed at Renee. She looked up, her eyes a startling shade of light blue, made even more so because of her mocha complexion, daring him. He lowered his hand and started building with his blocks.

Jasmine sighed watching her offspring. So damned different, each of them. Little Renee had been aptly named since she seemed to have her aunt's don't play with me' attitude at times. She was quiet as long she had something in her hand to draw with, otherwise, she'd raise a stink until she had her coloring implements.

Jackie was inquisitive. Give her a stack of puzzles and she'd work each one until she mastered it. Even if that meant dumping the pieces out and starting all over again. Unfortunately, she refused to share any puzzle in her stack and all the puzzles in the room wound up in her stack. Jasmine was grateful Adam and Jackie never fought over the pieces, but she knew it was something she would need to deal with as her daughter grew older.

Adam was a happy-go-lucky prankster. He loved to play and found joy in almost anything. Because his sisters were usually preoccupied with their own thing, he required a lot of his mother's attention. Sometimes she would prop David up so he could watch Adam play, and every once in a while he might hold a block or two. Adam would get excited and expect more from his brother, but it was obvious Adam's overabundance of energy wore David out.

Adam crawled up on her stomach and rubbed David on the back, mimicking her movements. Experience taught her sitting up was the best position when Adam was in help-mommy mode. She picked up Adam with one hand and held onto David as she scooted back against the chair for support. Adam gave her a grin, his tiny teeth gleaming in the light. His jet black curly hair fell to his shoulders. Whiskey-colored eyes and a small dimple on his right cheek might fool someone else into believing he was a sweet innocent, but Jasmine recognized the smile for what it was and moved David before Adam's teeth found their target.

She wagged her finger at Adam. "No biting your brother."

He grinned at her unrepentantly.

David looked down at his brother with a bored expression. Out of all of them, he was the most alert, constantly watching everything and everyone in the room. Despite his health challenges, Jasmine knew a sharp mind worked behind those eyes.

Adam held up both hands to her. Jasmine nodded to his nurse and the woman picked him up and sat with him on the floor. Jasmine glanced at the large clock on the opposite wall and released a breath. Adam was normally the first to get sleepy. Renee yawned but continued coloring. Jasmine knew Jackie wouldn't be far behind. She nodded to the other two nurses, who went, held the girls upright by the hands as they returned the puzzles and drawing materials to their proper place. Adam's nurse released him so he could put up the blocks and toys he'd been playing with back into the large plastic tub. Tired, he put up his usual fuss, but Jasmine remained firm and he eventually put everything back.

Adam was crying and reaching for her, so she exchanged David for him with the nurse as Silas walked in. The girls started yelling and raising their arms toward him.

"Rock star Dad," Jasmine teased as he took both Renee and Jackie in his arms and kissed them on the forehead before kissing David and Adam.

"Busy night?"

She shrugged. Tonight was not that much different from the other nights. The kids were fighting sleep, becoming irritable, but she was used to it.

Adam was the first to fall asleep, all that energy he used tormenting his brother and sisters took a toll. She laid him in his crib and took David from the nurse. He was normally the last one to close his eyes and the first to wake.

Silas placed Renee in her crib, then placed Jackie in hers. He took a moment and stared at their peaceful faces with a slight smile. It amazed Jasmine how much the children looked like Silas. It was as if his seed used her as an incubator to pop out little Silases. All four had black, thick wavy hair like his. Renee's eyes were a piercing blue and Jackie's were more blue-greenish. They had his full arched brows and it looked as though they'd even have his cheekbones and chin.

Basically, the girls were small, female Silas Knights. The boys were a combination, thank goodness. David's eyes were a piercing shade of golden-brown, but it looked as though he'd have her rounder face and fuller lips as he grew older.

"Maybe the next —"

"Don't say it," she snapped with a warning glance.

"Next —"

"I'm not playing don't say it," she said, laying a sleeping David in his crib.

"Maybe —"

"How do blue balls sound to you?"

He pulled in his lips and made a zipping motion.

"Thought so." She pulled the cover over David and did a quick check on the other three before turning to the nurses, who were preparing their beds for sleep. "Thank you, ladies, call me if you need me."

They nodded as they did every night. Silas grabbed her hand, nodded to the women, and left the room.

"Are you mad at me?"

"No. But discussing having more children with a mother of six after a very long, tiring day with four babies is not a wise move, Mister. You should know that."

He kissed the back of her hand. "I stand corrected, you are right of course." He pushed open the door to their suite and followed her inside. Once they cleared the door, he wrapped his arms around her waist and pulled her close for a sizzling kiss. It was so soft, sweet, and hot, her heart melted a wee bit. He released her mouth and dropped his forehead to hers. "You are the best part of my day," he whispered across her face, breathing life into her tired bones.

"Ummm." She pulled up his shirt, exposing his ripped abs and rock-solid chest, and ran the flat of her palm over him before placing a kiss on each of his nipples, enjoying him squirm. "Take it off," she murmured, her breath teasing his pebbled nipple.

He leaned back and pulled off his shirt in one swoop, then placed one hand on her hip, and the other on the side of her face. His firm lips brushed against hers. "My mate."

Hungry for more, his tongue pressed against the seam of her closed mouth. Eyes closed, she gasped at the sensual feel as he slid inside. Squeezing her ass he pulled her closer, deepening the kiss. When he dropped his shields, she almost buckled beneath the onslaught of his strong emotions. If love had a texture, it flowed over and around her, cocooning the two of them together. Her heart greedily absorbed everything he gave and returned it to him full measure. The cool air brushed against her skin. He'd undressed her while placing kisses up and down her neck.

She wrapped her arms around him, never wanting to let him go. "My mate," she whispered, reveling in the knowledge of what it truly meant to be one with this man. He filled all of her empty spaces. She was whole, lacking nothing.

He laid her on their bed, kissing her face, neck, breasts, and finally taking her tender, ultra-sensitive nipple into his mouth. She reached for his hardness, but he'd angled himself in such a way the most she could touch was his arms and parts of his chest. Settling for the limited contact, her hands held onto his flexing biceps as she lost herself in the feelings he evoked.

"I've been thinking about you, this, all day," he murmured.

She nodded. "I know. Seeing you, talking about us, it just lit something in me."

He stopped and stared at her. "I felt it. There was something different when you kissed me in the condo. I've been simmering from that kiss since then," he said raggedly. "I don't think I can prolong this, I need to take you, claim you." He leaned up, jerked down his pants, and kicked them to the side.

Holding onto her tight, he looked at the landscape of her body. She wiggled a bit, loving the clenching of his jaw, the way his nose narrowed as he scented her need. When he met her eyes, his were glowing blue.

She swallowed hard and grinned. Her man was borderline feral. That she could bring him to this after recently giving birth to four babies brought tears to her eyes and a song to her heart. She widened her legs in welcome. His fingertip traced the length of her inner thigh, traveled across her sopping wet center and down the other leg. He leaned forward and like the wolf he was, devoured her. The man licked and lapped her clean. Before she could holler or catch her breath, he crawled forward and slid home.

She arched her back and released a pleased sigh. Her man filled her to the delectable brim. "Ummmm," she moaned as he breathed fast and hard.

"Look at me."

She opened her eyes, saw his grimace, and knew it was on. He was trying hard to take it easy, but they hadn't let loose in a long time. That ended tonight.

"I need to reclaim you. I may shift partially but…I need to claim you."

She nodded. His gorgeous wolf was close to the surface. That part of his nature was ravenous. His wolf hadn't participated in taking her since before the birth of the babies.

"I need whatever you need," she said softly, meaning it. "Love all of me with all of you." He released a mixture between a howl and yell into the air. She had never been so happy that their suite was soundproof.

His eyes blazed and he pulled back, only to thrust into her again and again, picking up speed. She tried to continue looking into his eyes but heat coiled inside her lower regions as he slammed into her. She squealed in pleasure, lifted her legs, and wrapped them around his waist. She met him with equal fervor, needing to please him as much as gain her release. Their bodies slapped together making beautiful music. Her hand flew to his chest, grabbed his nipples, and twisted. His face morphed into the feral, lust-crazed one she loved. "That's right, Wolfie, give it to me," she said, urging him on.

She hung onto his arms as he pistoned into her, barely able to keep up with his pace.

Breathless, she closed her eyes to enjoy the sensations flowing from the top of her head to the soles of her feet. She cried out in pleasure as he took her with long, fast strokes, sending indescribable pleasure zipping through her body.

Her back arched. Her mouth opened but no sound emitted as her muscles clenched. She spiraled up and over into the blinding light of her release. Shuddering and gasping for air as ecstasy buffeted her.

"Shit," Silas grunted, his face wild in mid-shift, sharp canines crowded his mouth as he threw back his head and howled. The pleasure of his bite sent another shudder rippling through her.

Smug pride filled her chest as he surged into her over and over again. Seconds later he came with a loud cry, spilling his seed into her body.

Chest heaving, he slumped over and placed his forehead on the side of her neck. His raspy tongue lapped her neck.

"Ummm, feels good. You make me feel so damn good," she whispered, holding the back of his head as he licked and sucked on her bite. Tingles of pleasure shot through her.

"I need to see my mark on you. It looks good."

She laughed. "What time is it? You have to work, remember?"

"I'm the boss. I can push it back a bit."

He rolled over, pulling her close to his side. She placed her hand on his chest and breathed in his masculine scent. "Why are you working tonight? It can't wait until morning?"

He rubbed her shoulder. "Some of it will wait. But I need to search the rogues that set Rese up."

She stiffened. He tightened his hold and explained everything they had discovered, including how it tied into the bomb going off this morning.

"Oh my God, I bet Rese is blaming himself, isn't he?" She looked at Silas and saw the answer before he spoke. "That boy always did have a superman complex. He is not infallible. There was no way he could have known about the spy, hell, sounds like the spy didn't even know what his real job was."

"Calm down, Mama Bear. Tyrese is damn good at what he does. And he's smart. We didn't have the proper intel but are catching up. It won't be long before we're on the offense instead of defense." He placed a kiss on her forehead which helped calm her concerns.

"What about the Cop, I mean Detective? What's the plan to get him to back down, because the next time he disrespects Rose, she's gonna rip him a new one."

"He's infected."

"What?"

"His wolf's infected with something. I think his wolf is dying, but I'm not sure."

"Is that…possible? How can one exist without the other?"

He inhaled and her heart wept for him. It seemed there was one new problem after the other for him to fix. But this problem might impact her, no, their kids, so she wanted to know what was going on.

"Jazz, a year ago, I would have said you couldn't birth my litter or become my mate. I don't know what's possible or not anymore. Someone changed the rules and didn't pass out a rule book. At least I don't have one. So I can't answer your question without more information from the doctor and lab techs."

"But…what if someone tries to mess with Rese or Rone or Rose's wolves? Will that kill them?" she asked, voicing her biggest fear.

Silas shrugged and this was one time she wished he'd lie even though they promised never to lie to each other. "I don't know. You met Jenkins, did he look like he was dying?"

She thought of the tall, slim-hipped man with blue eyes and brown hair. "No. Quite the opposite. He was a jackass."

"See? There's no way to know what's really going on until after the tests are done." He rubbed her chin. "Be patient."

She nodded. "Are you still going to allow the Alpha challenge?"

"Yes," he said with a bite in his tone.

After silently accepting she beat that topic to death, she moved on to other things.

"Are we still waiting for David to be stronger before presenting the babies to your people? I only ask because I want my mom and Renee here for that. And I've been putting them off."

"You want your family at a wolf event? You sure they'll be up for that?" He looked at her. What does a presentation involve, she wondered.

"Maybe we're not thinking along the same lines because I'm thinking a presentation is similar to a baptism." He looked at her blankly. "It's when the priest offers blessings over the babies, asks the families or godparents to make sure the kids are taken care of."

"I will care for my pups, no one else," he said with a dark scowl.

She realized he couldn't fathom a baptism. "Tell me what is involved with presenting them to your people?"

"Normally, I'd travel to the four regions, and the Alphas from those areas would come meet the pups, renew their vows to include my mate and litter. Several days of celebrations would follow."

She waited for him to continue. When he didn't, she looked at him. "Okay, so you're not doing it that way, so what did you have in mind?"

He closed his eyes. "I don't know. I asked Jacques to handle it on his return visit."

Jasmine lay back and wasn't sure if she was offended or not. "So you have no plans for presenting the babies yet, and you shot down the baptism, which is a part of my culture."

He didn't say anything.

"Well, since you have nothing to say, I'll fill in the blanks and plan a baptism so that my children can be blessed in my faith. I will invite my mother, her husband, my sister and her lover, and the nurses who care for the children. It will be closed to immediate family only and the minister."

"What minister?"

She hadn't thought of anyone in particular, but she was sure she could work that out even if she had to fly in her former pastor. "I'll let you know."

"I'm not comfortable with a lot of strangers on the grounds near my pups. There are too many unexplained events happening now. Can you wait until the end of the year?"

She leaned up on her elbows. "You do realize that the babies are pulling up trying to walk and they're only six weeks old. By the end of the year, they might be driving me to the church or singing a song, or reading poetry. The thing is, nobody knows what things will be like in another six months, but right now, they are babies who can be held and blessed by my pastor."

"Everyone entering the grounds has to be scanned," he said, laying on his back and playing with her fingers.

"I know." She released a sigh at his tacit agreement to the event. Hopefully, Renee wouldn't put up too much of a stink over the tight security. "How much can I tell them? I mean, this place is huge and everything inside is top-notch. It looks like you're rich, what should I say?"

"Tell them the truth, I am rich and you're my bitch." He rolled over, pinned her down, and kissed her before she could react. The kiss turned steamy as he stroked her mouth and rubbed his hard length against her.

When they broke apart, she gasped for air but rose to touch his lips with the tip of her tongue. "Cancel the damn meeting," she said in a husky tone, licking his lips.

"I'm canceling the meeting." He sealed her mouth with another searing kiss.

Chapter 12

"Are you sure you need all of these people?" Silas asked Dr. Passen as he walked to the security point to scan the new arrivals.

"Yes, Sir." The man nodded a few times as if the extra nods would strengthen his point. "We are working feverishly on two projects instead of one. These five individuals were able to commit to working with me on short notice. They understand they cannot leave until the work is done and that communication will be limited. But…" He stopped and looked at Silas. "We need more help, not only to meet your deadline but to make sure there isn't a deadly chemical or drug out there that affects our wolves. That is of the utmost importance to every wolf in the lab."

Sensing the doctor's resolve, Silas nodded. Every time someone new entered the compound, even if it was a different wing from his private quarters and below ground, it was still too close to his mate and litter for him. But as

Patron, he needed to put aside those feelings and do what was best for the Wolf Nation. There were times when his role as Patron and Alpha of his den, or Daddy according to Jasmine, clashed. He didn't think that would ever change.

"Okay, we'll do this then." He walked into the room and greeted the four men and one female. As the doctor introduced each person, Silas shook their hand and did an in-depth scan of their bodies and mind. The third man smelled familiar but Silas couldn't place it, but the fool was hiding something. Silas poked a bit. The man winced. Silas let it go and finished the scan. When he finished with the last person, he went over the rules.

"You can all follow Dr. Passen, except you, Dr. Chism." Silas pointed to the tall, lanky red-haired male with the secrets. The color left Chism's face, making him look guiltier.

Silas motioned for him to follow him. Chism's green eyes widened, his mouth opened and then closed with a snap. With a swipe of his tongue across his lips, Matthew Chism stood, glanced at a frowning Dr. Passen, and followed Silas out of the main room into a much smaller one.

"Take a seat," Silas said as he took one at the small wooden table.

Matthew sat down and looked at him. Silas sensed his nervousness and didn't prolong the issue. "You're hiding something, what?"

"S-s-s-ii-rr?" the man stammered.

This was not the way he'd planned to start his morning. When Hank contacted him regarding the new arrivals, he and the twins were preparing to pick up the trail of the rebels. It would be slightly harder to do this morning than last night when he'd canceled the meeting, but everyone agreed it was in their best interest to bring the group in for questioning.

"I will say this only once. Tell me what you are hiding in the next minute or security will be carrying you out of here in a body bag." The man jerked back, his face devoid of color. "I…my mate and I, we...." He exhaled. "My mate and I took a chance answering Dr. Passen's urgent request for assistance. I specialize in tissue identification, did my dissertation on it in fact, and when he sent word for me to come, I said no. Then he mentioned there might be a virus attacking the wolves of the half-breeds. And I knew I couldn't live with myself if I didn't help. I am the best in my field, not bragging, it's just the truth," he said in a rush before inhaling.

Silas leaned forward. "Why is *that* so important to you? You're a full-blood."

"My mate…he um…well, his sons are half-breeds. And even though they don't, you know…uh, talk to each other, he…we want to make sure they are safe."

Silas blinked, inhaled again, and closed his eyes. *Hell, no.* Wasn't the bomb and virus more than enough yesterday? It's not like this week didn't already hold the honor of the absolute worse ever, he did not need this complication. Not today. He inhaled the man's scent again to be certain and released it with a muttered curse.

"Who is your mate?" Silas growled, needing to hear him say it. As much as he prayed to the Goddess that the devil hadn't risen from the dead and walked through his front door, he knew he wouldn't be so lucky.

"Please, Sir. There are complications… people could be hurt. If it's alright with you, can he remain anonymous?" The man's face tightened in fear.

Remain dead you mean. "It's not alright, now tell me his name," Silas said in a low timbre, unclenching his fist beneath the table.

"Davian Bennett."

Silas allowed the name to roll through his mind until it settled and solidified in his brain. This had the potential for all kinds of fucked up shit to jump off. "Wait here." Silas walked out and met Dr. Passen in the hall, who was waiting on Chism.

"Do you really need him?" Silas asked harshly, hating the position he was in.

Dr. Passen frowned. "Yes…yes, we do. He is the foremost authority on the physiology of half-breeds. He's years ahead in research, started it before anyone else. It's an honor to have him here." He paused and then straightened. "Sir, he's our best shot at discovering what's happening to that wolf. I've done all I can, and the wolf is still unresponsive. We need his expertise on this."

Silas nodded. His mind raced to calculate the fall-out. The twins might be a little upset, but nothing major. But Jasmine, he didn't want to think about her reaction when she discovered Silas had known all along Davian was alive and his mate worked on a cure for the sick wolf. He closed his eyes and prayed to the Goddess for guidance.

He could lose Jasmine behind this. Human breeders were not tethered to their mates like full-blooded bitches were. She could leave him, if not physically, then emotionally. Either way would cripple him. He clenched his jaw and inhaled.

"La Patron?" Dr. Passen called out. "We need to get started with the testing."

Silas looked at him for a moment and made a decision. "Go ahead, I will accompany Dr. Chism. There are a few things I need to go over with him."

Dr. Passen looked like he wanted to argue, but wisely nodded and walked off. Slowly, Silas gathered his thoughts and returned to the room. Matthew watched him enter with wary eyes.

"Is everything okay?"

Silas nodded. "Where is your mate?"

Matthews's eyes widened. "Why? Is he in trouble? Is this about Davian?"

"No. I just need to make sure he is safe so you can work without distractions."

Matthew stared at him a moment longer. "Capital Inn in town."

Silas sent a message to security to keep Davian under surveillance, the Bennett clan was supposed to be coming to town, and if they wanted a family reunion they needed to do it away from West Virginia.

"La Patron?" Matthew said when Silas didn't say anything for a few moments.

"There is a problem, Matthew." He looked at the man sitting in front of him and wished for all of their sakes things were different. But he had to play the hand dealt him and so did everyone else. Things were about to get sticky, but what else was new?

"Problem?" There was a thread of panic in the man's voice. His mouth opened slightly and he appeared tense.

"Yes, Tyrese and Tyrone Bennett are here. They are on my security detail. The only reason they aren't with me now is that I have them handling other duties." Silas watched the other man's reaction and felt bad for them both.

Matthew's eyes widened at the mention of the twins. He took a deep breath, looked at his intertwined fingers on the table, and then glanced at Silas. "Okay...well, they don't like me that much. I guess they feel I broke up their family. But that's not true, Sir. Davian and I are mates." He looked pleadingly at Silas.

Normally, when wolves found their mates, it was cause for celebration, and as Patron, he would be the first to pat these two wolves on the backs and wish them well. But these were not normal times and patting Davian and Matthew on their backs was the furthest thing from his mind right now.

He nodded. "I understand. I don't think the twins feel you broke up their family. They hate that Davian didn't just let their mom go so she could have a better quality of life, maybe meet someone else. But because he never did that and was with you, they were mad he cheated on her. If he'd come clean, divorced her, I don't think they'd mind you one way or the other."

Matthew looked thoughtful for a moment. "You're probably right. For whatever reason, he never thought to do that." He gazed at Silas. "Do you want me to leave?"

"Dr. Passen believes you can find out what's going on with the wolf and clue me in on how he came to such a state. Most importantly, he believes you can find a way to make sure it doesn't happen to any other wolves." Silas eyed the man. "I hope you are as good as he says because we are all going to pay a high price for you solving that riddle."

Matthew nodded. "I'll...I'll do my best, Sir. But Davian has to be safe, I won't be able to function if he's hurt or in danger." He swallowed hard as if it was difficult getting the words out of his throat.

Silas nodded in total understanding. "I'll make sure of that. I'm not going to lie to you, there will be distractions and disruptions."

"The twins didn't want me around before, but they are older now. Surely they'll understand I don't mean them any harm and I'll be gone as soon as we finish this project."

Silas chuckled. It was a dry mocking sound that did little to ease his burgeoning anxiety. Plus, there was nothing remotely funny about the situation he was in.

"I'm sorry, you misunderstood." He looked at the frowning man and sat forward, his tented fingertips on his lips. "It's not the twins I'm concerned about."

"Then...Who?...What?"

"Jasmine Bennett is here as well."

Matthew's brows rose to ridiculous heights as he leaned back in the chair as though someone had knocked the wind from him. "What? Jasmine...she's on the west...no...oh my God. What is she...." He ran his hand through his hair and closed his eyes. "Oh shit."

Yeah, that about summed it up. "She thinks her husband is dead," Silas said, in case the man in front of him forgot the crazy scheme he and his mate cooked up.

"But…I'll tell Davian to leave. She doesn't…"

Silas shook his head, sorrier than he would ever admit. "I cannot lie to her. And the lies have to stop."

"But…he wanted her to have the money from the military. He said she deserved it after all the years the military had him deployed away from his family. That's why he faked his death." He looked at Silas with desperation in his eyes. "He would have stayed with her, unhappy as they were; he loved her as much as a wolf could love someone who wasn't their mate."

Being mated, Silas understood. "But he found his mate and that changed things. I get that, but the lies…they end today. Once she knows…there will be some fall-out. It's not every day a woman discovers her husband is alive and with someone else." Or that her mate didn't tell her that information a year before, Silas added silently.

"And a man," Matthew said in a despondent tone.

Silas hadn't thought about that. He couldn't imagine how that nugget of information would impact her. His plate overflowed, so he refused to add her reaction to a male lover to his thoughts.

"She may come to see you. Probably ask all kinds of questions. She may even want to see Davian. I don't know what will happen, I am just warning you."

"But…but how can she do that? I'll be in a restricted area. Can't you keep her away?" He looked confused.

Silas offered him a sympathetic smile. "I cannot restrict her movements in this compound, she has complete access to everywhere, can open any door."

"How is that possible? Does she know her sons are breeds?"

"Yes, she knows." Silas paused. "She's my mate." He thought the man would faint.

Matthew's eyes widened. "Oh shit."

"Yeah. That about sums it up."

Chapter 13

After settling a shaken Matthew in the lab with instructions to keep their conversation confidential, Silas instructed the twins to meet him in the gym in twenty minutes. He needed time to think through everything that'd happened yesterday and today. Plus, he needed to rehearse his confession to Jasmine.

He walked in to find them shooting a few hoops with Stephen, the Alpha training manager, and laughing. Watching, he took a seat on one of the benches and waited for them to finish. Tyrone grabbed the ball and headed off the court.

"Finish the game," Silas said, being in no hurry to go upstairs and face his mate.

Tyrone tilted his head to the side and took a seat next to Silas. "He told you huh?"

Silas gazed at Tyrone, wondering if he was talking about Matthew or someone else. He was betting it was something new.

"Cameron," Tyrone said.

Silas frowned. He hadn't talked to Cameron since yesterday. He figured the young man was busy wooing his mate.

Tyrone shook his head and turned away. "Forget it."

Silas snorted. "You know that's not going to happen. What's Cameron going to tell me?" He watched Tyrese walk away from Stefan and join them.

"Hey, what's going on?" Tyrese asked as he sat next to Tyrone.

"Rone was about to tell me what Cameron wants to tell me."

Tyrese snorted.

Silas's eyes darted to him. "What happened?" He looked from Tyrese to Tyrone.

"Cameron wants to participate in the Alpha challenge next month. He thinks it'll help change the way Lilly sees him," Tyrese said.

Silas stared at Tyrese. He hadn't seen that coming. "Did you mention the challenge?" he asked Tyrone.

"No. Thorne heard it in the gym from some of the guys. Lilly and Rose were talking about it. Lilly thought the challenge was great, exciting. Rose didn't. Cameron asked me about it and I told him I was participating."

"Did you tell him I gave you that position?" Silas asked.

"Yes."

"And he still wants to challenge you?"

"Yes," Tyrone said. "And…I understand his reasoning. He wants his mate to see him as someone strong who can protect her instead of what she's seen so far. In all honesty, if I have to fight him, my heart won't be in because I understand why he's doing it."

"Plus, he's like family, your brother-in-law. You can't try and kill your mate's sister's mate," Tyrese chimed in.

Disgusted with all the talk of family, Silas shook his head. Things may have been boring before, desolate even, but he was rarely confused on how to proceed. Back then, the only people who mattered were his wolves. Now…the waters were muddied. He'd wait until Cameron presented him with a request to join the challenge and make a decision then. In the meantime, he had a mate to talk to.

"I wanted you to know one of the doctors that came in today was Dr. Matthew Chism. According to Dr. Passen, he is critical in discovering what's happening with the detective's wolf, so I allowed him to stay and work."

"Speaking of the detective, old man Merriweather arrived at the gate this morning, asking to speak with you. Rose told him you were unavailable. He put up a fuss, telling the guards how important he was and that they hadn't seen the last of him." Tyrone shook his head.

"Good job, I need her to clear my schedule today." Silas stood and sent Rose a message. He had a feeling he would not be any good after talking to Jasmine.

"Why? What's up?" Tyrese asked, his brow creased.

"I have to go tell my mate that the mate of her supposedly dead husband is working in the lab and pray she forgives me for not telling her Davian Bennett is alive and staying at a hotel in town."

Tyrese jumped up. "What? Matt's here? Why?"

"What's he doing here?" Tyrone asked, frowning.

Exasperated, Silas looked at them. "I just told you. Dr. Matthew Chism is here working on the virus to save wolf-kind. Supposedly he is an expert on half-breeds. Seems he's years ahead of everyone else in his research." Silas's brow rose at them.

The twins stared at him as though he were speaking Latin.

"Dad's in town?" Tyrone whispered in a shocked tone.

"Yeah, I have security watching to keep him safe in case the Bennett clan rides into town. Everything in place to snatch the rebels?" he asked in an attempt to change the subject.

"Yes, Sir," Tyrese answered, but Silas could see his mind was elsewhere.

Holding back a sigh, Silas returned to his seat. "Look, I know you want to see Davian." He raised his hand at their protests. "He's your father. That will never change, I understand that. But I can't allow either one of you to go into town, not until we lock down this virus and the bomb deal. Good news though, we are close to being able to detect the bomb."

"Mom is going to be hurt because of this," Tyrese blurted, looking at the concrete floor.

"That's the understatement of the year," Tyrone muttered. "All those years she thought he was dead and to have him show up…here, of all places." He shook his head. "Unbelievable."

Tyrese looked at his brother. "They never divorced," he whispered.

Silas straightened, a bit miffed at being ignored. Tyrone spoke before he could. "She is not going to handle this well." He closed his eyes and shuddered. The twins' response to Jasmine's possible reaction sent a wave of dread through him.

"She's mated," he said to get their reaction.

"Yeah and she does have the babies, that should help," Tyrone said thoughtfully.

Tyrese shook his head slowly. "She's going to blow." He looked at Silas. "You don't know how sad she was about the quality of her life. Now she's going to find out her husband's been living it up with his mate, happy all this time…maybe if you remind her of the mating pull that might help, but…he should have been honest." He looked at his brother. "We should have told her he might be alive even if we weren't sure. She's going to think this is something else we hid from her."

"Damn," Tyrone said softly, looking off into space.

"This is not helping," Silas snapped as he stood, stomach tied in knots as he headed for the entrance.

He was La Patron, leader of the Wolf Nation. Men quaked beneath his anger and coveted his favor. Yet with each step toward the stairs, his heart ached, and tendrils of apprehension wrapped around him. By the time he reached the nursery where his mate sat on the floor playing with his litter, his nerves were twisted like several pretzels. He stood just inside the door and watched her roll over as Adam crawled toward her. David was propped up in his bouncy chair, watching the byplay, and the girls were drawing and working puzzles.

Two years ago he would never have imagined this scene. But as the Goddess instructed, he had embraced the truth. The wave of change was a rough ride, but looking at his pups and his mate, it was worth it.

"Silas," Jasmine called to him. "Come see what Renee drew."

He smiled and walked toward his daughter and stooped beside her. There was a mixture of colors on the paper that resembled nothing he recognized.

"Good job, Renee. It's pretty, like you." He brushed a kiss against her forehead and received a large smile in return.

Jackie held up a color wheel wooden puzzle she had completed for his inspection. Her garbled words signified she was encouraging him to enjoy her work. He cooed and ahhed over it and then kissed her forehead. When he stood, Jasmine was looking at him with a raised brow.

"What's wrong?" she asked, rolling a small ball to Adam.

Silas sat next to her on the floor. Adam abandoned the game, crawled onto his lap, and started pulling at his shirt buttons.

Absently, Silas grabbed his son's hands and held them as he rocked the youngster. "We'll talk when they go down for lunch." He made sure she couldn't read him, he suspected she had been trying since he walked in the room.

Frowning, she picked up David, checked his diaper, and stood. With an economy of movements, she changed the boy and handed him to Silas in exchange for Adam. Releasing Adam, Silas held David close and placed a kiss on his chubby cheek.

Jasmine handed Adam off to his nurse, who sat him in the high chair to feed him. She changed the girls before handing them off to their nurses as well. Then she took David from him and sat him in his high chair, motioning for his nurse to feed him. Stepping back to leave, Silas prepared himself for the conversation. But Jasmine oversaw the children's meal before placing them into their cribs for a nap. They were all covered and asleep before she ushered him out of the room while holding his hand. In silence, they walked down the hall to their suite. When they entered, she walked over to the small kitchen and poured them both glasses of sweet tea. Returning to the living area, she passed him a glass and sat on the sofa. She patted the space next to her while offering him a tiny smile.

"You're nervous, so that means I'm not going to like whatever you have to tell me," she said, watching him closely. His jaw clenched. He took a large swallow from the glass to ease the tightness in his throat.

"Jasmine."

"Wait," she said, stopping him. "Sit down. Whatever this is, I want to see you, your eyes. Sit with me." She patted the sofa again.

He sat in the chair across from her and stared into her concerned eyes. Clearing his throat, he spoke. "There is a doctor I admitted on the grounds today, Dr. Matthew Chism. He's a specialist of some sort in his field and Dr. Passen is convinced this is the guy to crack the virus thing if it is a virus. Whatever is affecting the detective's wolf, this doctor supposedly is the man who can fix it."

She frowned. "That's good, right? You were worried about this last night, at least now you're on the right track."

"Yeah," he nodded and took another swallow of the sweet beverage before meeting her eyes again. The tightening in his throat mimicked the restricting muscles in his chest, even now his heart slammed against the shrinking confines of his ribs with such force he was sure she could hear the sound through their link. His tongue swept across the scaly dryness of his lips in preparation to utter sentences that could return him to the cold arid places in his mind. His barren world before she brought warmth and color into his life.

"What he's doing is important and will save a lot of half breeds, so…he's mated. His mate is in town at the Capital Inn and the reason this is important is that his mate…his mate is Davian Bennett."

It took a moment for anything to register on her face, first, there was a small furrowing of her brows, then it deepened as if his words were being weighed and judged. Then her eyes widened and stared at him. Her mouth opened, closed, and then she flopped back, wide-eyed against the seat, her hand on her chest as she sucked in large gulps of air.

"Say that again," she asked in a brusque voice.

His skin tightened. He swallowed hard and repeated the last line.

Her eyes narrowed and he'd swear he saw golden flames in their brown depths. "What the hell do you mean his mate is in town? Davian Bennett died four damn years ago. I buried him," she said shaking her head and pointing her finger at him.

If the situation weren't so dire, he'd appreciate how glorious she looked in her rising fury. Chest heaving, nostrils flaring, and eyes narrowed into slits, *just beautiful*. "He wasn't dead, he faked it so you could have the money from the military," he forged on immersed in the knowledge that each word he spoke was the equivalent of poking a hole in the boat of their relationship.

She stood so fast, her finger barely missed his nose. He leaned back and stared.

"I buried my husband four years ago, Silas. He is dead."

He took the shaking finger in his hand and covered it with his. "Okay. He's dead. It's okay."

She snatched her finger away from him and walked away a bit. "He's mated?" she murmured. "Davian has a mate? A mate he's been with all this time?" She stopped and looked at him. "Answer me!" she yelled.

Fascinated with the movement of the curtains from the wind of her anger, he spoke. "Yes."

"How long have they been together?" she ground out.

He paused. The knowledge that words from his mouth and his actions caused her pain rippled across his skin. They both shared the misery of the moment. "Seven or eight years I think."

"What?" She gasped. Spinning around, her hand flew to her mouth. His chest ached with the horrible pain he saw in her eyes.

"He was with him while we were married," she whispered. "Married…we're married." She gazed at him like he was a monster. "I'm married. He's not dead."

In his mind, the marriage meant nothing. She was his mate, which took precedence over a legal procedure. He had the presence of mind to keep his thoughts private.

"I have babies from you," she said in a horrified whisper that concerned him. She walked off mumbling.

"When…when did you know he was alive. I know it wasn't today. You're too damn thorough for that. No, I bet you knew before you ever touched me." She pivoted and glared at him.

He exhaled as he answered. "Yes, I knew."

"Why didn't you tell me?" she asked in an agonized whisper that tore at his heart.

"Because he was dead to you. He'd found his mate and had no choice but to be with Matthew."

"He damn well could've divorced me first," she yelled. "I was miserable thinking I was lacking, that something was wrong with me. Did you know that? Huh? …" Her eyes blazed a liquid bronze. "He wouldn't touch me. No damn sex, lived like a eunuch, for years…damn it. He treated me like a damn roommate. I thought something was wrong… with me," she whispered. "I thought something was wrong with me." She slapped her chest and turned from him.

His heart ached for her. He reconsidered his promise to keep the doctor's mate safe.

She placed her palm on her forehead. "No wonder he was gone so much the last few years, he was fucking his damn mate and leaving me at home wondering what the hell I was doing wrong. I bought new lingerie." She ticked it off her fingers as she heaved and wiped the tears from her face. "New perfumes, worked my ass off so I would look good for that bastard, and all the fucking time he had a man on the fucking side?" she yelled and a vase hit the floor from the force of her anger, smashing into small pieces. "I will kill his ass. He'll be good and dead when I'm finished with him."

She spun around and pointed at him. The room heated a few degrees but she didn't notice. In fact, he was positive she had no idea she was pulling energy from him which fueled her anger as she approached. "You... how could you have kept that from me? I'm married. I had kids with you and... I am married."

"We're mated. That's a deeper bond in my world." The flimsy excuse sounded weak beneath the weight of her pain.

"I am not a damn wolf," she screamed. "I'm human. You keep forgetting that and it keeps coming up. I am human. By human law, if Davian is alive, I am married." She nodded repeatedly.

He clenched his jaw and looked away, ashamed. There was little he could say to refute her.

She leaned closer and met his stare. "You should've told me. Allowed me to be the woman I am and make my own damn decisions. I would've divorced him and been free to follow my conscience." She closed her eyes and opened their link.

He flinched beneath the barrage of hurt, pain, and disillusionment swirling through her. It was such a stark contrast from yesterday's adoration, it slammed into him with the force of a falling boulder.

"I cannot believe you did that to me," she said softly.

Her pain wrapped around him until it pierced his core. Understanding dawned. He made a gross error. His decision violated her moral code, a part of the fabric that made her uniquely herself.

"I was wrong to keep it from you. At the time I thought it was for the best. Now I see I was wrong. Forgive me, please." He was wolf, as such he saw things in black and white, but this was one time he should've searched the gray area.

She huffed as she looked at him and shut down their link. "Forgive you? Why? You thought it was for the best. It was a decision you made based on the information you had, right? It never occurred to you that sleeping with a man who wasn't my husband would bother me, right? Because wolves do that all the time and you…you're a wolf. So no biggie."

This was getting worse. "Jasmine, that's not true." He hadn't considered her marriage valid because her husband had gone to great lengths to terminate it. Their marriage had been dead for years, it simply hadn't been buried with a divorce.

"Or maybe you thought I'd be just fine accepting money for my husband being killed in combat when he wasn't. I guess I'm just that kind of woman to you."

"No… that's not true." Truthfully, he'd never thought of the illegality of her accepting the money from the government. He could wring Davian's neck for this mess.

She snapped her fingers and placed them on her chin. "I get it. You thought I'd be perfectly fine having babies from one man while my husband was banging someone else." She waved her hand. "Yeah, because I'm that kind of woman, so there's no fucking need to tell me he's alive, just wipe that tidbit beneath the mat." She paused, wiped the wetness from her face, and glanced at him. "Guess what genius, my last name is still Bennett and now that means something because he's still my fucking husband in a court of law. And the law matters to humans, damn you," she screamed.

The lights flashed on and off.

Her words sliced through him. He stood and took her in his arms. She fought him, tried to push him away, and although she was strong, he was much stronger. He wrapped her in his arms and held on tight. She was slipping away from him. He sensed it in his bones.

"I'm so sorry…Baby, forgive me…I was wrong…I'm sorry…Please, forgive me…I love you so much…I was wrong…" he continued until her sobs lightened and her breathing normalized.

"Jasmine, believe me, if I had to do it all over again, I'd handle it differently. I never thought less of you for any reason, you know that."

"You didn't want to mate a human."

He closed his eyes. "That was before I knew you. You are the best part of me. I messed up. I admit it. I'm asking you to forgive me."

She mumbled something against his chest.

Frowning, he leaned back. "I didn't hear you."

"I said get out." It wasn't the words but the utter lack of emotion that accompanied them that ripped through him. He looked down into her face and when she looked up at him, there was no warmth, no gentle humor, and no loving glances. Loathing filled the depths of her eyes. A chill slid through him as she pushed him and stepped away.

"Either you leave or I will."

He didn't know what to say or how to deal with this cold person. It was as if she had reached inside him and took the worst of his attributes.

"Baby, don't do this…"

"Get out," she snarled low and rumbling, sounding like him.

He exhaled as he raked his hand through his hair. She didn't recant or release her narrowed stare.

Moving slowly, he walked to the door. When he reached it, he glanced over his shoulder. "I love you, Jasmine. That will never change."

"The cost of your love is too high. Get the fuck out."

He left, shutting the door behind him. His stomach roiled as her words reverberated in his mind. *The cost was too high?* What did that mean? They could work through this, they had to work through this. She was it for him, for life. Didn't she understand she was his mate? He leaned against the wall, resting his head on the canvas wallpaper. After a few deep breaths, he was still clueless about how to fix this. She was right; he had dealt with Davian's situation like a wolf. Listening to her, he realized she should have been told, should have made her own decisions.

"Everything okay?" Cameron asked, coming down the hall toward him.

He nodded. "It will be, eventually. How're things with you?" he asked, not caring one way or the other. His mind and heart were behind those closed doors behind him.

Cameron looked up and down the hall. "This mate thing is driving me crazy. This need for her…" he tapped his chest. "I feel it deep, so deep sometimes I can't think straight. But…she's like moving at a different speed." He leaned closer his dark brown eyes brimming with confusion. "I don't think she feels the same about me, how's that possible? I mean how does this work if we both don't want each other the same?"

Silas exhaled and forced himself to change the trajectory of his thoughts. Talking about half-breed mating habits was just the thing to keep him occupied for a while. Jasmine needed a little time to think through things. He had no choice but to give it to her.

"You've been gone for a while and I haven't had a chance to bring you current, especially about dealing with half-breeds."

"Jasmine's a half-breed, right?"

"No, she's not. She's human and has no wolf."

Cameron jerked back, searching his eyes. "That's not…how'd that happen?"

Silas looked at the closed door one last time, slung his arm over Cameron's shoulder, and walked off. "Let's get you caught up. There are a lot of things going on around here and I'm going to need your help."

"Yes, Sir."

Chapter 14

Jasmine walked to the window and looked out over the complex. To her right was the north wing where Tyrese, Cameron, and his mate, and a lot of offices were housed. To her left was her former wing, where Tyrone and his mate, along with Thorne, lived. She and Silas were in the largest wing; their private area occupied the top floor, giving her an excellent view of the mountains.

The sun had just risen and kissed the peaks. She stretched as the panoramic view soothed her tortured thoughts and soul. Her sleep hadn't been peaceful, it never was without Silas. It had been two days since he'd told her Davian was alive. Two nights she had slept alone. Because they were semi-connected, his distress over their situation kept her half-awake through the night.

He had honored her request, albeit grudgingly, to back off and give her space. They spent time with the children separately and had no further communication. Yawning, she went into the kitchen, grabbed a bottle of water, and guzzled it down. It had taken a few hours after Silas' announcement about Davian being alive and mated for her to get over her shock and anger. Davian hadn't loved her, not the way she needed to be loved anyway. She was still pissed and planned to tell him about himself one day, but…eh, in the grand theme of things, he didn't really matter.

Hell, she was content to allow him to stay dead. No skin off her back. There was no valid reason to drag him to court. Why divorce a man who's legally dead? The real issue, the thing that kept her from returning to the warmth of her lover's arms yesterday was how Silas handled the situation. Her marriage with Davian had been one-sided and she'd be damned if she'd ever do that again.

Silas hadn't treated her like his equal partner and that burned. He made a high-handed decision on her behalf and she refused to live that way. Granted, he probably knew Davian was alive before they mated, but he should have told her before they'd committed to each other. Silas had a long history of disliking humans and thinking they were inferior beings. There were times she wondered if that was the reason he refused to recognize her as a human.

For them to make it, he had to accept her for who she was at her base level. Neither of them could change the fact she couldn't shift into a wolf or have fangs or even think like a wolf. It was a discussion that needed to be dealt with soon.

But first, she wanted to talk to Matthew Chism, Davian's mate. She strode to the bedroom to dress and go see her babies. She would contact Hank and tell him to set up a room for her and Matt to talk privately, with no audio.

She knew better to ask for no video, Silas would never permit her in a room with anyone other than himself or the twins without security watching.

Her cell rang.

It was either Renee, her mom, or Mandy, her sister's mate. Needing a sunny voice in her darkened mood, she moved quickly to answer it.

"Hey, Renee." She smiled, genuinely happy to hear from her sister.

"Hey. Thanks for the pictures, they are beautiful. All four of them." She paused. "I can't believe you have six kids. It's hard to comprehend."

Tell me about it, Jasmine thought beginning to doubt the wisdom of answering the call. "Yeah, I know right. Never would've guessed it. How's Mandy? You talk to Ma lately?"

"Mandy's at work, but doing good. After seeing the pictures of the babies, she backed off the baby talk. She's petrified that multiple births run in our family. I should thank you for that."

Jasmine laughed.

"Last I talked to Mom she got married again They were traveling to his home-town, somewhere in Italy. She says he's the one, the real deal, and then got mad when I reminded her she said the same thing about Chris and Rafael."

"She did say that, didn't she? Well, at least she hasn't given up her search for true love."

"No, because she keeps finding it, over and over again," Renee said with a chuckle. "I told her to take her stone with her this time and maybe this new man will last."

Jasmine's stone was in her bedroom on the dresser. She had forgotten and wished she had used it the past two days. "I hope it works for her this time. How are your classes coming along? Any interesting students this semester?"

"No. Not yet. They are all sniffing about, trying to determine how tough I am. If I mean what I say, that type of thing. It won't get interesting until the flakes drop the class. That's when I get to teach and play hardball."

Jasmine shook her head. Renee was a real softie beneath the tough shell. Few people took the time and effort to look deeper.

"I have some time off next month, Mandy and I want to come see the babies and the boys. That okay?"

"Yeah, that's great. I'll do the christening then so you don't have to make another trip or miss it. I'm thinking about flying in Pastor Wells to do the service."

"Who's that?"

"He's from my church back home. I haven't found a church here yet."

"Oh."

Renee believed each person created their own destiny, and as such were their own gods. After a few tense discussions through the years, religion and faith were topics they agreed to disagree on. "I have a stone for each of the kids. I'd like to present it to them and when they are older, I want to show them how it works if that's okay with you."

"That's fine. I'll have to explain how a gratitude stone works to Silas first." Jasmine walked into her bedroom and picked up her stone. It was no more than a smooth rock similar to those you buy in a craft store. But it acted as a focal point to channel thoughts. Closing her eyes she rubbed and thought of all the things she had to be grateful for.

"Thanks, I appreciate it. Maybe I'll bring him one, you think he'll use it?"

"Yeah, I think a gratitude stone might be a nice gift for him. Thanks."

<<<<<>>>>>

Jasmine entered the secure room and looked at the large glass in front of her wondering who was on the other side. Tyrone? Tyrese? Silas? Because of how personal this was, she knew it would be one of them. She bit back a smile, the twins had avoided her for the last two days, just sticking in their heads in the nursery to say hi, and kept moving. It would be good to see them, check out their reactions to Davian being alive. Although he was no longer important in her life, he would always be their dad. And for the most part, he had been a decent father.

Butterflies raced in her stomach as a door from the other side opened and she released a pent-up breath. She had no idea what she thought Davian's mate would look like but it wasn't the tall, redheaded, man who stood just as nervous near the door. Matthew wasn't handsome, in fact, Davian probably outshone the man whenever they were together. He offered her a hesitant smile and his whole face changed. His green eyes were cautious but they also lacked guile, the brackets around his mouth said he enjoyed a good laugh.

In a patented diva move she learned from her sister, she inclined her head. Not quite sure what she expected from this conversation, but committed to seeing it out.

"Matthew?"

"Yes, Jasmine?"

She took a seat at the table, interlocking her fingers together to hide her nervousness. He took the one across from her. They studied each other for a moment in silence. He was as tall as Davian, which had been a surprise. Maybe it was the pale skin and green eyes. Davian was very light-skinned although he tanned quickly when he spent a lot of time in the sun.

"So you are Davian's mate?"

He rubbed his chin. "Yes, I am."

She nodded.

"This is awkward. I mean ever since La Patron told me you were here and might want to meet with me, I've practiced what I would say. I had a litany of reasons why Davie and I are together, why he faked his death, why he returned to you so many times before making the final break." He paused and released a breath. "But…now, looking at you." He shook his head. "You are beautiful. I understand why it was so hard for him to leave."

She glanced at the Kelly green and white short-sleeved shirt and matching pants she wore and wondered if he were giving her a line.

"Hard for him to leave? He left quite often if you've been mated for eight years."

He nodded. "You're mated. You know how hard it is to deny your mate, and he did that for a few years because he was torn. He wanted to be with you and his sons, but the mating call pulled him in a different direction. There were times I thought he'd end it all for real."

She didn't want to hear how hard it was for Davian to leave her and the twins. "Davian is gay? How long has he known? Did he date other men while we were married?"

Matthew frowned. "Neither one of us is gay. We're mated and that's not a gender thing. No one was more surprised than me when he walked into the hospital where I was working in Iraq. I was dating one of the nurses at the time, and I liked her. A lot." He chuckled and something eased inside her.

"The only man I've ever been attracted to is my mate. He never cheated on you, with a man or woman. He's not that kind of man. This mating thing…" he raked his hand through his hair. "The only way to understand the intensity of it is to experience it. I don't think anyone can truly explain the joy of being irrevocably connected to another person at a cellular level. It is mind-boggling."

Jasmine thought of Silas and had to agree with him on that point. She leaned forward, elbow on the table, and held the side of her face in her palm. "I hate him, you know."

He released a breath. "I know."

"He should've divorced me."

Matthew nodded. "You're right."

"That was a high-handed move. He left me at home while he spent time with you."

His face twisted in a grimace of distaste. "Huh, he should've stayed at home. He only sat around feeling guilty when he was with me."

"We didn't have sex the last few years."

"Honey, he couldn't get it up for anyone but his mate, that's physiology. But I wasn't getting any real sex either." He looked at his hand, opened and closed it a few times, and then winked at her.

She laughed. She couldn't help it. Matthew was a likable guy.

"Seriously. I got no real loving until after his death. Then, well let's just say it's all good."

"Good?" She shook her head wondering if he had low standards because Davian had never been that good of a lover. Especially after being with Silas, her ex didn't even rate.

"Most definitely." He paused and leaned back watching her. "Can I tell you something? I mean I know we're being watched, I was warned within an inch of my life to remain respectful and not to upset you."

She wasn't surprised. "What do you want to tell me?"

"He was scared of you. Davie."

That surprised her. "Why?"

"You're human. He's a big man, in many ways. He was always afraid he would hurt you. But if you're mated with La Patron, you could've taken anything he could've thrown at you. I'm glad for all of our sakes he didn't know."

Jasmine wondered if Matt knew she was a human breeder. "You're right. I can't imagine what would have happened if I was actually happy with Davian and he left me for you," she said in a sarcastic tone.

"What if by some twist of fate, you were happy with Davian, and then you met La Patron? Huh? What if he realized you were his mate? That would be a disaster of gigantic proportions."

That was unimaginable. "He would have brushed me off as some human," she said dismissively to see if he knew anything about breeders.

"La Patron is a wise man. Telling you about Davian was a hard decision for him. The man was torn. I offered to leave and take Davian with me, to keep the lie in place. To keep you blissfully unaware. But he refused. Said he could not lie to you and the lies needed to stop. He made that decision knowing it would cause problems between the two of you. Not that he admitted that, but if I were you, I'd be mad as hell."

She tipped her head in acknowledgment but remained quiet. It wasn't often she heard this side of Silas's decisions.

"He warned me that you might want to talk to me or Davian, and when I asked him to keep you away, he refused. He said you had access to any room in this place; no one could lock you out of anything, or something similar. I was impressed and then scared to my toes when he said you were his mate. So… that was my rather long-winded way of saying, La Patron might have fought the bond for a while, maybe even tried to respect Davian's human claim as your husband. But at the end of the day, you would be right where you are, a woman who is loved by her mate and sons."

Touched, Jasmine swallowed hard and tried to smile. "Thanks."

He nodded.

"I'm still going to kill him, though."

Matthew laughed. "Oh please don't do that, I've just about got him trained the way I need him."

Heart lifting, she smiled. "Okay, I won't kill him."

"Thank you. You are as kind as you are beautiful."

She sobered. "But I am going to talk with him, for closure."

He nodded. "I understand. Plus, he heals super fast so feel free to slap him around a bit, just nothing permanent please."

Jasmine laughed. "I'll try and restrain myself." She paused. "What do you know about the breeders?"

"Not much, I've just started including them in my research. It's been hard getting the half-breeds to say who the women are. From what little I've gathered, they are unique beings. It's as though someone spliced the best of the wolf and human and came up with breeders. It's fascinating research." His eyes were lit with an almost fanatical glow.

"We have a breeder locked up. The one with the bomb is also a breeder."

"Was."

"Huh?"

"She died when they removed the bomb. It was connected to her heart."

"Oh." Jasmine didn't know how she felt about that. Julie was the one she normally talked to. She had just recently met Siseria in the caves.

"Good news is, they've discovered a way to identify the bomb and nullify the detonation."

"Okay." He talked fast when he was excited and it took a moment for her to understand him. "That's good. What about the wolf?" Seems like a lot had gotten done the two days she had been on lockdown.

He smiled. "That was my baby. The reason that wolf was impacted by the shot was the fool hardly ever shifted. So the wolf was weak and timid to begin with. The shot was a simple compound that I was able to recreate in the lab. If La Patron hadn't discovered the sick wolf, it would've gotten worse."

"Would that have killed the man?"

"I don't know…we caught it in time and I prepared an antidote. The wolf is getting stronger, and eating again. But I am going to petition La Patron to allow me to study some of the deceased shifters to see if there is a possible connection."

She nodded, knowing Silas would welcome the assistance. "Does the virus only attack half-breeds?"

"No, I don't think so. Based on my findings it amplifies whatever is already in place. So if the wolf is weak, he becomes weaker."

Jasmine tapped the table. "But if a healthy wolf gets a shot of this, he gets…what? Stronger?"

"Yes, I believe that's what happens. I have only tested the formula on three people and they all said they were stronger, faster, and their reflexes were quicker."

"Sounds like steroids."

He frowned. "That's the problem with dabbling with chemical enhancements; you don't know the long-lasting consequences until someone uses the drug for a long time. By then all you can do is record the results, it's too late to do much else."

"So what happens now? With the wolf?"

"I'll watch him a little longer, but he should be fine."

That wasn't what she was asking but realized he had no idea who the wolf was or why he was there in the first place. She sent Silas a message. *"I want to talk to Davian."*

"Jasmine..."

"Either you can bring him here or I'll find a way to meet him in town. Your choice."

"I have sent someone to retrieve him, but...you cannot meet with him alone. You cannot touch him. He cannot touch you. My wolf would not allow it."

She heard the regret in his voice and melted. Glancing at Matthew, she stood. "It was nice to meet you and I'm sure I'll be seeing you around. Thanks for talking with me."

His eyes widened and then he smiled brilliantly. "The pleasure was mine. Thank you for not hurting me." He grinned as he stood and left the room.

She walked out the opposite door, glanced at security, then headed for her wing. *"Silas,"* she whispered through their link.

"Jasmine?"

"I understand and I won't meet with him alone. But this conversation is for closure. He's the father of my sons. I thought he was dead and I never had a chance to say goodbye."

"I am asking you to say goodbye without touching him or he will be dead. It will be difficult for my wolf to allow your former lover anywhere near you, let alone touch you. Please tell me you understand."

When he put it that way, there wasn't much to say. *"Okay."* She hesitated. *"I love you, you stubborn, pigheaded man. I will always love you, but you hurt me and*

I cannot live like that. We have to be partners or this will not work."

"*We are partners, we are one. You are in me and I am in you.*"

She realized he didn't fully understand and decided to wait so she could explain clearly. "*Let me know when Davian is here.*"

"*You forgive me?*" His voice held too much hope and longing in it for her to ignore.

"*I'm working on it.*" She disconnected and headed for the nursery.

<<<<<◇>>>>>

Silas turned from the huge blond wolf sitting shackled to the chair and smiled. His heart leapt joyously. He wished he was done with the interrogations of the rebels so he could go see his mate. He missed her smile, touching her face, and holding her close. The past two nights, he'd stayed in his office unable to rest. He missed her warmth. His need to be close had driven him to the door of their suite many times. But he was determined to prove he would honor her wishes no matter what it cost him. Most of all he wanted, no needed, her to see him as she had the night before everything went to hell.

He glanced at the camera in the corner ceiling. There was one just like that one in each rebel's holding room, where they watched their comrades on a monitor while awaiting their turn with La Patron. He'd started with Leonidas since he was the biggest and more importantly, Silas needed to release some pent-up frustration. Once he rifled through the rebel's mind, he relayed the information to Tyrese, who verified the data, which gave Silas time to slap the large wolf around.

After Tyrese confirmed the information was true. Silas walked up to Leonidas, ignoring the horrified fear in his eyes, grabbed his head, and pretended to snap his neck. What he'd done was sent the man to sleep, but the other prisoners wouldn't know that. He had Leonidas' monitor turned off as he walked into the next room. Silas crossed his arms and glared at another big guy who had already wet his pants. It has been too long since he'd toyed with anyone, he had forgotten how entertaining it was.

"I am going to ask you one question, one time. Answer me truthfully."

The man nodded so fast Silas thought he might dislocate his head or something.

"Who sent you to attack Bennett the other night?"

The man frowned.

"In the alley of the club, remember, he kicked your ass."

"Yeah…he was a tough fighter. I don't handle contracts or nothing like that. I was told to jump him when he came out and I did. I swear that's all I know."

Silas rifled through his mind and found nothing useful. "Stand up." The man stood and Silas released his cuffs. The man frowned as he massaged his wrists.

Silas stepped back and punched him in the face. The guy spun around and hit the ground. "Stand up," Silas growled.

"Please, no." The man covered his head and rolled into a fetal position. No matter what Silas said, he whimpered and remained curled in a ball. Silas sent him to sleep and stormed into the next room.

"I don't know anything, honest, I don't. I would tell you if I did. That's why they never tell me anything," the man cried before Silas spoke.

"Who is 'they'?" Silas asked before rifling through the man's memories. There were some shadowy images but nothing concrete enough to matter. Silas punched him in the stomach on general principle and then did the same to the next guy. By the time he reached the female's cage, he knew she had been the brains behind the entire operation. Thinking of his mate, and the human females below, he concluded too many males underestimated the ingenuity of women. They could be an angel or the devil in disguise.

Security had just contacted him that they were on their way with Davian, ETA thirty minutes. Since he was running out of time, he strode into her room and immediately searched her mind. She was the initial contact. A rebel to the core, she'd set everything up. Just as Silas was going to pull out and exterminate her, he sensed something in the corner of her mind. He poked it and she winced.

Whereas she'd been haughty up to this point, she now looked petrified. Her mouth opened and closed. "Please don't," she whispered with tears in her eyes.

Silas wrapped protection around the small globe and then penetrated it. He watched for her reaction and when there was none, he watched as an alternate memory unfolded. She'd been taken at an early age to someplace where they'd worked on her. She was a trained assassin, they kept her family to keep her in line. All in all, the wolf in front of him had been tortured, given a new reality, and sent on this mission.

Holding onto her memory, he searched the other four and uncovered another set of memories in Leonidas. The wolf thought he was mated, and someone held his mate and pups to make him do their bidding. A blinding rage tore through Silas. Someone was experimenting with full-blooded wolves, altering their realities.

A popping sound went off in the minds of Leonidas and the unidentified female. Silas realized the balls containing the memories were set to destroy the wolves if tampered with. No wonder she had pleaded with him to stop.

Quickly he rid their systems of the poison the mini-explosion released and eliminated it. When he left the female's mind, she frowned, and then her eyes widened. "You got rid of it. They said you couldn't help, no one could."

Silas sat at the table in front of her. "What's your name?"

She wet her lips as her eyes darted around the room. "Asia. Asia Montgomery." She grinned and it made her look even younger. "That's my real name. I remembered."

"Who took you? Who experimented on you? Took your memories?" He prayed to the Goddess they were getting closer to solving at least one unknown piece of the puzzle, hopefully, it'd lead to solving the human breeder mystery.

"I don't know anyone's names." She frowned. He was still in her mind and saw the large warehouse before she mentioned it.

"They kept us in some kind of building underground, really good security. I had a small apartment. They said I had a baby." She placed her hand on her stomach. "But that's another lie, isn't it?"

He scanned her body. "You have not given birth." Since she'd opened up and started talking, Silas flowed through her memories, searching for landmarks or clues to the facility. He found it when she had been at rifle practice at an outside range. There was a sound that he recognized, and it was only found in one place. He opened up and did a memory dump to Tyrese. Finding Asia had been like finding the mother lode. A few minutes later he was done. He glanced at the clock. He had another fifteen minutes before Davian's arrival.

"Rest. I will be back later and we will talk."

She nodded.

The mental transfer had drained her and she should be out for a little while. He took her hand and completed another in-depth scan to make sure she wasn't locked and loaded. After checking her restraints, he left to check on the other four men.

Three of them were dead. He called the lab and had them take the men downstairs to be checked. He wanted a report of what was used and how it worked.

He stepped into the room with Leonidas and took hold of his wolf. "Wake up, Leon." Tawny eyes blinked and then focused. Silas waited a moment for the man to catch his breath before he sorted through his memories. Leon had a visual of the same warehouse, except there was more detail to the building. Leon had been in areas Asia had not.

"I didn't die," he whispered as though the idea was alien to him.

"I didn't break your neck, I put you to sleep," Silas said, flowing through the memories and sending them to Tyrese.

"No…no, you changed something and it was supposed to kill me." He looked at Silas with a confused frown.

Silas met Leon's eyes and spoke tersely. "I am the Patron, leader of all wolves. There is nothing about you, baring death, which I cannot fix. You should've come to me immediately," he snapped.

The man rubbed his brow. "I know that, at least I used to know that…what the hell happened to me?" He glanced at the steel cuffs on his arms and legs. "What did I do?" he whispered.

"You were involved in a plot to overthrow the Patron, me." Silas finished pulling the information and looked into the slack-jawed face of the man in front of him.

"No. They wanted information on your son, or is it sons?" He shook his head as if to clear it. "You have twins somewhere. You've been hiding them until now." Leon closed his eyes, thinking.

Silas tried to help make sense of the scrambled information. Leon's eyes popped open, the irises were translucent gold. Silas held onto the man's wolf while hovering inside Leon's mind on the lookout for deception.

"You had two sons, twins from a human. They wanted to see what a breed from La Patron would look like, how he thought and fought. So when the guy claiming to be Bennett showed up, he was all wolf. But we'd been told some breeds could cloak their human side and not be fooled. Rumors had it that your son came to that club occasionally. I think someone followed him to the condo and he never came out."

"You getting this Tyrese?"

"Yes, Sir, talk about mixing things up."

"Do you know who wanted to see him in action?" Silas asked Leon.

Leon scrunched his face. "No, I never met the two men in charge of the operation. The doctor who worked with us called them Batman and Robin under his breath."

"Same two who wanted mom killed?" Tyrese asked

"Sounds like it."

"Tell me everything you remember about the operation. It looks big and well-funded," Silas said.

"Yes, Sir. They've been around for years. I met a couple of service wolves who lived their entire lives in that compound, some fifty plus years."

Silas's heart sank. How could he hope to catch up with that much lead time? "Are the men in charge human or wolves?"

"Most of the doctors were human. No wolves though, but a few other species. Like I said, I don't know who the real leaders are."

"How did they see the fight?"

"Asia held up her phone and captured it." He paused, frowning. "Asia? Is she okay?"

"She's asleep. The other men didn't make it." He watched as Leon scowled.

"Good riddance," Leon spat, literally. "They were our guards, dumb as rocks, but wouldn't veer from their instructions, not the tiniest bit."

"They were full-bloods."

"I know, still dumb though. All muscle, no brains. I know two of them had been born in the compound and were only taught to fight and follow instructions. When Bennett whipped them so fast, they were the first to report the wolf had to be your son to have beaten all four of us so quickly."

"Really?"

Leon snorted. "They train every day to fight, that's all they do. And he whipped all four of our asses without breaking a sweat." He glanced at Silas. "Is it true? Is he your son?"

"One of them."

"Thank goodness. I would hate to think a regular breed whipped my ass like that."

Before Silas could respond, security informed him Davian Bennett was in one of the holding rooms, and that they had walked in on him fighting two men who had broken into the hotel room. It was only the mention of the man's mate that had made him come peacefully. So they were after Davian? Why? The man was reportedly dead. Too many questions and the answers were coming too slow.

Silas looked at Leon and then at the clock. *"Jasmine, Davian is here, he's in the same room where you met Matthew. Please do not go in before I get there."*

"I won't."

He exhaled, glad she hadn't given him a hard time. Hopefully, they'd be able to get through this closure session without bloodshed.

Chapter 15

Silas placed Leon and Asia in a deep sleep before leaving them. Tyrese was nearby, monitoring the pair while filtering through all the data Silas sent.

He chuckled at the idea Tyrese and Tyrone were his sons simply because of how well they fought. It must have been the Texas fight the unknown men had seen. The breeder had been taping that fight with the twins against the group of half-breeds as well. He was certain that's when they came up with this theory.

Exiting the lift, he strode to the holding room. Jasmine stood next to the door and his heart stuttered at the sight of her. The green pants hugged her rounded hips and the matching wrap-around blouse emphasized her small waist. Her braids were pulled back from her face into a small bun on the back of her head, emphasizing her faultless facial features. A stab of jealousy hit him as he wondered who she'd dressed for. Also, knowing the man on the other side of that door was the only other male to have sex with his mate made it hard for his wolf to settle.

He caged his beast as he approached her. Jasmine always dressed; even when she rolled on the floor with his pups she was neat and well-groomed. If she looked any other way, it would have been odd.

She glanced up and offered a small smile. Unable to do anything else, he took her into his arms and held her tight for several moments, inhaling her scent. Leaning back he searched her eyes and saw it, that tiny spark that was always there for him. He hadn't realized how much he'd come to count on it until it was missing.

His lips pressed against hers. She opened her mouth, allowing him in. Her warmth soothed him. His wolf urged him to reclaim her. He soothed his beast with a promise of later, now he had to allow his woman to have closure with the man who'd left her years ago.

He placed a few more kisses on her face, not wanting her to leave the circle of his arms. It had been days since he'd held her.

"Silas…Silas, I want to get this over with so I can get back to the nursery." She pushed him back and cupped his cheek. "Dinner? Let's have a dinner date."

"Okay," he said, breathing hard.

"Can we go in now?" she asked when he didn't move.

He stepped back and rearranged his pants to cover his raging hard-on. Leaning around her he opened the door. She placed a quick kiss on his lips and entered the room.

Davian Bennett was his height, with a muscular build and chiseled features. His wolf scented the air and didn't like the other wolf so close to Jasmine. He fought back the growl that rose in his throat.

"Jasmine?" Davian's jaw unhinged and then snapped shut. He blinked and looked at her again. "Whaaat are you doing here?" He glanced from her to Silas. Then looked at Silas again and straightened to attention. His eyes slid from Silas to Jasmine, but he remained standing and quiet.

"At ease," Silas said. "Have a seat. Jasmine just discovered you aren't dead, she talked to Matthew earlier and wanted to talk to you. Do not touch her, this is not a reunion, she has a few things to ask and get off her chest."

Davian nodded slowly, pulled out a chair, and sat. He pulled his eyes from Silas and looked at Jasmine. A little too long in Silas' opinion.

"Jazz," Davian began in a soft voice. "I'm sorry. I have no excuse for being such an ass. I thought things would be better for you if I disappeared after I met Matt. I didn't plan for that to happen. I'm sorry."

"Why didn't you just divorce me? You were with that man while we were married. I could've moved on, met someone else. Someone who'd love me," she asked.

"I loved you and the thought of not having you in my life, I…just couldn't bear it. For a long time, I was so angry about Matt. I rejected him as my mate. He's a man, Jazz. A man…I didn't like men…" He closed his eyes and shook his head as though the idea was too hard to believe.

"I had a wife, kids, a home, responsibilities. And poof, just like that it was all gone because of something out of my control. I couldn't believe the fates would do that to me. Matt wasn't all that thrilled at first either. There was this nurse he was really into. After we met he couldn't…you know, get it up. And she grew tired of his mouth and … well, you get it. It was a hard thing to accept.

But I could see how miserable you were. You tried to make it work." He closed his eyes. "You'd bought that purple and black lacy thing, and I wanted to—"

A low growl escaped Silas's lips. This was not the kind of closure he'd agreed to. His wolf strained at the leash as it was.

Davian's eyes snapped open. He glanced at Silas with a frown and then looked at Jasmine. "Anyway, I'd never hated being mated like I did that night. Every time I was near you was torture. I wanted you, but my …my equipment wouldn't work, and you weren't into much else." He paused and looked at her. "You were so unhappy, it tore me apart. I couldn't tell you I was a mated wolf or explain why I couldn't be your husband in bed." He released a breath. "You were already entitled to half my pension but I wanted you to have more. So I faked my death and cut myself out of your life."

"What about the boys?" Jasmine asked.

Silas glanced at Jasmine. She didn't seem moved one way or the other by what he had just said. And since their link was closed he had no idea what she thought or how she felt about all of this.

He looked away. "They hate me for making you unhappy. Tyrese..." he shook his head. "That boy is one tough sucker. After a couple of years of going back and forth, I introduced Matt to the boys on one of our camping trips. I planned to explain what mating was and how it would impact their wolves. I got as far as the introduction, Tyrese jumped me and Matt, and neither of us is small. I had bruises the next day," he said proudly, as though congratulating his genes for their part in procreating such a fine specimen.

"They still missed you."

"Hell, I missed my wife, my sons, my life. But it was out of my hands. You were a passionate woman who deserved to be loved. If I could have given that to you, I never would have left."

Silas read the sincerity in Davian's eyes and was happy for Jasmine's sake that the man had a damn good reason for being an ass. He waited for Jasmine to thank Davian and leave the room.

"I hated you," she said, looking at Davian.

"I know."

"You should've told me. I probably couldn't have handled the wolf thing back then, but you faked your death. I felt guilty for hating you. I would have let you go, no drama, no strings. A divorce would have worked better, for me."

She sighed. "I convinced Silas to let us talk for closure. I like Matthew by the way; he gave me permission to slap you for the heartache you caused."

"I deserve it." He looked around. "He was in this room, this chair earlier. Is he okay? I mean he had nothing to do with me leaving. It was becoming harder and harder to function when we were separated."

"I'm mated."

Davian's brows rose and he snapped back. His eyes slid from Jasmine to Silas and then back to her.

Silas straightened, wanting the man to know she was indeed his mate.

"So now I understand. But I didn't back then and that's what I needed closure on. Thanks for explaining what happened. I wasn't sure what I expected, but... thanks. Be happy, Davian." Jasmine stood and in Silas' opinion, appeared regal.

"Wait," Davian said, reaching forward to stop her.

Silas growled and his eyes burned, no doubt the color of his wolf.

Davian's hand fell as he glanced at Jasmine. "You're not a wolf. How can you be mated?"

"How could I have babies who turned into wolves?" she countered.

He nodded. "So you're a human breeder. We were so young back then when I heard about that possibility, I ignored it. And all this time you were one of those lucky women who can handle a wolf and give him pups."

Scowling, Silas looked at the man.

Davian threw up his hands in a placating gesture. "Well, we only had the boys, so I thought it was a fluke."

"No, Davian, it was birth control pills and an IUD. After a few years of marriage, I wasn't taking any chances on another oopsie."

"When did you first hear of human breeders?" Silas asked.

Davian placed his fingertip against his lip and closed his eyes. "It was right before that party you threw for the boys at the skating rink." He looked at Jasmine and she smiled softly.

A flash of jealousy hit Silas at their shared memories. She glanced at him and replayed scenes of the two of them with the babies which eased his spirit.

"That would've been when they were just turning eight." She looked at Silas. "That's been a while."

"Umm." Davian looked at Jasmine and then Silas. "So the two of you are mated. Is that why you're here?"

"Yes," Silas said before Jasmine could answer.

Davian smiled broadly, stood, and stuck out his hand to Silas. "Thank the Goddess. I prayed she'd meet someone worthy of her and she has."

As much as Silas didn't want to like the man, he found himself shaking his hand and doing a scan. Just as he thought, there was no subterfuge in Davian Bennett. He loved his mate, but he loved Jasmine and his sons as well. Most importantly, he was genuinely happy for Jasmine.

"She completes me," was all Silas could say, watching the color rise on her cheeks.

"If you could put in a good word for me with the twins the next time you talk to them, I'd appreciate it. We live in Arkansas near the University. I'd love to have them visit. Or call me, just to catch up."

"They live here with us. Both of them are on Silas personal security detail," Jasmine said, pride ringing through her voice.

Davian's eyes widened before he looked at Silas. "They are good pups. Smart, strong, loyal, you couldn't have chosen better." He looked at Jasmine. "In your mate or security detail."

Silas nodded. Ready to remove his mate from such close confines, he opened the door and called Tyrese. There was no response. *"Tyrese?"*

"Tyrone?"

"Yes, Sir?"

"I cannot connect with Tyrese. Do you know where he is?"

"One moment." Tyrone came back on the line. *"He's unconscious. Wherever he is, he can't respond."* There was a rising note of concern in Tyrone's voice.

"Calm down, Rone. Let me in through your connection," Silas said and piggybacked through the intimate connection of the twins, which was much closer than the one he shared with them.

"What's wrong?" Jasmine asked when Silas remained still without speaking.

He held up one finger even as he threw out a security net around the building and did a body check. *"Hank, we have two men down in the tunnels leading to the holding rooms. I left two rebels in chains there, check them first."*

Jasmine pulled his arm and stared at him. "Tyrese is missing."

"What?" Davian said, moving too close to Jasmine. Silas growled and his eyes heated again. "Back up, Bennett."

Davian returned to the other side of the table, gripping the chair tight. "I can shift and pick up their trail. I'll contact you through Rone as soon as I find out something."

Silas held up a finger for quiet.

"He's in a trunk and he's not alone," Tyrone said.

Silas inhaled through the link. "Asia, they took Asia."

"Asia?" Jasmine looked at him.

"One of the rebels I interrogated earlier." He spoke to Tyrone. *"Anyway to determine their direction?"*

"Give me a minute."

Silas looked at Davian. "Follow me. I'm going to let you out to see if you can pick up his trail."

Davian nodded.

They moved at a clipped pace to the stairs and went down two levels until they reached the holding areas. "Contact Rone the minute you know where he is. Do not engage them. They may be your family."

Davian's head whipped around. "What?"

"The Bennett clan has it out for my mate and her sons. Supposedly they are on their way to kill them. I don't intend to allow that to happen, of course."

Davian's eyes glowed with the force of his anger and the eagerness to change, it pulsed through him. Silas understood his raging need to protect and defend. "My family, except for my son, is in this building. The rest of them are dead to me."

Silas nodded.

Davian changed into a large brown wolf. He padded around the area a bit before entering the room Tyrese had been working in and the room Asia where had been locked up. He followed the scents down the stairs, past the dead security guard who had driven him to the compound, and out of the building. Silas watched on the screen as Davian cleared the grounds. He motioned Jasmine forward while he continued to monitor Tyrese with Tyrone.

Jasmine placed her smaller hand in his and squeezed it. Her large gorgeous eyes said it all. *Please don't let anything happen to my baby.*

Silas kissed the back of her hand. "Rone has merged with Rese. We're going to try and push the drug out of his body so we can get a better understanding of what's going on. Cameron is on his way with Lilly to meet you at the nursery. I want you and the pups to move to the emergency rooms below ground. I will come to you when things are stable."

She opened her mouth, and then closed it, releasing a long sigh. "Okay. I love you, Silas Knight. Handle this." She patted his ass and walked off.

Satisfied that the compound was secure and the dead were en route to the lab for examination, Silas focused on finding Tyrese.

"I… can't… push… through the drug," Tyrone said, groaning beneath the strain.

"Let me help." Silas worked with Tyrone to stop the drug, but it was a fast-acting concoction. It had already spread through Tyrese's system. Silas tried to reach his wolf, but the animal growled sluggishly. Whatever they shot Tyrese with was strong enough to knock out both sides of his nature.

"Your dad is tracking the car and will contact you as soon as he gets a location. I've called in my honor guard, a hundred or so will be here within the hour. As soon as we know where he's been taken, I'll dispatch the men."

"Dad is an excellent tracker," Tyrone said.

Silas didn't respond. A battle raged within him, he was torn. This was the first time he'd ever sent his honor guard out to battle without him in the lead. His wolf strained to fight those who challenged him. It was his nature to prove his right to his position of Patron. But his wolf also refused to leave his mate and pups, believing that he alone could protect his precious litter. It was a bittersweet struggle, one in which his human side had no say.

Agitated but resigned, his wolf remained to protect his den and that settled the matter. He would be active from here, running interference and calling the plays. He would trust Davian and his honor guard to handle this situation on the ground. And while that was a less than an ideal solution, it was one both his natures could agree upon.

"Rese's wolf is fighting the drug and is restless. Can you calm him down?" Tyrone asked.

Silas stroked the beast until it stopped fighting and rested.

"I don't like this."

Silas agreed with Tyrone. *"Bastards came here, to my turf. I guarantee they won't be leaving,"* Silas growled as his energy surged through Tyrone's link, searching for clues. Whoever was driving wasn't talking. There was no music, no sounds other than the steady roll of tires on pavement.

Shit. He was working blind and needed eyes on the situation. Silas threw out a call to any nearby wolves and was answered by a man walking down a path not far from the main road. Silas pulled his wolf and sent him after the car. Pretty soon he had three wolves following the vehicle.

"Tell Davian it's not a car, the bastards took one of our vans after disconnecting the tracking system. It just turned onto the dirt road near Buff's Creek." Silas said, conveying the information from the wolves. Once the van turned off, Silas bid the wolves to hide and watch the road. He wanted to know if more cars accessed the area.

Pulling up a map, he pursed his lips. *"There's an old mine shaft there...Darson's. No telling how far below ground it goes."* Silas contacted Hank. *"Pull up anything you've got on Darson's old coal mine near Buff's creek. The van just turned down a dirt road leading to that building."*

"Yes, Sir."

"*Dad's almost there, he wasn't that far behind.*"

"Good." Silas contacted Rose.

"Sir?"

"*The honor guard?*"

They are waiting for you in the gym."

"Thank you." Silas left the bunker and headed to the gym. Still connected with Tyrone, he strode through the tunnels to the gym while going over all the clues. How had someone accessed the lower levels, shot Tyrese, and carried him out without being seen?

"Hank, recalibrate the security monitors. I want new eyes and playback on the lower levels. Someone tampered with the system; I want to see what happened, bunker area, last hour."

"*Yes, Sir. I uploaded the mine's schematics and information to your tablet. The good news is this drawing is one you commissioned five years ago when the mine closed. There are no utility records, so they must be using generators.*"

"*Fuel bills?*" Silas pulled up the mine on his tablet. Six possible exits needed to be covered. But the damn place was a death trap. It had been closed down because it was unstable. He hoped whoever was using this place had at least fortified it to some degree.

"Sir?"

"Go ahead, Hank." Silas waited at the lift, sifting through the information Hank had sent. A glimmer of a plan began forming in his mind.

"There have been three propane deliveries from an out-of-town gas company within the past month."

Silas snorted. *"Make sure we send them a letter expressing my displeasure for not being informed someone operated this close to my compound."* Every company in the state knew Silas was to be informed of any business performed within a thousand miles of his complex.

"Yes, Sir."

"Trace whoever receives the bill, let's pull every thread. I want air traffic records, who's been visiting in the dark? Pull some of your lower levels. I want an all-out search. Rese was working on something. Let me see if he sent it to me yet." Silas checked his in-box and smiled. *"I'm sending you a file, verify and then look for clues. I want to find these bastards. They've been working on this for over 50 years. Time for them to retire."*

"Yes, Sir."

When he walked into the gym, the noise stopped and the men snapped to attention. A loud, "La Patron, Sir," filled the room, and then the men kneeled. Looking over the crowd of loyal men, a wave of emotion filled him. Their way of life was under attack for no good reason. Honest, hard-working men and women were being taken and used for unnatural experiments. Rage, remorse, and yes vengeance, twisted into an unbreakable braid and filled him with indignation.

Silas raised his arms in acceptance and spoke. "Rise, Honor Guard of La Patron." The men and women stood.

Each wore a tattoo with his brand and the HG initials on their left arm. They watched him intently, waiting for instructions.

"Once again the enemy has brought the fight to my door. Change has come to our people. The Goddess has granted life to some who are different, and I will not discriminate between a full-blood and half-breed. We are all wolves."

The guards cheered and raised their guns and fists in the air.

"The rebels would kill and destroy those we call brothers, sisters, and friends because they are different. But when we shift, are we not all wolves?"

"Yes!" the crowd yelled.

"Then we fight as wolves and crush the enemy. La Patron protects all wolves."

"All wolves," they cheered.

"I have given your team leaders their assignments. Today, we honor the Goddess, the giver of all life as we fight for our brothers and sisters."

"Goddess Bless," the wolves yelled and gathered in their groups. Within five minutes, those who were assigned outside the compound had dispersed and were headed to the various points he had dictated.

Silas threw out his energy and searched the compound. He touched every heartbeat to insure they had permission to be on the grounds. Afterward, he contacted Hank.

"Do a roll call, make sure no one left the lab who could have passed on some chemicals or shot Rese. Whoever took him had help from inside."

"Yes, Sir."

"Jasmine?"

"Yes?"

"Are you locked down?"

"Yes, the kids and I are locked in the tunnels. Don't worry about us, focus on finding Rese and kicking some ass."

"Bloodthirsty bitch."

"You love it."

"Yes, yes I do," he said, entering the lift to head upstairs to his control room.

"*They came too close, Silas. I can't have them coming this close.*"

"*I know and I promise you, I will take care of it.*"

"*Thanks, baby.*"

Chapter 16

Jasmine released a stream of air to quell her jittery nerves. Her gaze landed on Lilly holding David while he slept. Adam lay across Thorne's lap, laughing and trying to grab the small ball from Thorne's hand. Renee looked through a picture book with Rose, and Jackie worked on her puzzle.

Cameron returned after checking all the other rooms. "Everything looks good, do you need anything?" he asked her while glancing at Lilly.

"Silas, but I'll have to wait for that."

Her answer had him doing a double-take before he smiled and nodded. "Yeah, won't be long though." He picked up the remote and turned on one of the TVs in the corner. The reception wasn't the best, so he looked through the DVDs and put in a movie. Jasmine smiled at his choice, *Finding Nemo*. As soon as it started, Adam, Renee, and Jackie turned to stare at the screen. She smiled as Cameron slid into the seat next to Lilly, placed his arm around her, and pulled her close. Those two were going to be fine.

"I'm going to lie down for a minute," she told Rose as she moved to the opposite side of the large area to lay on the sofa. She worried over her sons. Tyrone was so connected to Tyrese that if anything happened to one…she wasn't sure if the other would survive. Closing her eyes, she sought her mate. Seconds later, she watched him enter a large room she had never seen before and kneel in the middle of the floor. He clasped his hands together and bowed his head.

Oh my God, he's praying, she thought.

The heaviness of his heart for his people touched and humbled her. She was stunned by the enormity of the weight of his confusion over the past events as he asked for guidance to do the right thing, to make the best decisions. He asked for protection of his family and those who worked diligently by his side daily to govern the Wolf Nation.

Jasmine lay in utter shock as Silas communicated with the Goddess and asked nothing for himself, other than wisdom and knowledge on how to better take care of the wolves. She exhaled and joined with him. He stiffened initially and then merged with her as they asked for guidance as one.

Opening all her senses, she was filled with Silas's absolute confidence that the Goddess would be with him and guide all of his decisions in this fight. She was lifted along with him into a place where worries were released and left at the feet of someone greater. Bright ribbons of color swirled around them binding her closer to him until their hearts beat in one synchronized rhythm. A curious lightness invaded her being, filling her until there was no room for fear. And then, she heard his words.

"I and my mate humbly seek your guidance. Thank you, Goddess, of light." She was touched that he'd included her in his benediction and sent waves of love and support through their link.

"Thank you, Jasmine. I've always done this alone. But it is good you are with me."

"We are stronger together. I can stay merged with you until we kick their asses."

Silas chuckled. *"Not a complete merge, love. I trust those with you, but I need you alert to everything around you and the babies."* He paused. *"Thank you for your trust."*

"I've got your back, Silas. I'll give you a lil' room, but I'm close if you need me."

"Okay."

Rejuvenated, Silas exhaled and turned on all of the monitors in the room. One by one, he opened files, turned on surveillance cameras, and reset all his links to the outside world. Within minutes he had eyes on his honor guards. The small packs with clothes and weapons they carried on their backs made their progress slower, but they'd soon reach their positions. They could not enter the mine, it was too dangerous. Their jobs were simple, no one was allowed to leave the mine alive.

"They've stopped. The van stopped. I still can't wake him," Tyrone said.

"Lie down and close your eyes. Just support him, don't try to work through the drugs, they will pass through his

system eventually." Silas flowed through their link waiting to hear something.

"You got him?" a voice asked after a door opened.

"Yes, Sir."

Silas swept the area, all human.

"Good. Leon and the girl? Did you see the meat-heads?"

"Didn't see the other three. Got the girl, couldn't get Leon out, it would've taken more time. She was locked down but it was easier to slide her wrists through and she didn't have ankle cuffs."

The man snorted. "They always overlook women and this one…" The door opened, the men were near Tyrese and came in clear. Silas could smell the speaker's nervousness.

"She's the best assassin in the ranks, probably the world. Can shoot a tick off a dog from yards away or maim a man in three seconds. Mind like a trap, sharp. Higher-ups spent a shitload of money on her and the Lion. They want them back."

"I brought in these two, and we're out." There were other footsteps, Silas thought there were at least five men in the immediate area.

"Okay…you sure you don't want to get the other one?"

"Yeah, come back, I'd love to meet you," Silas whispered.

"No. We're done."

"Thanks. Job well done."

There were footsteps, a popping sound, and then the sound of flesh hitting the concrete. "Get them outta here. Take them down to the incinerator."

"Pull the van into the lift, send it downstairs. We have a lot of work to do before the plane arrives. Move it, people, I want to leave this dumbfuck town before sundown," he yelled.

The van moved forward and stopped. There was a whirring sound.

"It's moving down. They're taking him down, where are you, Dad?" Tyrone asked.

"I'm here but I don't have a weapon yet, and they're hot. I'm trying to get in a better position," Davian whispered.

Silas looked at the screen. There were men with guns walking the perimeter, and his guard still hadn't arrived. *"Davian, a guard is walking near the northwest corner of the property, right now he's alone.*

Silas watched as the guard walked by a small bush. An arm reached out and pulled him into the bushes. It happened so quickly it was a blur. *"One down,"* Davian said as he stepped from the bushes dressed in the borrowed uniform and holding a firearm.

The van jerked to a stop as it reached the bottom. Once again Silas threw out his senses and smiled. There were two half-breeds nearby. One worked the communications console and the other worked security.

"Put them on the gurney and follow me," the same voice from outside spoke. There was some jostling. "Get two more men, do not drop him. It's your life if you do."

"Good, now lay him here." Tyrese was placed gently on a smooth surface and wheeled away. After a few minutes, they stopped. "Ready?"

"Yes," another man spoke with eagerness.

"Shit, shit shit," Tyrone yelled. *"They injected him with something that burns like fire. Oh my God, they poisoned him."*

Silas clenched his fist to maintain control. His wolf wanted to hurt someone. Frantically he checked Tyrese's vitals, and other than his heart racing, he seemed stable. He inhaled and exhaled a few times to calm down.

"I can't go in. He needs me and I can't go in," Tyrone said, distraught.

"I'm still in, it's okay. I'm not leaving."

Tyrese's body bucked and his eyes flashed open. At that moment, Silas saw two men standing back watching. One wore a white coat, the other a denim shirt and jeans. Silas flashed their images to every wolf he was connected to. These two men had just been named enemies of the Nation and would be killed on sight no matter where they went.

Tyrese collapsed back onto the gurney, closing his eyes.

"Did it work?" one of the men asked.

"I don't know, it needs some time."

"It worked immediately on all the rest."

"You want to call it in, Trigg?" There was a note of derision in the man's voice.

"No, we'll wait a few minutes. I guess being the Patron's son might make a difference."

"You think?"

Footsteps were leaving.

"Fuck Trigg, screw all of them," someone whispered harshly to Tyrese. "They have no idea what you can do, do they, son of Silas Knight. They watched the video and think they know you. They know nothing. This drug may weaken your wolf, but it will make your human side ten times stronger. I hope you kick their asses," he finished.

Silas guessed the man speaking was the one in the lab coat and wished he could talk to him. He sent Davian instructions to save the man in the lab coat if he could. Next, he booted up the remote laptop and grabbed the wolf of the half-breed working communications. It was weak like the detective's, but that didn't mean Silas couldn't control the human through the wolf.

Within moments, he was online to their entire communications system. Silas got his first look around the mine. It was dim everywhere except the main area. Bright floodlights provided the necessary illumination to move around safely. The area where they staged the operation had been the loading area for the carts going down into the mines. There was a small flat cleared area where they worked. Four steel posts held metal beams creating a square to support the ceiling. Silas felt better seeing those although this area was still below ground, just not that deep.

There were a few areas, like communications, that were cleared as well. Pallets of supplies were stacked in random locations and a makeshift mapping area was near the van. The amount of trash made it obvious they had been there a while.

"Hank?"

"Yes, Sir?"

"You got someone good who can run traces?"

"Yes, Sir."

"It's on the remote. I don't want this coming back to anything here."

"I will bump it off-site to a fellow I keep around for just this type of thing."

"I'm sending it to you, send it to him and then get out, have him clean behind you. I want locations and names."

"Yes, Sir."

Silas checked on Davian. The man had entered the lower grounds. Silas switched on all the screens. *"Stop Davian."*

The man stopped just as two guards walked past him. *"They gave Tyrese some sort of drug, he's not as deep as before but he's not conscious yet. I'll get you closer to him."*

Davian nodded but didn't speak.

"I'm back in," Tyrone said.

"I'm leading your father to him."

"You have eyes?"

"There was a breed working the consoles. Another one walking around as security."

"You need help?" The note of hopefulness stopped the automatic 'no' that sprung to Silas' lips.

"I can always use a smart pair of hands. I'm in my control room, you've never been here. Go to the elevator next to my office and I will clear you once you're in."

"Thank you, Sir."

Busy watching Davian creep down the dark corridor, he grunted. A ding alerted him to an elevator being used without authorization. He glanced at the monitor and frowned, he didn't recognize the person. Silas allowed the elevator to moves and stopped it between floors. Using the elevator camera, he did a scan. Human. The person slapped the walls searching for a way out. The box was solid, made to contain wolves.

Silas pushed the intercom button on the console. "Security?"

"Yes, Sir."

"Elevator 5 has an unauthorized human, they are locked between floors, I'll send the box to the lower level, proceed with care. Feel free to exterminate if they give you any problems." Chances were they found the connection to Tyrese's capture.

"Yes, Sir."

"Tyrone?" Silas looked at the monitor and scanned the young man.

"Yes, Sir?"

"I'm bringing you up." He hoped the human didn't give security any problems. He would love to talk with him or her.

Silas stood, punched in some keys on the keypad, and waited. Tyrone looked like he hadn't slept in weeks. His eyes were red and puffy as he walked silently into the room.

"Sit here; there was a human sneaking around the gym tunnel area. I don't know if they came in when I opened the shield for Davian's car or not, but I've got to handle that. Time for some exterminating," Silas said, returning to his chair.

"What?" Tyrone sat in another chair and watched the monitor. "They're taking him or her out now. What do you mean exterminating?"

"Tell them I said take it to the bomb shelter, strip it, and toss it in. We'll deal with it later, I've got a hot situation on my hand." Silas worked the console, closing down specific areas in the compound as he issued a level three warning throughout the compound. "I've been Patron for decades, this is not the first time I've been under attack. But with new technology, my systems get breached from time to time." He shrugged as he pressed a few more buttons and waited. "So every year I have the security systems tested by professionals and they make recommendations how to stay secure based on the most current technology."

"So you've got an extermination system? I'm assuming it's not the Orkin man." Tyrone said. And then he relayed a message. "It's a woman. They cuffed her arms and legs and are taking her downstairs. Okay, she's in, they locked the door."

"Good. Now I'm monitoring Davian's progress. He's almost to Rese, but two men are arguing over what to do with him. Whatever they shot him with isn't working," Silas said, preparing to create a diversion.

"I just issued code yellow. My people know what that means. When this light blinks, let me know. And no, it's not the Orkin."

"Will do…I think he's coming around," Tyrone said, his voice rising.

"Rese, if you hear me, don't open your eyes. Just listen. They are talking about something they just injected

into your system, Rone says it burned like fire. So if you're feeling uncomfortable, that's what it is."

Silas sensed Tyrese's confusion.

"Rone, sorry man," Tyrese said in the lightest whisper.

Tyrone cleared his throat and wiped his face. *"We got this Rese, whatever you need to get out of there, we got your back. Silas is riding shotgun, so he has eyes and ears on the place. Dad is inside on his way to you."*

"Dad's here?"

"Yeah, so is Asia," Silas said. Noticing the blinking light, he placed his palm on the pad, waited for a second, and pushed a button that released noxious gases throughout the unsecured areas in the compound. The gas would knock out a wolf but was deadly to humans. His no trespassing signs and security guards warned everyone of the consequences of entering his domain uninvited.

"They got her too?" His voice came through a bit stronger.

"Yes, they have invested too much money into training her as a premiere killing machine to let her walk. It'd be nice to get her out of there," Silas said, remembering the young wolf was as much a victim as the others.

"No doubt."

"They are getting ready to contact somebody, whatever he shot into me isn't working."

"I'm going to say hello. Keep pretending you're out of it," Silas said, happy to be communicating with the intense young pup again. *"Davian?"*

"Sir?"

"Find cover, I'm going to shake things up a bit."

He waited until he got the all-clear. Closing his eyes, he envisioned a storm, felt it churning within him, building, growing stronger and stronger. When it reached its peak, he corralled the energy and targeted it. Above the building, the wind blew wildly as if in preparation. Silas flung his energy toward the Darson building, lashing at it until the roof and walls of the old building collapsed. The exterior guards fell and were crushed beneath the debris. Silas knew the lower level should have minimum impact because of the steel beams, but still worried that something might go wrong below ground.

In between deep breaths, Silas muttered. "Welcome to West Virginia." He and Tyrone watched the horrified gazes of the people inside. They were trapped.

"I'm here, Silas," Jasmine whispered as she merged with him. Immediately his breathing eased and he was able to think clearly. He had released more energy than he realized.

"Where the hell is the back-up?" Trigg yelled, brushing dust from his face.

"Well, that cut the numbers down nicely. If I have the breed guard take out the guards on the ramparts, and Davian hit the rest on the floor, that might work," he said to Tyrone.

Tyrese how you feeling?" Silas asked.

"I've been better."

"Oh shit," Silas said, watching the monitor as Davian was dragged in between two men and propped in front of Trigg.

"Caught him lurking in the corridor, probably had something to do with that cave in." Trigg whipped a gun from another guard standing next to him and shot Davian point-blank.

Tyrone gasped as his father folded to the ground. "Dad!"

"I've got him, be easy, Rese. I've got him, Rone. Watch the monitors for me Rone while I work on your dad."

"Yes…yes, Sir."

He called Jasmine. *"I'm going to need you on this, I need to recharge and I don't see that happening within the next hour."*

"Whatever you need to do, let's do it," she said as they merged fully.

Tyrese watched in shock as his father lay on the ground. He listened intently to Silas as he worked hard to save his father's life.

"They were using bullets tipped in silver. I'm sending energy to surround the poison before it spreads throughout his system. Once the poison's contained, I'll neutralize it."

Tyrese tensed as two guards grabbed Davian's arm and started dragging him away. Tyrese blinked to clear away the fog milling around in his mind. He caught the backs of the guards and saw the soles of the boots his father wore before they disappeared around the corner.

"Sir?" he called out to Silas. He didn't want Davian to die because he came to help him.

"Still working," Silas said.

"They are moving him outside," Tyrone said.

"I found the bullet in his chest," Silas said. There was silence and then, *"Out…out you go."*

"Everything okay?" Tyrese whispered along their link, trying to control his panic.

"Yeah, the bullet fell onto his shirt. I sent additional energy to speed the healing. That should hold him until he shifts. Come on, Davian wake up and kick some ass," Silas growled.

Tyrese's lip curved at the edges. He released a breath and looked around from lowered lids. His heart was racing and he couldn't understand why. Silas said someone shot him. Was that how they got him here? Closing his eyes he retraced his steps but each time he ran into a dark wall. What the hell? He pressed forward, trying to remember how he got here, wherever here was. A stabbing pain in his head, followed by uncontrollable spasms ripped through his body. Rivulets of sweat rolled off his face and puddled at the back of his neck.

Closing his eyes, he chanted a calming verse his dad had taught him and Rone as boys. Within a few minutes, he could think a lot clearer and move his arms, his legs. Inhaling, he checked his wolf and was met with a low snarl. He was pleased with the response.

"Damn, dad kicked ass. Threw them in the incinerator and locked the door. Sweet."

"What?" Tyrese tried to follow his brother's excited chatter. *"Who threw who, where?"*

"Dad. Silas and Mom healed him. He grabbed the two guards by the arms and slammed them together. I think he broke their necks. Too much blood to tell. Anyway, he's got their guns and is on his way back to you. You okay?"

"Woozy, it's getting...better." He tried to find a comfortable position and couldn't. *Wait, did you say Mom?* The thought slipped away before he could question it.

"He's on his way to you, and he is pissed. I feel it through our link."

Tyrese clenched and unclenched his fists, preparing to move when his dad arrived. He didn't want to think about the last time they saw each other. If the Goddess was willing, he'd have time to apologize later.

"Wake up, Rese, time to get out of there. I am going to rouse Asia's wolf, see if I can wake her as well. I don't like the plans they have for her," Silas said.

Tyrese opened his eyes and blinked fast, thinking it was his imagination. His dad loomed over him, looking him up and down before extending a hand to help him get up. Shaky, but standing, he handed him an automatic. "Ready?"

"Silas said to get Asia," Tyrese said in a low voice. His dad's palm on his back helped support him.

"You're not getting anyone," Trigg said, standing across from them. He looked at Davian and frowned. "Didn't I—"

A round of gunfire rang out and Trigg fell forward. Davian and Tyrese dropped to the floor for cover. There was silence as everyone tried to find the source of the gunfire.

"I'm releasing the half-breed guard and sending him upstairs with the other breed. I can't find Asia," Silas said. *"Check around, see if you see her. I can't explain why, but she must be saved."*

"I'll check the van," Tyrese said, moving out while his dad covered his back. Either everyone was busy covering their backs or they no longer cared about the mission, because there were no attempts to stop him.

"Empty," Tyrese said, looking in the back as his dad signaled the front was empty as well. He leaned against the van to catch his breath. Tingling prickles of warmth slid across his chest from right to left, he scratched the itch and ignored it.

"Hold on, let me search again." Silas pushed through Tyrese and searched for the female. *"They are trying to exterminate her. She's in the back in a cave with the man who gave you that shot. Hurry, get to her before it's too late. Her wolf is weakening, barely responding to me."*

"Why are they trying to kill her?" Tyrone asked, sounding puzzled.

Tyrese didn't answer. He and his dad tiptoed to the back per Silas' instructions and stopped outside a small cave. His father waved him to the other side of the rough-hewn wall. Tyrese moved silently and leaned against the wall waiting for his dad to signal the next move.

"I'm giving her wolf my energy to keep its heart beating. They've stabbed and shot her, yet she lives. Get her the fuck out of there."

Tyrese nodded at his dad when he pressed his hand down signaling Tyrese to go in low. His dad pivoted, sent some shots up high toward the ceiling, and returned to the side as a volley of bullets split the air.

"I've got her, but she's losing too much blood. Something is stopping her from shifting," Silas said. Tyrese looked at his dad, nodded as he stooped to his knees, rifle up and ready. Davian swung around and released more shots and slammed back against the rock wall. The gunmen returned the shots above Tyrese's head. He leaned in and shot both men holding the guns. They dropped to the

ground. The doctor ran to the wall. He was holding some kind of knife, but he opened his hand and it clattered to the rocky floor.

"Take the silver noose from her neck so she can shift and heal," Silas told Tyrese.

A moment later, nothing was preventing her from changing. But she didn't shift. Silas pulled at her wolf, commanding it to shift, and nothing.

"She needs to shift, so she can heal," Tyrese said, stating the obvious.

"I'm trying." Silas scanned her body. *"There is a silver dart in the back of her neck, pull it out,"* he told Tyrese.

She gasped the moment she was free of the offending piece of metal. *"Shift,"* Silas commanded and she flowed into her animal.

"Do you have a plan for us to get out of here or do we just leave them behind to rot?" Tyrese asked, watching his father stalk the shaking doctor.

"No one leaves that building except the two breeds. I've separated them in the communications area. I'm controlling their wolves."

"Yes, Sir." Tyrese turned and watched Asia return to her human form. She was firm all over with a tight round ass, and dark quarter-sized nipples tipped the end of breasts just large enough to fill a man's palm. His dick hardened at the sight of the sexy bitch.

She glanced at him, turned, and pulled clothes off one of the dead guards. Her long legs were well-formed; she was a magnificent bitch.

"You got another gun?" she asked as she dressed with quick efficient movements. The shirt was too big. She tied it around her small waist and rolled the pant legs up before sliding on the black boots.

"Here." Tyrese passed her the one they'd taken from the man she had just stripped. She checked it and then nodded. Davian approached with the doctor. He'd secured the man's hands behind his back with plastic ties.

"Silas asked me to keep him alive for questioning," Davian said, pushing the hapless man behind Asia, while Tyrese took lead. With silent steps, he moved outside the door and checked the area. It was dark and quiet. He searched for human heartbeats and heard none. He waved the others out. Asia went to his left and then crept forward, gun at the ready. The doctor came out next and Tyrese grabbed him and pulled a stethoscope from his pocket. Grinning at the irony of using the man's tool to secure him, he tied the doctor to the steel post for safekeeping until he returned to question the guy. Sliding down, the doctor sat on the dirty floor, leaned back, and closed his eyes.

Davian waved to Tyrese to move ahead of him. Tyrese took three steps, turned to the left, and pulled the trigger. The guard fell from behind the wall. Tyrese looked at his dad and patted his chest. *"Listen for their heartbeats."*

Davian nodded and walked in the opposite direction. Every once in a while gunfire would erupt and Tyrese would take cover. After an hour or so it stopped. *"Did we get them all?"* he asked Silas.

"Hold on, I'll scan. There are two more. One in the dumpster, just close the lid. It's too heavy for him to lift it. And one more hiding…looks like a few feet from Davian beneath that pile of rubble."

Tyrese strode forward and emptied a clip into the debris. The man yelled and then went silent. His dad looked at him and nodded.

"Get the doctor, he didn't sound too happy with management when he gave you that shot. How are you doing by the way?" Silas asked, sounding more like himself since the immediate danger had passed.

Tyrese inhaled. His heartbeat still moved at Mach speed, his skin itched in places, felt a little tight, and warm, otherwise, he felt okay. "I'm good." He retraced his steps to the doctor, pulled him up.

"How you feeling, doc? I got a few questions for you, hope you don't mind the piss-poor accommodations," Tyrese said into the man's ear as he marched him to the communications room where Asia was talking to the breeds. He sat the man down and secured him to the chair, not that he thought the man would try to escape, they were below ground. But he didn't want the man to get any ideas and try to jam the communications channels.

Tyrese waved the breed aside and looked at the system, tapping in some keys. "Good," he murmured when he accessed the internet. After typing in a password on a particular site, he ran a scan to make sure the data was clean and then downloaded a popular virus. Within minutes, all the data that had passed through the system was now headed to numerous wolf sites around the world. The enemy had just been exposed.

That done, he looked over his shoulder at the doctor. The man sat with his head bowed, chin on his chest. "Strip him, make sure he's not wired." He looked around, searching for something to scan the doctor with. If this dude was packed and loaded, he needed to take a one-way trip down the mine shaft without a cart. Tyrese looked around at the steel beams that had been hastily put in place. He doubted they could withstand a direct blast.

"Where do they keep the scanners?" he asked the half-breeds.

"I don't know," the small communications guy said.

"If they had any, they'd be in Trigg's bags and those were buried when the wall fell." He pointed to an area that had at least a five-foot-high collection of debris.

"Sir, can you scan him for bombs, please?"

"R. J., how you doing?" Asia asked the doctor, leaning against the desk.

"I don't sense any bombs like the ones we've been exposed to lately. However, the good doctor has all kinds of locks in his mind. When he talks it will probably kill him, literally."

Tyrese shrugged. *"He's going to die either way. Maybe we can learn something useful before he does."*

"What's going on, R.J.? I thought you stopped working for those assholes," Asia said, leaning against the small console.

"You know better than most, they never let you quit. Not and live," he said bitterly as he rolled his eyes at her.

"Why are you in West Virginia?" Tyrese asked. The doctor had a limited amount of time and there were more important issues to be tackled.

"We came to get La Patron's son." He eyed Tyrese. "It's a known fact his son's a breed, we saw you fight in Texas before the breeder was destroyed."

Tyrese's eyes slid to his dad and returned to the doctor. "You thought to use…me as a bargaining chip against La Patron? He's the leader –"

"Who loves his son. He would do anything to get you back. Even step down."

Tyrese looked at the man a moment longer. "*Sir?*" Stunned and at a loss, he called out to Silas for the next question.

"One moment, we got some vermin being exterminated in the house. I'll be with you in a few…"

He searched his mind for another question. "What did you shoot me up with?" He crossed his arms and waited for the answer.

"It's a new drug, well it's not new, it's been around awhile and we finally worked out the bugs. It's supposed to kill your wolf."

"What?" Tyrese and Davian roared as they jumped toward the man.

He didn't flinch. "Except it only works on wolves who are already undeveloped, like those two." He pointed at the two half-breeds. The guard scowled at the doctor and the other man turned away looking at the floor.

"So nothing's going to happen to me?" Tyrese asked, feeling a little better, although the idea that he'd been given a shot in the first place pissed him off.

The doctor chuckled dryly. "I didn't say that. The drug amplifies everything inside you. If your wolf was mean before, he'll be ten times meaner. Even in your human form, you'll be better, faster, stronger, a mean son of a bitch." He looked up at Davian. "What time is it?

"Why?"

"Because it takes thirty minutes for the serum to irrevocably change the cells on a healthy wolf. For them," he nodded to the breeds. "They have to take a series of shots and then exercise their wolves to reverse it."

"So you're trying to create super wolves?" Davian asked.

"No, they scrapped the program, this was the last test. Having stronger wolves for the Patron to control soured the higher-ups."

"Can a man live if his wolf dies?" Tyrese asked.

"No. None of the test subjects were able to."

Anger ripped through Tyrese at the mention of innocents being used for research. A trickle of blood ran down the doctor's nose. They were running out of time. He looked at Asia, she appeared to be deep in thought.

"Why were you trying to kill her and why didn't she die?" Tyrese asked, nodding at her.

Asia looked at him and smirked.

The doctor's lips moved in a parody of a smile. "She's a complicated mystery for us, well, for them now, I guess. She was the prototype who broke all the rules. Asia was in the program way before I joined. She's been operated on so many times it's amazing her wolf still functions." He sniffed but the blood continued to roll down across his lips to his chin.

He glanced at her. "I know they replaced one of your arms and legs with titanium. They thought it would kill her wolf and stop her from shifting. There's a tracking device in her skull with a kill mechanism. It failed, which pissed them off big time. The only reason she was allowed on this mission is that she's black and they felt she'd have a better chance connecting with you." He tipped his chin to Tyrese before peering at her. "How many researchers have you killed or maimed, Asia?" He coughed, spitting up blood.

"Obviously not enough, they're still operating," she said with a sneer.

"Does he know who started the human breeding?" Silas asked. Tyrese was glad he was back and asking questions.

Tyrese asked the question.

The doctor looked surprised. "Is that what they wanted that wolf for? I wondered about that."

"What?" Tyrese asked.

"There is a pack of wolves in Oklahoma. They weren't the brightest, but they were tough, mean, strong, could withstand torture, wouldn't break. Good full-blood stock. They used the seed from that pack to start a separate half-breed program to see if genes made a difference in the quality of the wolf."

Blood trickled faster down the doctor's chin. "Plan failed though. None of the wolves bred half-breeds. That pack's hard to control, hates the very idea of breeds. So they're using the Bennetts to stir up the rebels against the Patron."

"Why? Why do humans care about wolves and our Patron?" Tyrese asked, frustrated. Why couldn't they just leave them alone?

The doctor chuckled and coughed. There was a gurgling sound in his throat. "Humans? I don't know if I'd call them that. They're power-hungry monsters." He gasped as more blood ran from his nose. "The wolves are at the top of the power chain," he panted, sweating. "And every man wants to be at the top. But…but no one can be top as long as…Patron…lives." His chin fell against his chest as blood dribbled from the corner of his mouth onto his chest.

No one spoke for a moment.

"I didn't catch the beginning of the interview, we had some housekeeping going on here," Silas said. *"That was an odd comment about Asia being a prototype. What is she the first of?"*

Tyrese sent the recorded conversation to Silas. The two breeds stood and stretched their arms and legs. Everyone ignored the dying man tied to the chair.

"My men should be reaching you in about five to ten minutes."

"Yes, Sir. Did you get the part about coming after me because they know you have a son?"

"No, I missed that. I'll listen to this in a minute"

"Help should be here soon," Tyrese said to his dad.

"Aren't you curious about what the drug is going to do to you?" Asia asked, searching his face. "It's been longer than thirty minutes."

"I'm very curious, but you heard him. They get this stuff wrong all the time. Nothing may happen or I might fall apart when I shift or cry like a baby." He shrugged. "I just have to wait and see."

She nodded.

"What are you the prototype of?"

She looked at him from the corner of her eyes. "Let's talk about this when we get back to La Patron. I would prefer to explain it once."

He nodded. *"Is she returning with us?"* he asked Silas.

"*Yes, her and Davian, Matt is getting antsy. He felt the pain from the shot and almost tore up the lab trying to get to his mate. Let the breeds go home or wherever they want.*"

He walked to his dad and hugged him. "*Thank you…thanks for coming,*" Tyrese said through their link.

"*You are my son. I would die for you or Rone. I've made a lot of mistakes, many your mom pointed out to me a few hours ago –*"

Tyrese pushed back in surprise. "*You talked to mom? At the compound?*" He looked his dad over for bruises. "*The Patron allowed it?*"

Davian smiled. "*He was in the room and there was some growling, but for the most part, I got to explain and apologize. It had been eating at me for a long time. I am happy you and your brother took care of your mom when I couldn't. I'm very happy she has a mate who loves her.*"

Tyrese nodded. Glad his dad had finally come clean.

"*I am so proud of you and Rone. Living with the Patron and on his security team. I thought I would hit the floor when I heard that.*"

Tyrese's heart leapt at his father's praise. He stepped aside as someone stepped forward and looked at his dad.

"Is he the Patron's son?" the communications guy asked Davian, who stared at the youngster for a minute.

"Why?" Davian asked, frowning.

"Because that's what this whole thing was about, grabbing the Patron's son to use as a bargaining chip. I just wondered if they got the right guy."

Davian smiled and didn't answer. Tyrese placed his hand on his dad's shoulder and squeezed.

Chapter 17

Silas watched for a moment later and switched monitors. Security zipped up four body bags and lined them up in the tunnel on the floor.

"Is this from the extermination?" Silas asked through the mic.

"Yes, Sir. Three were in the HVAC ducts and one had been hiding in a supply room. All human, Sir." Silas sent a silent thanks to Jacques for instituting their current security check program. The toxic gas he had released in the unsecured areas throughout the compound had been a costly venture, but looking at the bodies on the ground, it was worth it. No telling what these people had planned to do. He sent a message to Rose to have the gas tank refilled and the duct system checked.

Silas exhaled. "Good work, stand front and center." They all stepped in front of the bodies. One lagged a bit and then joined the line. Silas scanned each hooded guard. "The one on the end is human." The security guard next to the human whipped out his gun and shot the perpetrator. The man fell to the ground. The other guards helped strip off his gear, leaving him naked and exposed.

"Did they have any tattoos or anything identifying them as belonging to a group or something?"

"No, Sir. We have collected their weapons. There weren't that many. They had a lot of surveillance equipment."

"Institute full searches by quadrants after I air out the area. I want no bugs in my house."

"Yes, Sir."

Silas returned to the conversation with the doctor and Tyrese.

<<<<>>>>

"We're almost there," the lead honor guard told Silas, who repeated the information to Tyrese.

Disturbed more than he wanted to admit over the human invaders, Silas watched the various monitors of the hallways in the compound, the lab, the gym, and the grounds.

"Jasmine, everything okay?"

"We're good."

"Davian got to Tyrese, they're waiting for the guard to dig them out, and then they'll be on their way."

"Rese is okay?" He heard the nervous quiver in her voice and sought to ease her fears.

"They gave him a shot of something. Rone said it burned like fire through Rese's system. I was monitoring him and the only thing I noticed was his faster heartbeat."

"You might want to check with Matt. He told me the detective received a shot of something, and based on the previous condition of your wolf, it will amp it up. Kind of like a steroid shot."

Silas hadn't had a chance to go over the reports from the labs or receive a personal briefing. He was sure there was a lot more going on than what Jasmine said.

"Will do," he said, looking at the unopened file from Tyrese with the doctor's conversation.

"It's just a good idea to know as much as possible about this."

"Speaking of ideas, I wonder when I'll be treated to a purple and black treat." He was jealous knowing she'd dressed specially for her ex and hadn't for him. At least not yet. Normally he preferred her naked, but the image of her sexy curves and smooth skin in wisps of satin and lace had taken root. Now he wanted to see her in seductress mode.

"Really? You'd like that?"

He shook his head at the question. *"Most men like that. Except, not in those colors, dress for me in a different color."*

She giggled. *"I only did that to get things moving with him. We've never had that problem. But I'll dress for you if you want me to."*

"I want you to," he purred.

"Oh, okay. Damn you sounded so sexy just then. Do it again."

"Jasmine," he said her name in a soft purring sound.

"Sir?"

Silas closed his eyes at the interruption. "Yes?" he said without looking at Tyrone.

"There's something wrong with the remote's monitor."

He looked over his shoulder and the screen blinked on and off, followed by a series of rolling codes and symbols. Something was going on with the laptop.

"I'll get back with you, baby."

Silas watched the display, wondering where it was headed. He punched in a few keys and inserted a tracking device into the USB port. The screen blanked and a picture of a large black wolf, which looked remarkably similar to Silas' wolf, jogged across the screen and was hit with a bolt of lightning. It was a grisly sight with body parts flying everywhere, which merely stiffened Silas' resolve to find and eviscerate the fuckers.

He scooted to his main computer to ensure he hadn't lost control of his network. Everything was good. He released a breath and waited to see if there was anything more to the animation.

"I hear something, they must be getting close," Tyrese said through their link.

Silas looked at his other monitors and although the honor guard moved fast, none of the groups were close to the area with Tyrese. Perhaps the noises were amplified and echoing off the walls.

"It looks like it'll be a while," Silas said while watching the laptop. A message, with large white letters on a black backdrop, scrolled from bottom to top, reminding him of the beginning of Star Wars.

"SILAS KNIGHT YOU ARE NO MORE A LEADER OR PROTECTOR OF THE WOLVES THAN THE PRESIDENT OF THE UNITED STATES IS A PROTECTOR OF HUMAN LIFE. BOTH OF YOUR DECISIONS ARE COUCHED IN THE APPROVAL OF

OTHERS. THE VERY NATURE OF WOLVES WAS CHANGED BENEATH YOUR NOSE AND IN YOUR ARROGANCE, YOU MISSED IT. CHANGE CAME OVER A DECADE AGO AND YOU WERE ASLEEP ON YOUR POST. THOUSANDS OF WOLVES HAVE DIED OVER THE YEARS AS LAB RATS AND YOU ARE CLUELESS. YOU SIT AND MAKE JUDGMENTS WITHOUT KNOWLEDGE OF THE FACTS. AS A RESULT, YOU HAVE BEEN JUDGED AS UNWORTHY. YOUR HOUSE OF CARDS WILL TUMBLE. YOU HAVE FAILED. YOU WILL FALL."

The picture of the dead wolf grew larger and larger until it eclipsed the screen.

"That's some bullshit," Tyrone said from next to him. "Cowards won't show their faces, they hide behind a fucking computer saying all kinds of shit." He slammed the top of the console and rolled back to his monitors on the other side of the room. Silas felt the young pup's anger and let him be.

Silas watched the blackened screen unsure of his feelings. There was a certain amount of truth in the words. He hadn't been aware of the breeding program, it had caught him unprepared. A queasy feeling filled his gut at the possible number of wolves it had taken to perfect the cross-breeding process. He was late to the game.

But you are here now," the soft words from his mate blew across the acrid places in his soul, watering and softening the landscape.*" Your heart beats true. You govern the wolves from a position of service to your Goddess. You gotta trust you were kept unaware for a reason and continue to serve with the same commitment,"* Jasmine whispered through their link. *"You are a man of honor. My man of honor,"* she continued. Her words filled his mind, healing his bruised heart. *"Don't stop being the baddest wolf around because of someone who hides behind vague expressions."*

He smiled. Her words strengthened his determination to finish this fight. Knowing she believed in him, believed he had done his best to serve his people, girded him in ways nothing else could. Her unwavering faith soothed his battered ego and lifted his flailing spirits.

*"You are a good man, a great leader, and an awesome Father to your children. Do **not** allow assholes who don't know you cause you grief. Put that BS where it belongs, in the toilet, so we can kick their asses."*

His smile morphed into laughter. The screen blanked and the dim interior of the mine returned. *"Bloodthirsty Bitch."*

"Only when my man or family comes under attack. You have my permission to eliminate them in any manner you wish. Just come back to me in one piece."

"Yes, Ma'am."

"Rese, how's it going?" Silas asked, and then frowned when there was no response. He glanced behind him at Tyrone. "I just tried to contact Rese but it didn't go through."

"I know. There's been interference since that crap rolled up. I've been trying to reach him and Dad. No luck with either of them."

Silas panned the camera and saw the five of them standing near the van. Asia talked to the communications person, while Davian and Tyrese stood to the side chatting. Silas rebooted the laptop; the video came on immediately, but no audio and no way to contact the wolves. Stunned,

Silas watched with a sinking feeling in the pit of his stomach. Problems were on the way and he couldn't warn his people.

Shit.

<<<<>>>>

"I can't reach, Rone," Tyrese said to his dad, hoping he would realize that meant he couldn't connect with the Patron either.

"I've been trying to reach him too, but all I get is static," Davian said, picking up his gun and moving away from the noises coming from the outside. *"Let's move up so until we're sure those are friends out there."* He nodded to the small space above the beams connected to the steel posts, which helped the ceiling remain in place.

Tyrese eyed the beams with uncertainty; they didn't look steady or strong enough to hold him or his dad. Asia pulled her rife across her shoulder, and after a series of jumps landed gracefully on the side of a beam, pulled herself over, laid down with her weapon pointed at the opening.

The breeds' eyes widened as they watched Davian do the same thing on the opposite side of the cleared area. Tyrese slung his weapon onto his back and picked up the breeds, one beneath each arm. He leapt over the short ledge and landed on the platform that housed the communications area. He set them down and pointed to the small space beneath the console.

"Wait here, remain still, and don't talk." They huddled close together and leaned as close to the makeshift wall as possible. Satisfied he had done all he could for them, he turned and leapt up. The rocks on the wall were unstable and fell beneath his weight. He landed hard on the ground with a grunt.

Winded, he leaned on both arms, and shook his head, realizing he wasn't back to one hundred percent yet.

"You okay?" his dad asked through their link.

He pushed up and stood slowly. *"Yeah, just a bit disoriented. Give me a sec."*

"We don't have a second," his dad said as the rapid-fire of guns split the air. Hit, Tyrese slammed backward and he fell on top of the tumbled wall. Another bullet hit his chest, and then several more hit his arms and legs. Each entry point burned and he smelled the stench of his seared flesh.

He sought Tyrone and there was nothing but static. In the background, he heard the battle ensue but had no idea what was going on. *"Hold on, Rese,"* his father said.

"Okay," he said automatically, not sure how to carry out that demand. He closed his eyes to distance himself from the agonizing pain in his body. His wolf snapped and snarled at the invading pieces of silver. Tyrese's thoughts went to his mother. She was going to be so pissed. The thought brought a smile to his lips. If she had any idea he was laying on the ground, full of bullets, bleeding out, there would be hell to pay. Her love eased his pain. Knowing how distraught she would be strengthened his determination to not die on the dirty floor of an abandoned mine.

Rough hands grabbed him by the arm and pulled him up. He bit his lip to keep from screaming in pain. Someone grabbed his jaw and shook his face. Opening his eyes, he looked into a dark pair that looked eerily familiar.

"So this is the son of La Patron?" the man sneered and then spit in Tyrese's face. Next, he punched Tyrese in the stomach so hard he lost his breath and the world went black for a moment. The next hit to his jaw had Tyrese spitting out blood.

"Stop, if you kill him, we all die," someone yelled from behind the man holding him.

"Then I die and take a piece of La Patron with me." Out of the corner of his eye, Tyrese saw the glint of steel and stiffened.

"Stop," Davian's voice rang out.

Tyrese inhaled a bit as the hold on his arm loosened slightly. "What the hell?" the man whispered as if shock. "Davie?"

His father stood a few feet from them. Tyrese met his agonized gaze and swallowed hard.

"What? ...they told us you were dead. Why didn't you contact us? Let us know you were alive all this time?" The man sounded happy and angry at the same time.

Tyrese's mind raced even as it filled in the blanks. The man holding him was kin, a Bennett. *Don't tell him I'm not Patron's son. Please,*" he said to his dad. "*I have to protect my brothers.*"

His dad gave him a subtle nod. Tyrese sought Tyrone again and received static. He needed an energy boost to dispel the bullets so he could shift and heal. His wolf snapped again, snarling and howling louder, gaining his attention. That's when it dawned on him that he was no longer bleeding. The silver tips of the bullets should've prevented his body from healing. An inexplicable heat swept through him, his stomach clenched and he was sure he was going to be sick. Beads of sweat popped on his forehead as the temperature in his body increased. He gritted his teeth against the firestorm racing through him. Bit by bit, his wounds healed and the pain dissipated. His wolf snapped and growled, demanding release. Confused by what had just happened, Tyrese looked up and noticed his father on the ground on his knees, hands behind his head with a gun to his forehead. Operating on instinct, Tyrese grabbed the knife from the man in front of him who was spewing vile, hateful words to this father, threw it, and hit the man holding the gun on Davian right between the eyes.

Tyrese spun in and kicked one of the men holding him and punched the other. Both hit rock-solid walls with a crunch and slid down, their necks broken.

"Fuck!" The man who had punched him yelled, trying to grab him from behind. But Tyrese avoided his arms by jumping over him and landing behind him. He wrapped his arms around the thick neck in a chokehold and squeezed until the man went limp. Then he grabbed his head, twisted, and broke his neck. Bending down, he grabbed the rifle and ammo and returned fire.

Some of the men shifted and Tyrese noticed his dad had as well. The small space stank of blood and death. Three wolves jumped over a pile of debris toward him and Tyrese shifted. Only instead of a full wolf shift, his body stopped midway. Or at least that's what it felt like. He was much taller and wider. His claws were twice as long and his teeth crowded his elongated jaw. He didn't have any time to wonder what his body was doing; his wolf took charge and swung his large paw at the first wolf. The animal flew across the room with gaping holes in its side and hit the wall. The next two wolves attempted to attack him from different sides. He waited until they came at him, and jumped up. The wolves hit each other and were stunned. Landing, he grabbed them by their necks, breaking them before tossing them aside. Tyrese waded full throttle into the fight. Although it was just him and his dad, together they destroyed the other pack until there was only one man left heaving on the ground.

Tyrese called his wolf and shifted to all fours. To say he was relieved was an understatement. It had been in the back of his mind that he might never be able to run on four legs again.

He released a howl. There were echoes of his howl beyond the walls of the mine. The honor guard was close. He released another howl. This one was answered by his dad, Asia, and the two breeds.

Returning to his human form, he realized his dad stood looking down at the man on the ground. Curious, he walked over to see what the delay was. The man looked at him through hate-filled hazel eyes.

"What's up?" he asked as Asia landed next to him, her weapon on her arm.

"That's Josh. Joshua Bennett," Davian said, glancing at him. "*My father,*" he added through their link.

Tyrese clapped his dad on his shoulder. "*Whatever you decide to do is fine with me.*" He stepped back to find a place to sit. Now that the fight was over, his system was on overload. Adrenaline pumped through him like a train. His eyes burned, his skin itched. He needed to run or fuck. He eyed Asia; she met his look with a glimmer of a smile.

Good.

The half-breed guard walked toward him slowly and stopped. "I'm Hamus. This is Shaun," he said in a low voice. Wide-eyed, they bowed to him.

Confused, Tyrese crossed his arms and waited for them to explain. "What're you doing?"

"You must be La Patron's son. No one has ever done what you did except the Patron," Shaun said.

"Keep it quiet, we don't want anyone to know, okay?" Tyrese said, going into damage control mode. As soon as he returned he would have Matt check him out. The shot altered him somehow, but he wasn't exactly sure how just yet.

Both young men nodded seriously as though they had just passed some type of initiation and were in an exclusive club.

A lone shot rang out and Tyrese spun around, his gun aimed toward the sound. His dad stood at the far side of the mine. Asia held the gun on Josh and then broke his neck. The look she sent Tyrese clearly said, 'he wasn't related to me and he had to die.' Silas had said no survivors.

His heart went out to his dad and once his father said he was okay, he left him alone. It was one thing to turn your back on your pack and family. But quite another to see your former pack and relatives dead by your hands on a dirty mine floor.

Tyrese couldn't grieve for his kin, he didn't know them. Besides, there was no doubt in his mind they would have still killed him for being a breed even if they knew he was Davian's son. Fuck them.

He looked at Asia and waved her over. He was still jacked from the fight. His body was on fire, he needed to lose himself between the coolness of her thighs.

Laughing, she shook her head. "Wait, I'm too dirty."

He looked around; he had seen some bottled water earlier. When he found the pallet, most of the bottles had been squashed beneath the debris. Lifting five bottles, he waved them at her with a grin. She moved in his direction. His eyes were glued to her swinging full hips and the vee between her thighs.

"Up here is where you'll find my answer," she said once she reached him.

"I know your answer. I'm working out the details."

"You went through a serious shift. I've never seen that before. You need to get checked out, make sure you're okay."

He frowned. She sounded like his mom. He didn't need or want her in that capacity. "Right now I need to fuck or fight. I prefer to fuck. You game?" He'd never begged a bitch or human for sex and today would not be the first. Her arousal teased his nostrils, she was game.

She released a long sigh, picked up the remaining bottles of water, and headed toward the van. Like a damn puppy on a leash, he followed her rolling hips to the vehicle, fully prepared to help her clean herself.

Frowning, Davian looked up at them. His eyes widened when Tyrese held up the water bottles. *I need a release.* His dad smiled nodding and headed to the other side with Shaun and Hamus to wait.

Chapter 18

By the time Tyrese rounded the back of the van, Asia was stripped and pouring water over her face and wiping it with the inside of the dark brown shirt she had removed. Tyrese stepped forward, took the material from her hand, and cleaned an area she had missed.

He poured the rest of that bottle over her neck and chest, enjoying the sight of water trailing down her flat stomach onto her hairy pussy. Taking the shirt, he cleaned the dirt from her neck and grabbed her breast with his other hand. The dirt from his palm left a smudged print on her chest.

She laughed. "You're supposed to be cleaning me, but you're making me dirtier."

"You're right." He didn't bother apologizing; she was the one who wanted to get cleaned up first. Instead, he took her nipple into his mouth, rolled it around his tongue, and bit down on it slightly.

She released a low moan, followed by a sensuous sigh. Her hand held his head in place as he teased her hard nipple. He gave the other breast similar treatment and then backed up. Opening another bottle of water, he poured it over the front of her and cleaned her with her shirt. When he was done he placed the pants she had worn on the floorboard of the van, lifted her, and placed her on it.

"You okay?" he asked, widening her legs so that her glistening core was on display.

"Um-hmm," she said, watching him.

He opened another bottle of water and poured it between her legs, covering her lips, clit, and opening.

"Oooh," she said, trying to move.

"Stay still." He held her in place with the flat of his hand as the water pooled and then trickled to the ground. Next, he poured water on his hands and wiped them clean, or as clean as possible. Finally, he poured the remaining water on his hard erection and wiped it. She watched his movements with a hungry gleam and he was glad. This wasn't going to be slow or remotely intimate. They were both scratching itches.

He pulled her to the edge of the van, placed her legs around his waist, and lifted her ass slightly so it lined up with his cock. His fingertip played in her cream for a second or two before he placed his tip to her opening.

She widened her legs further, permitting him to ravage. And with one strong push, he entered her tight sheath. He paused for a second to fully enjoy the feel of her, and then he slowly withdrew and surged back inside. He took her hard and deep, the van creaked as it moved in tandem with his thrusts.

"Take all of it," he growled as he pistoned into her. His fingers gripped the sides of her thighs to keep her in place as he sped up.

The sounds of her pleasure and his grunts echoed throughout the mine. He was beyond caring. The need to exorcise whatever inside drove him to find his release. His wolf howled, nearing the surface as he increased his pace, slamming into her with violent abandon.

Stiffening, she screamed. Her walls tightened around his cock as her body shuddered through her release. She came too quick. He kept her in place as he continued his thrusts. Moments later, a euphoric feeling rolled up his legs. His balls drew up. Close, so damn close, he thought as he thrust into her again and again. And then it hit him. He arched his back, threw his head back, and howled as he thrust one final time.

"Arrghh." His body shuddered and convulsed as he shot his load into her welcoming warmth.

Inhaling, he fought to catch his breath. He rubbed the area on her thighs that he'd been holding before releasing each leg. He placed his palms on the floorboard of the van next to her and dropped his chin to his chest. The endorphin rush eased the immediate needs of his body and cleared his mind. He looked at the slumberous expression on Asia's face. She hadn't joined the fight, not until the end when it was safe. He stepped back. A look of apprehension crossed her features before she masked them. He wondered what game she played.

"Patron?" He was met with that damned static again.

"Why didn't you fight?" he asked her when he couldn't connect to Silas.

Her eyes widened a fraction and then she lowered them. Scooting back, she sat up, took another bottle of water, and poured it over her puffy flesh. "Ummm," she moaned as the tepid water flowed over her as she removed his jizz from between her thighs. She took the shirt and patted herself dry.

His eyes followed every move. Now that he wasn't in the throes of a post-battle adrenaline rush, he couldn't help but think her movements were calculated to change the discussion. He glanced at her face to try and read her. But she was busy pulling the pants over her hips as though she needed some type of cover. He noticed a body not too far off and stripped the clothes from the dead man. He handed her the shirt and he pulled on the pants and boots. She replaced the boots she'd worn earlier.

Once dressed, he pulled her to the front of the van, opened the door, and gestured for her to get in. She searched his face for a moment and then stepped up into the van.

"Why didn't you fight?" he asked again.

"I did, I fought from the beam."

"No. You watched from the beam. You came down after. Why?" He didn't fault her for not getting involved, the Bennetts turned out to be a nasty, dirty fighting bunch who didn't believe in surrender. He just wanted to know why a highly trained assassin with titanium body parts didn't get involved.

"I can't afford to get captured," she said, turning away from him.

"What?" That wasn't what he expected to hear.

She looked at him for a second before looking away. Her reddish-brown eyes were serious. "I'm a mutt, okay. I've had so many experiments done to me that even I don't know what I can do half the time. But I know every time I go back to the lab, they do something else to me." She looked out the window in the direction of his dad, Hamus and Shaun. "They are so innocent. Do you know Shaun has never shifted, has no real relationship with his wolf?"

He didn't know. Shaun hadn't talked to him. "No."

She snorted. "They have parents, both of them. A mom who loves them and a dad who provides. They have no idea of the shit-storm headed toward all breeds."

Suddenly, he didn't want this woman anywhere near his family. She had too many secrets and he wasn't sure he wanted to travel down her dark and twisty roads to discover them.

Dragging in a deep breath, she looked at him. "I'm a breed, a special experiment gone wrong on so many levels. For some reason known only to the Gods, my body tolerates an unusual amount of pain and is flexible."

He frowned. "Flexible?"

"Very flexible. In other words, I became the perfect specimen. The latest experiment?" She looked at him with a raised brow. "They were trying to kill me. Not because they wanted me dead, although I don't think that mattered to the head guys, they've put so many alien things into my body and given me so many shots, they think they've created a monster."

Tyrese saw the flicker of shame in her eyes as she said the word monster. "Have they?"

She shrugged. "I don't know. La Patron saved me before they were done. But I thought I was dying, welcomed it. He knows."

"What? Who?"

"La Patron knows what I am, whether he will tell me or you is another matter. So… I froze. The thought of being captured and taken back to the lab…" she looked at her balled fist. "I froze, sorry about that." She inhaled while she looked out the window. "I met my mate." She tipped her head to the side and then looked over his shoulder. "Maybe a decade ago. It caught both of us by surprise. He'd been captured and brought to the labs. One day we passed in the halls and scented each other."

Tyrese could imagine how her mate had reacted to seeing her as a captive.

"Whew, his reaction was explosive. He killed about five workers before they gave him a shot, and later decapitated him. I never told them who he was and they never understood why he went berserk."

"What are your plans now?" he asked to change the trajectory of the conversation. Silas had read her and would decide her fate. Hopefully, she was redeemable, otherwise, she'd never see another sunrise.

She looked at him strangely. "I don't have any plans; it's up to La Patron. I have to return to the room he left me in for debriefing and exams. He was very clear about that."

Tyrese shrugged. "Okay."

"I've never seen anyone shift as you did. You stood on two feet but had super-sized wolf traits. When you batted that wolf, it didn't look like you put any effort in it at all, but he flew across the room with deep gauges in his side.

I've seen you fight before and you're fast, but today you were a fucking blur. I mean, you ran into those men like a Mack truck and mowed them down. There were at least forty of them against you and Davian."

Tyrese was shocked there were that many. Which meant his dad had been prepared to die when he walked out to face the Bennett pack leader. His mind reeled.

"Do you think it's because of the shot R.J. gave you?"

"Has to be. That never happened before." Of course, he'd never smelled death so close to his door either.

"They gave me that shot before sending me on this mission. I can't imagine shifting into some super wolf. Not that it matters. Now that they know the formula works, they'll be shooting up more wolves to try and control them."

"La Patron controls all wolves."

She sighed. "They are working on a device, something to block his transmissions. If they can do that, then he cannot access the wolf and control them."

Tyrese stared at her as understanding dawned. All of this, the mine, the injections, the fighting, the loss of lives, was nothing more than a test, some kind of research. It boggled his mind.

"They were watching the fights?"

She nodded and looked down. "I'm positive there are cameras here. Somewhere far away and safe, a group of men and women watched everything that happened today and are making notes on how to improve their research." She looked sad when she glanced at him. "Despite what R.J. thought, that project has not been scrapped. When you changed into that hybrid form, I can assure you somewhere a bottle of champagne is flowing with the knowledge. Life as you knew it has changed in more ways than one. They were already curious about you, but now…now they'll be more eager to study what they consider the jewel in their crown."

"Bullshit." There was no way he would become anyone's lab rat. He'd die first.

She shrugged and the conversation lapsed. He thought of everything she said and wondered if those assholes had any way to know he couldn't reach Silas.

A howl in the near distance sounded like music in his ears. "Back away from the front," a voice shouted. Tyrese and Asia cleared the van and joined Davian across the mine.

"I think this is our crew," Tyrese said to his dad.

Davian nodded, his jaw clenched tight.

Tyrese realized that he'd gotten release after the fight, but his dad had not. *"We'll be out of here soon and you can get to your mate."*

His dad eyed him before nodding.

Chapter 19

Silas waited in the bunker beneath the gym with an anxious Matt and Tyrone for Tyrese and Davian's return. The doctor examined Leon and assured Silas the full-blood was free of any threatening devices. Silas wasn't sure what he planned to do with the hulking man yet, so he sent Leon to assist Froggy in training the detective's wolf now that it was healthy and recovering.

Dealing with the detective once his wolf was strong would be interesting. Silas contacted the police chief to explain the detective had been found wounded and was receiving medical care. He would return to work once he was on the mend. It was a testament of his authority that the chief sounded relieved and accepted Silas' explanation.

Based on the blood work Matt had done on Leon, there was nothing to indicate he had been injected with whatever Tyrese or the detective received. Silas still couldn't believe Tyrese's transformation. He and Tyrone had stared open-mouthed as the huge man-wolf mowed down the wolves in his path. As a breed, Tyrese shouldn't have been able to shift partially and Silas had a sinking suspicion it had nothing to do with the drug.

Silas hadn't morphed into his man-beast in years, so seeing it replicated in Tyrese brought back disturbing memories. He knew the reckless thirst for vengeance that accompanied the shift, the utter lack of compassion against one's enemies during the fight. When in that form, there was only one thing on your mind, destroy whoever was against you. Sometimes, the enemy wasn't always so clear and others got hurt. That was one of the reasons he had abandoned partial shifting years ago. Perhaps the Goddess felt the time was right for a champion like Tyrese and had granted him that ability. He would talk to Her about it.

His thoughts remained on the fight and the tenacity of the Bennett pack. There was something in the Bennett line that made them a little different from the rest. The doctor mentioned they had been in tests years before, perhaps that's why Davian's seed had taken root in Jasmine. Or why the twins were better fighters than most full-bloods. Plus, they could merge with each other, something normally done between mated pairs. Certainly, not all half-breeds were natural predators like the twins. Silas didn't even sense the heightened level of ferocity in Davian, although the feral look on the man's face when Tyrese was punched in the stomach was borderline rabid.

After Tyrese and his father left the mines, Silas had his guards decapitate the deceased and throw their heads into the incinerator first and then the bodies. It was a long process but Silas wanted no more research done on the individuals who died today. He also had the guards search through the rubble for any supplies, or more importantly, medicines. A black case with vials of liquids was on the way in so they could be tested. Several cameras were located and destroyed as his guards methodically searched for anything of importance to prevent strangers from setting up camp again in their state.

"*Silas, do you want us to remain here tonight?*" Jasmine asked through their link.

He thought about Asia, Leon, the detective, even Davian, and Matt, and felt uncomfortable with so many new people in the compound. "*Yes, I will bring Rese and Rone when I come down after we clear things up here. It may be late, so we'll grab a bite before we come. Make sure you move to our private quarters, I want to spend time with you in the underground spring. You game?*" He knew she would be, she loved the moss-lined cave and whenever they had a chance, she'd drag him there to relax in the warm bubbling waters.

"*Always. I'll see you soon.*"

Security alerted Silas of Tyrese, Davian, and Asia's approach. He watched as each walked through the scanning device and then underwent a more thorough scan. Silas smiled at the primitive look in Davian's eyes as he watched his mate. Perhaps there was more to the man than he'd realized. Davian was the first to get the all-clear. He gave Silas a cursory glance and salute before wrapping his arms around his mate and kissing him with obvious hunger.

When they broke for air, Matt's wide grin showed he was more than ready for some alone time with his mate. He looked at Silas, a question in his eyes.

"Security will take you to one of the condos we have prepared for you. We'll debrief tomorrow, Davian."

Davian turned, his arms still around his mate. His wolf bled through his eyes as he nodded. Silas stroked the mans' wolf to ease him. Davian had been apart from his mate too long; add his recent adrenaline rush in battle, and the man was jacked.

"Good job, we appreciate your service."

Davian straightened a bit, looked at his sons, and then Silas. "It was an honor, Sir, and a privilege. We'll see you in the morning. Matt needs to check Rese out…tomorrow."

Silas nodded as the two left the area. Tyrone grabbed Tyrese and the two men embraced, slapping each other on the back. Silas had no doubt they were communicating about everything that just happened and gave them a moment of privacy while watching Asia's reaction to the scene. Her eyes had widened when she saw Tyrone and now she was frowning. Silas scanned her closely and had security bind her arms from behind. He took a bandana from the guard and covered her eyes.

"Thank you, Patron," she said through their link. *"I'm sorry they can now positively identify the twins. If I could cut my eyes out I would."*

Silas understood.

"We will talk, get some rest." He had security carry her to a more secure room and place her inside. They removed the cuffs and bandana. Silas watched through the camera as she found the bed and lay down. He heard her soft weeping through their link. If any person had been abused and misused, he suspected it had been Asia. He wasn't sure why the Goddess wanted her spared, but he would do his best to make her comfortable until he knew more about her and her abilities.

"She's got a lot of problems," Tyrese said, standing next to Silas watching the monitor. "They have done all kinds of experiments on her, even injected her with the same thing they gave me. I locked up that black case by the way. If it's okay with you, I'd like to stand security when it's being tested. I'd hate for anything to go missing."

Silas nodded. "Okay. I want you to undergo a full check-up with Matt tomorrow. And then Asia, and then your dad. I didn't sense anything but I want to be sure you didn't pick up anything in the mine."

"What happened to Hamus and Shaun?" Tyrone asked.

"They went to a hotel. They plan to rent a car and leave in the morning. Shaun plans to finish school so he can work for the Patron. Hamus tried to talk to the honor guard to see what it takes to become a member," Tyrese said with a slight grin.

"They did well," Silas said.

Tyrese nodded. "Rone told me about that bullshit note they sent you. It's all bullshit."

"Organized bullshit," Tyrone said as they moved to Silas' office.

"Yeah, you're right about that." He told them what Asia told him and his conclusion regarding the root cause of what he had gone through.

"You think they did all that to test the drug?" Tyrone asked, frowning.

"Yeah, I do. They heard La Patron had half-breed pups, they saw us fighting in Texas, but we were so fast, they weren't sure if it was one or two."

"They know it's two now," Silas said, agreeing with Tyrese's premise.

"What? How?" Tyrese asked.

"Asia. Her eyes have some type of lens in them. I noticed something was off with her while she watched the two of you. I'm still waiting on Jayden to send me a complete file on her and Leon. We should learn more about those two in a day or so."

Tyrese nodded. "She watched the fight, didn't get involved. Said it was because she couldn't be captured and returned to the lab," Tyrese said his brow creased. "So they got what they wanted? They saw me shift into that…that thing as a result of the shot." He sounded disgusted.

"You did a mid-shift, or hybrid shift, part man, part wolf. I've never seen a breed do it, but then again half-breeds are new to me."

Tyrese faced him with an eager look. "Full-bloods do partial shifts? I've never seen or heard of that."

"I do partial shifts. I stopped a while back because…my animal was too violent. I haven't done it in over a hundred years. The blood-lust grew harder and harder to contain, so I shut it down." He stared at Tyrese. "You have to work hard to control your wolf at all times or he will take over. It's not good when you can't think rationally."

Tyrese nodded. "Will you help me?"

Silas nodded, pleased with Tyrese's level of maturity. "Yes." He looked at the twins and stretched. "I know you found release and are relaxed," he said to Tyrese. "But I have not seen my mate or pups since you were taken yesterday. She misses me."

Tyrese laughed as they all stood. "I had to report to you first, but I know and you know, I have to go let Mama check me out. I'll try and be brief."

Silas smacked his shoulder and they left the room.

"Mom tell you, Aunt Renee, Mandy, and Grandma are coming next month for the Christening?" Tyrone asked Tyrese.

"Next month? Before or after the challenge?" Silas asked.

The twins looked at him and laughed. "You should be telling us," Tyrone said as they entered the elevator.

"She's planning this. I will show up of course. But…I've been busy with other things and don't have all the details," he grumbled.

"It's in two weeks," Tyrone said.

"Okay, before the challenge," Silas said, his mind on the upcoming fight.

"Have you decided Cameron?" Tyrese asked as they left the elevator and headed to the below-ground living quarters. Silas placed his palm on the scanner and was admitted. The twins repeated the process and within moments the wall moved and they walked down another hall.

"No. Not yet. He talked to me about it, but winning the admiration of your mate doesn't seem like the best reason to become Alpha of a state. What happens when she wants something else? Move to live near water or snow or sunshine, what then? I will decide soon and let you know if you are off the hook or not," he said to Tyrone, who nodded.

They reached the door and Silas punched in his code and spoke a word. The door opened and they entered. Jasmine unfolded from the chair and walked toward them, her eyes locked on Tyrese who opened his arms. She ran and hugged him tight.

Tears leaked from her eyes and Silas noticed moisture in Tyrese's eyes before he closed them while rocking her from side to side. When they broke apart, she cupped his cheek in her hand and smiled.

"I am so happy to see you. I was so scared when they took you. Silas called me bloodthirsty when I told him to teach them a lesson about taking one of ours…" she nodded. "But I'd have neutered them myself if I'd have caught them."

"Mom," Tyrese said, groaning and covering his private parts.

Laughing, she slapped his shoulder and pulled her to him again. Silas met her eyes, she mouthed, "thank you" to him. He'd have to give a full accounting later as they soaked in the spring. He hardened just thinking about getting close to her. Not wanting to appear selfish or brutish, he left them alone and entered the area where his pups rested on a large mat. Rose and Tyrone broke from a tight embrace as he entered.

"Good night, Patron," Rose said as she left the room, pulling an eager Tyrone behind her.

He waved not wanting to wake his pups. A soft mewling sound from the bed had him reaching for David. His fingertip brushed across his son's lip and David grabbed it and bit down hard.

"Hey, that's not food, buddy," he whispered, surprised David sucked his finger. Was that normal, he wondered as he pulled his finger out gently. David's eyes widened and then his face split into a grin showing smudges of red on his teeth from the bite.

"Da," he said and took Silas' finger again.

Immobile from the burst of love and pride careening through him, Silas didn't realize his son had bitten him again and was sucking on his finger. When it dawned on him that David sucked his blood, he pulled his finger away, again.

His son grinned and in an unprecedented move, crawled up his chest and touched his face the way the other kids had done numerous times.

"Da."

"Did he just…oh, is he standing on you?" Jasmine asked with wonder in her voice.

Silas hadn't realized the boy was standing and now bouncing on him without assistance. The glow of excitement from David's smile was catchy and he found himself grinning right along with the boy.

"I can't believe this," Jasmine whispered through the fingers covering her mouth. "What happened?" She looked at him.

Silas was clueless. "I went to pick him up, he was making some noises, you know how he does."

She nodded and stroked David as if his bouncing on Silas' lap were a mirage that she needed to make sure was real.

"I missed his shoulder or something and my finger grazed his lips. He grabbed it and bit down." He glanced at Jasmine. "Has he bitten anyone?"

"No." She frowned, stroking the babe's hair. "Adam is my biter, not David."

"He sucked my blood."

Her eyes widened and her hand froze in mid-stroke. "What?" she asked in a horrified whisper.

He had to remember she was human and the idea of blood exchanges grossed her out. "He marked me, I guess." Silas tried to sound offhanded about it.

"But…he's…just…why did he do that?"

Silas thought about it. The Goddess's words came back to him. "Maybe that's the way I'm supposed to heal him." He shrugged. It was good seeing the pup with a bit of life in him and if his blood was the catalyst for that, he'd feed the boy a steady diet. Jasmine took David and rocked him until he fell asleep.

"He's resting." Grinning widely, she looked at Silas. "Truly resting."

He placed a kiss on her forehead and assisted her up with her bundle. "Glad I could be of help, should have thought of it before." He shook it off, feeding his sick pup his blood never occurred to him. "Put him to bed, the real test will be if he sleeps through the night."

She nodded and returned David to his spot between Adam and Renee. Silas spared his pups another look, took her hand, and pulled her toward the bathing area. They had just entered the space when the chime rang, signaling someone at the front entrance.

Silas looked at Jasmine. "It's one of the stooges. Rone, Rese, or Cam."

Chapter 20

Jasmine chuckled as he patted her hip and left the room. David started crying and she went to check on him, visions of a rough ride from her sexy mate going up in smoke. When she walked into the room, David looked at her, his small lips quivering as he rolled to his side.

Unsure why he moved that way, she touched his thigh and then checked his diaper. He whimpered and then yawned. He was damp, not wet, but she changed him anyway. When she lifted him to place the diaper beneath him she stopped, leaned down, and then stood straight again.

"Silas?"

"Hold on."

She traced the pattern of the birthmark on David's outer right thigh. It was a purplish mark, but as she watched, it faded to his skin's natural complexion leaving just the outline. "Yeah?" Silas said, placing his palm on her neck.

"Look at that." She pointed to the new mark on David's thigh. That wasn't there before."

He leaned closer and then straightened. "You're right."

"Have you ever seen anything like that before?" she asked, perturbed. He was a little too blasé about this for her.

David had fallen asleep. Silas finished changing the diaper. He then took her hand and led her into their bedroom. "Yes, I've seen that before."

He walked into the bathroom.

She remained in the bedroom waiting for an answer. The man had had a long day, she understood that, but something strange just happened to her baby and she was not going to play twenty questions. She crossed her arms and stopped her feet from tapping.

He re-entered the room. "I just saw it for the first time, on Tyrese."

Her arms fell and her mouth opened. "Whaaat?"

"That's what he wanted to show me, there was a burning on his right thigh, same place as David, and when it stopped, the mark was there. "I don't know that it's a birthmark, because it just happened."

Jasmine moved forward, "David's was changing into an outline," she said. "You think this is what Julie was talking about?"

"Tyrese's is not an outline, it's filled in. As far as Julie and her predictions, David is my seed. As much as I wish it, Rese is not. They both received these marks at the same time. I think whoever is supplying Julie and her companions with information has a lot of it wrong." He placed his fingertip on her lip when she started to speak. "I will seek the Goddess' help, but not now. We are constantly interrupted and I want to spend some time with you, away from everything." He ushered her forward.

"Yeah." She realized he was right, they kept getting interrupted.

When they stepped through the gold inlaid Spanish tile to the rawness of the grotto, she stopped and breathed deeply, and pivoted in slow motion with a wicked grin.

"It's always so fresh and alive smelling in here." She spun and gazed at him. "I love how wild and untamed this room is…like a certain somebody I know."

He watched her intently. A slow seductive smile crossed his handsome face.

She backed away from him as he advanced.

Silas's brow rose. "Yeah?" he mocked as he caught her around the waist and pulled her snug against him. He slid his mouth over hers and tasted the inner sweetness between her soft lips.

"Yeah," she said against his lips before wrapping her arms around his neck and taking his lips again. His fingers slid beneath the straps on her dress and pushed it from her shoulders. The cool fabric brushed against his legs on the way down. She was naked. His cock rose in acceptance of her questing hip movements and returned them with a few of his own.

"Off, take them off now," she insisted, her hands were everywhere pulling on his pants.

"Slow down, I'm not going anywhere, you've got me for the rest of the night," he whispered, placing kisses on her face. He loved the soft texture of her skin, and the sweet lilac fragrance wafting from strategic points on her flesh drove him mad with desire.

It had been a long, life-changing day, and she had been his solace. Throughout the entire ordeal with the mine, the honor guard, Cameron, Jasmine had been there for him, close but not too close. Ready to offer encouragement, soothe his bruised ego and bring a much needed smile to his face. All he thought of was this moment when he'd be able to hold her tight and never let her go.

Her fingertips brushed against the tip of his erection, canceling his thoughts. His mate hungered for him and refused to wait.

"You want it right now? Like this, raw? No build-up?" he asked in a gravelly tone as he pushed his pants from his hips and slipped out of them. Pulling her close, he rubbed his long length against her.

She pushed back, jumped, and wrapped her legs around him. "Yes, you've kept me waiting all day while you took care of everyone else, now take care of me," she demanded as she rolled her hips against his hardness while holding his eyes.

The heat and juices from her core seared him. He held her ass, leaned back slightly as she gripped his thickness.

"Ahhh, don't play with me, put it in."

She placed the tip at her entrance and moved toward him as he thrust forward. "Yes," she said on a long sigh. "I need this."

Remaining still, he looked around at the natural stone walls. That would never do for what he had in mind. He headed for the inner bathroom's smoother walls. This coupling was going to be hard and fast.

"Ooooh, somebody's up for a challenge," she said, rolling her hips on his pulsing rod.

He smacked her hips and then rubbed the sting. "Be still, I don't want to drop you."

She snickered at the hollow threat and continued driving him crazy. Once inside, he backed her against the cool marble on the walls and pushed into her as far as he could.

"You want me?" he asked huskily, needing to hear it. On one level he knew she was his. But right now, at this moment he was a man who'd been hit with uncertainties over the past forty-eight hours that burned in his gut. He didn't know when this need materialized; maybe it was seeing her with Davian and listening to the intimacy of their conversation. Davian and Jasmine had kids and history, something he was just now building with her. He could never compete with her past and needed to hear they were on the same page for their future. Or maybe the scrolling message on the laptop screwed with him on a visceral level, he wasn't sure. He just needed her reaffirmation that he was it for her.

"Yes."

"Look at me, say my name, and tell me. Do you want me?" There was an underlying sense of urgency in his voice. Being vulnerable was alien to him and he hated not being able to change it or shrug it off.

Her eyelids fluttered open and she searched his eyes.

Hopefully, she found whatever she needed because he laid it all on the line for her. Now he needed her to tell him that he was the one, the only one she wanted.

"Silas, I want you. I need you, baby. Only you."

He closed his eyes and dropped his forehead to hers as her words filled and warmed him. "I love you," he whispered as he slid back and then surged forward.

"I need you to give it to me hard and fast…no chase."

His heart slammed in his chest. His beast howled as he held her hips steady while he pistoned into her.

Jasmine growled as he took her in such a primal fashion. She couldn't catch her breath as his hardness slid deep inside her. She grabbed his hair, pulling his mouth to hers as he thrust repeatedly into her body, sending her spiraling towards her release. Her walls throbbed as he thrust faster and urged him to come with her, to meet her at the cliff. His thickness pulsed.

Like falling pins in a lock, her body tumbled over the precipice into a mind-blowing, earth-shattering climax. Her heart thrummed so loud she could barely breathe due to the intensity of the moment.

He pumped into her over and over again, then froze with a harsh cry as he shot his seed, coating her walls with his essence. In the aftermath, his body shook beneath the force of his release.

His reclaiming bite near her neck calmed her. His grip on her tightened as she stroked his hair.

Jasmine placed gentle kisses all over his face. This week had been one for the books, their relationship had been tested through fire. And yet, here they were, more solid now than before. Her heart clenched. "You chose us."

"Hmmm?" He didn't move.

Tears filled her eyes as her heart nearly burst with hidden emotion. "Today, you…you chose me, the babies."

He leaned back, his brow furrowed. "What?" He carried her to warm spring.

Leaning against his chest, she gloried in the solid beat of his heart as he walked them down into the bubbling waters. Once submerged to their chests, he separated them.

"Mmmm," she moaned as the waters soothed her woman's parts.

He tapped her nose. "What were you talking about?"

Moving closer, she sat on his lap facing him. "You chose us today. I felt your struggle. You're the top man, the leader. For you not to be in the midst of the fight and wondering how things would've turned out if you were there?... I know that was hard for you." Her eyes watered again.

"Jasmine, it was no choice, not really. I'd give my life for you, my pups." He lifted her chin. "For your pups as well. I count the twins as my own."

Her heart expanded and she couldn't stop the tears if she tried. "I know." She stopped to catch her breath. "I have wanted someone to love me… for me, for so long." She shook her head and looked away. "What you did with Davian."

He tensed and she patted his chest. "No, hear me out. That was hard. You knew I would flip, be hurt. You could have taken the easy way and kept the truth from me. But you told me the truth, dealt with the fallout, and waited for me to forgive you." She stared up at him. "Don't get me wrong, I was hurt and upset, but you told me the truth. Even when it caused us problems. I can trust you to be honest with me and I've…I've never had that before."

He pulled her close and they rested on each other. "I am wolf. I see things in black and white, at least I used to. You are pulling me into shades of gray. I don't know family like you're showing me. I have a pack mentality, but with so many half-breeds being raised human I need to change. It's difficult, and damn inconvenient. There's no way I could have made it this far, with the current political challenges in my world, without you."

He kissed her forehead. "This week…bombs, fancy equipment, viruses, the mine, now those marks, could be the birthmarks delayed and I have to wonder if they have anything to do with Julie's predictions…" He shook his head. "Can I tell you something?"

She nodded and gazed up at him.

"I thought I was going to lose it a couple of times. There was too damn much happening at once. There were a few moments, like when the bomb exploded, and then to find out the human breeder carried one with my name on it. Worse, the bitch had been in lockup all this time? My heart stopped when I thought what could've happened to you, my pups…I almost lost it," he whispered.

Hearing the despair and seeing the anguish in his eyes caused a deep ache in her belly. She touched his face and waited until glassy eyes met hers. "It was a shitty week, hands down. Folks tried to kill my mate, me, my kids. It was bad…but guess what, baby. I'm still here. You're still here. All our kids are still here and one of them is now healed."

The corner of his lips inched up. She had more work to do to convince him it would be okay.

"That means they failed. They threw a bunch of shit at you and failed. You're still La Patron. When it was just you, the risks you took kept things interesting, kept you from boredom. But now you have a family and that's what we are. Get used to saying it because in a few weeks, Mama and Renee will be here. Family. More people to use as a bargaining chip, more people to have safety concerns over, more people to take care of, but you know what?"

He shook his head. Smart ass.

"Family is also more to share the heavy loads or burdens at the end of your day, more people to come to your aid that you trust, more people to have your back, more people you can count on to help keep those you love safe, more people who love you. Family may be inconvenient at times, but when we work together, we rock, Wolfie."

He laughed. The shadows from his eyes lessened. She understood he'd always have concerns for the wolves he presided over, and change had stormed into his life, but he was handling it. Tomorrow would present a new set of problems but she was confident that they were strong enough to work through each and every one.

<<<<>>>>

Hello and thanks for taking the time to read my third book in the La Patron series. I love paranormal books and characters in general and shifter stories in particular. Throw in the romantic element, strong Alpha characters who bend beneath the power of love and I'm over the moon. Sighs…

I wanted an older heroine who'd had kids, experienced life in the "real" world first so that she could realistically handle an Alpha like Silas Knight. He's not easy but he loves fiercely and that's what Jasmine (and most of us) craves. Jasmine fit the casting call, with her set of twins, Tyrone and Tyrese. Their family dynamic blows me away every time the boys cater to their mom. Love it!

You're invited to journey with me through the six and counting books in this series. If you like fast-paced action, suspense, and great love connections like me, you won't be disappointed. Feel free to drop me a line, LaPatronSeries@gmail.com, or join La Patrons' Den, my Facebook group where discussions regarding Silas and the Wolf nation abound. Also, you can find me at my website, SydneyAddae.com.

La Patron, the Alphas Alpha is my first paranormal series and I'd like to ask a favor. When you finish reading, please leave a review, whatever your opinion, I assure you I appreciate it.

The following books are in the La Patron Series, enjoy!

Thanks again
Sydney

Birth Series
BirthRight
BirthControl
BirthMark
BirthStone
BirthDate
BirthSign
Sword Series
Sword of Inquest
Sword of Mercy
Sword of Justice
Holiday Series
La Patron's Christmas
La Patron's Christmas 2
La Patron's New Year
Christmas in the Nation
KnightForce Series
KnightForce 1
KnightForce Deuces
KnightForce Tres'
KnightForce Damian
KnightForce Ethan
Angus
LaPatron's Den Series

Jackie's Journey (La Patron's Den Book 1)

Alpha Awakening – Adam (La Patron's Den Book 2)

Renee's Renegade (La Patron's Den Book 3)

David's Dilemma (La Patron's Den Book 4)

Rise of the Wolf Nation Series
Knight Rescue - Rise of Wolf Nation 1
Knight Defense (Rise of Wolf Nation 2)

BlackWolf Series
BlackWolf Legacy
BlackWolf Preserved
BlackWolf Redemption

The Leviticus Club (The Olympus Project Book 1)
Altered Destiny
Family Ties

Booksets:
La Patron Series Books 1-3
La Patron Series Books 4-6
Sword Series
KnightForce Series Books 1-3
KnightForce Series Books 4-6
A Walk in the Nation (Three Stories to Tease Your Imagination

Other Books by Sydney Addae:
Last in Line (Vampires)
Bear with Me (Bear Shifter)
Jewel's Bear (Bear Shifter)
Do Over: Shelly's Surrender
Do Over: Rashan's Recovery
Secret of the Red Stone

www.SydneyAddae.com

Made in United States
Orlando, FL
06 December 2021